Atkinson's Administration

The Reaper Series
Book One

John Paul Bernett

ISBN: 978-0-9926173-1-8

Dedication

To my wife Beverly Gail Bernett, thank you for believing in me and your constant support and encouragement.

Acknowledgements

I would like to thank Gavin Johnson and Lee Coates from V-Edition Media for their work on the book cover.

Also, Hunter Gray Tate for my author Photograph.

Also my wife and muse Beverly Gail Bernett for all her help.

Foreword

To take part in this story, the following must be understood – Atkinson and Dewhirst had walked between the Plane of Existence and the Realm of Death since time began and always did the job they were created for perfectly; one gathered souls, and the other did the eternal paperwork. Both tasks had to be done if the life circle was to continue. Life and Death need each other. Many people believe in different meanings of this. Albeit religion or fate, it does not matter what you believe in – the only sure thing is, if it lives, then it must die, and Atkinson and Dewhirst are the despatchers of the latter.

John Smith was an accountant. He lived a boring life. He slept and worked, and that was all. Then things changed in a big way, as he began a journey into the past to save the future of mankind. This journey would take him into different realms of existence and, along the way, he would make friends who would help him try and save what we know of as Humanity.

Atkinson is Death...the fourth horseman of the apocalypse in modern guise. He and his brothers grow weary of Humankind and believe the time of the great prophecy is now.

The four horsemen of the apocalypse mount their steeds.

Let the battle commence.

Chapter One

John Smith woke from yet another night of broken sleep, his pillow wet with perspiration, the quilt at the foot of the bed. His nocturnal journey from bedtime until waking used to be simple – he slept, he woke. That had been the way of things for the past twenty-two years, but not anymore, something was about to change.

Today was Tuesday, but it was destined to be like no other Tuesday he had ever drudged through before. He rose from the bed and struggled to fasten his dressing gown. After the day's first technical breakthrough, he stood there with his dressing gown tied perfectly, and his brown carpet slippers on his feet. With a familiar feeling of dread for the oncoming hours, until he returned to his bed, he made his way into the sterile kitchen. Switching the kettle on, he wandered into the bathroom, and there it was, that same grey face looking back through the mirror. After the growth of Monday's hours was shaved from his chin, his face washed and hair combed, he looked back in the mirror and again, that same grey face staring back at him.

Having eaten his cornflakes and drunk his Earl Grey, he put on the clothes that Atkinson, Atkinson and Dewhirst, the accountancy firm he worked for, demanded – grey two-piece suit, white shirt, and the obligatory grey tie – then made his way down the stairs from his top flat at Number 3 Lindale Mews.

Opening his umbrella, he ventured out into the cold, raining December morning.

The crows seemed to be crowing, "Work! Work!", and a solitary magpie cackled. *Why was it always one magpie – never two, or four, always one for sorrow*, he thought to himself. The one magpie certainly matched his mood as he mounted the Number 12 bus to take him to the city.

The Number 12 was on time and delivered him to his desk by 08:30. He ran the gauntlet of the younger go-getting, upwardly-mobile employees, who took great delight in making his working life a misery. The female members of staff showed him the same amount of contempt as any woman he had ever met, and the bosses simply ignored him. The only reason he was still there was because of one special account. Alfred Winters owned that account...it was for a haulage business and he had insisted that John Smith alone would deal with it. He didn't know why this was; he had dealt with this account from his very first day, twenty-two years ago that Christmas, and by a strange coincidence, that was the very day the account started.

He turned on his computer, and like every other morning, his inbox was full of internal mail; this was the new way of sending him all the hurtful and spiteful office memos. It seemed that some of his so-called work colleagues stayed up late to think up the new insults for his arrival at work each morning. This normally didn't bother him, but, this was no ordinary Tuesday.

Without thinking, he retorted with sharp and hurtful wit, a thing he would never usually do, and he pressed the 'send to all' button. For the first time in twenty-two years, he did something spontaneous, and something stirred within him. He didn't know then what it was, he only knew it felt good.

Reginald Arthur Dewhirst, eighty-four years old and the only surviving founding member of Atkinson, Atkinson & Dewhirst, summoned Smith into the office. Mr. Dewhirst's office was a dark, foreboding place, rarely seen by anyone. Entering was like walking into a bygone age many centuries past; it had that certain smell that comes with age. Not a bad smell, just distinctive. The room was long, with a large, carved oak desk decorated with a leather inlay at its far end. Sitting at the desk was Old Man Dewhirst, as all the other members of staff called him.

"Come in, my boy," the old man croaked. "Take a seat." This was, without doubt, worrying; he sat down in the chair opposite with the same trepidation as someone on death row being strapped into 'Old Sparky'. He spoke with few words, but the ones he used were always well thought out. Recalling his witty e-mail that, in hindsight, he wished he had never sent, he readied himself for whatever was to come.

"Twenty-two years! Twenty-two years!" John recoiled, feeling increasingly smaller in his seemingly ever-growing chair, waiting for the payload about to drop on him. "After twenty-two years, you choose now to show yourself to them." That was the most Dewhirst had ever said to him. If John was worried before, he was in a state of confusion now.

"Mr. Atkinson Senior is unimpressed at your untimely intervention." John's first thought was, *Who was he talking to?* Dewhirst was looking straight at him, but he had no idea what his boss was talking about, and Mr. Atkinson Junior had been dead these past twenty-two years. The old man had clearly lost his mind.

He apologised humbly and Dewhirst told him to keep his head down. Mr. Dewhirst was assured that this would happen. Returning to his dreary desk, John read everybody's response, none of which came close to what he would have called a good comeback, but he did not reply. He had a lot of work in his 'in' tray. He was confused, and was looking forward to catching the Number 12 back to Lindale Mews.

The day seemed to drag more than ever; he was having one strange thought after another. He was feeling hot, his fingers missing the keys on his keyboard; today was proving to be the strangest day he had ever known. His co-workers kept looking at him as he fumbled with his collar, which seemed to be too tight. For the first time ever, he had taken off his jacket, and perspiration could be seen under his arms. When the 'end of the day' bell rang, he was the first to log off his computer and be out of the door.

On the bus, he noticed people looking at him, staring. *How rude,* he thought to himself. People seemed to be talking about him. This was strange — no one had even noticed him before, now this. Mr. Dewhirst's words were going over in his head — *who had the old man been talking to?* He had been looking at John directly, and there was no one else in the room, *but what did he mean?*

The tightness in his collar made him undo his tie; it had never been tight before. His head was pounding and he was perspiring again. *Get off this bus!* he was thinking to himself, or he thought he was thinking that — it might have been someone saying it, he didn't know. All he knew was he had to get off. This had become the strangest of days. He needed the boring comfort of his home surroundings and to get the thoughts of today out of his head. It was quite apparent to him that he had become scared, but of what, he didn't know.

With his bus stop now in sight, he depressed the stop bell and the bus came to a halt. He eventually got off what had seemed the longest bus ride of his life. He saw the reassuring comfort of 3 Lindale Mews in front of him and he was safe, and home.

Unlocking the door of his little apartment, he noticed, for the first time, how cold it had become. On any other day, the first slight drop in temperature sent him running for his warmest vest and overcoat. With his tie undone and suit jacket over his shoulder, he closed the door behind him and climbed up the stairs to what he thought would be his usual tea and countdown to bedtime.

Looking at the tins of beans and loaf of bread in his pantry, he began to prepare the Tuesday teatime feast of beans on toast. Sitting down in his late-eighties fitted kitchen with early-eighties wall décor and even earlier utensils that he picked up in a second-hand market, his mind tried to unravel the day's events – the computer e-mail messages, the strange audience with Mr. Dewhirst, the hellish bus ride home, and the discomfort with what seemed like his clothes tightening.

After eating he rose from the table, plate and cutlery in hand, and made his way to the sink. Staring blankly into the wall while washing the midweek silverware, he drifted back further, just short of twenty-two years to be exact, and his first day at Atkinson, Atkinson & Dewhirst.

At 8:25 on the seventeenth of December 1977, he walked nervously into the clerk's office of Atkinson, Atkinson & Dewhirst, his present employer. The elderly gentlemen already at their desks made it look more like a retirement home than an office. Mr. Braithwaite, who by far looked the oldest of the Sunny Acres Mob, slowly rose from his chair, and showed the young man to what was going to be his desk for the rest of the millennium. The first job he was given was a new customer of some importance. Mr. Braithwaite informed the new apprentice of this with a certain amount of unease. The apprentice would soon learn that there would be many things about his employment that he would not understand. "Look over this portfolio, and report your findings to Mr. Atkin...." He stopped abruptly and said, "Report your findings to Mr. Dewhirst...Mr. Atkinson died last night."

At those words from Mr. Braithwaite, he began thumbing briefly through the thick folio that would take up so much of his working life.

Bang! Bang! Bang! He was wrenched out of his daydream to a heavy knocking at his apartment door. Drying his hands, he gingerly made his way to the door – he never had visitors before.

With the chain firmly in place, he opened the door an inch or two. The small landing outside his door was quite empty, there was no one to be seen. He could see all the way down the steps; the bottom door was still closed, and, as far as he knew, locked.

A smell of dampness and decomposing leaves – the smell of the woods in early January – had filled the passage. Although not a rambler of any kind, he recognised that bittersweet, earthy smell. Closing the door, he unhooked the chain and opened it fully, letting the scent fill his apartment.

Walking out past his threshold, he tripped on something. It turned out to be a box – a plain, brown, paper-covered, ordinary-looking box. It was about twelve inches square; it had no seams and no obvious top or bottom. The address was simply his name, John Smith. Looking at his name on this uninteresting box, it summed up his life – plain and uninteresting. He sighed, picked up the box, and retreated behind the safety of his locked door. Once inside, he curiously observed his new acquisition. The brown paper turned out to be some kind of skin-type material; he pulled and tugged at it, but was unable to tear or break it. Also, his name had now gone from its side, and the word 'Atkinson' had taken its place. Like an excited child on a Christmas morn, he frantically tried to gain entry. After what had seemed a good hour, he ventured into the kitchen and returned with the sharpest knife he owned – unfortunately, it was as dull as he was. He placed the only sharp part of the knife – the point – into what he had now randomly decided was the top of the box.

The second that the point touched the box, it bled. Instantly retracting the blade, he dropped the box and fell motionless into his padded leather chair. Immediately, the bleeding stopped. By now, he understood what was happening; quite simply, he was losing his mind. 'If it was only that simple...' said the voice in his mind that he last heard on the Number 12 earlier that evening.

Looking at the large railway clock on the mantelpiece, he saw that the round, greyish-blue face showed that it was ten past seven; the distinctive ticking of that faithful old timepiece was all he could hear. He seemed to feel more alone and scared at that moment than he had ever felt in his life.

After about ten minutes, he returned to the box lying on the floor, and placed it on the coffee table in the middle of his small, cluttered living room. There were no stab marks on the box and no spillage of blood, again pointing to the fact that he was having a nervous breakdown. Instantly dismissing this notion, in order to pre-empt the voice bellowing back into his brain, he picked up the box and carried it to the door, once again checking the passage – it was clear. The smell of the woods had now diminished. Thirteen steps down and he was outside the door; just as he thought, it was locked. He unlocked the door, turned the rusty handle, and the box was evicted into the open waste bin. In a dramatic fashion, he clapped his hands in an up-and-down motion, like they used to do in old comedy movies. Turning back up the stairs, the door locked and double-checked behind him, he returned triumphantly to his living room. To his absolute horror, sitting proudly on the little coffee table, was the same twelve-inch square brown box. He felt a pain grip his chest; sweat started to collect in droplets on his brow and it was hard to draw breath. He was literally frozen to the spot, petrified. All he could move were his eyes, and they were fixed firmly on the box that he had just thrown out.

Be still, sit down, and relax. This voice wasn't like the other one. *Welcome to schizophrenia! (A lovely place that embraces all and their inner friends)*, he thought to himself. Of course that would have been a good, simple answer, but it would have been the wrong one. *The box will let you know when the time is right. Until then, be calm – all will become apparent at a later date.* This time, the stark realization was that the voice was not inside his head. It was all around him! He seemed to recognise this deep, scary voice...maybe it was scary because of the day that he had just experienced? What was he saying? Voices in his head, boxes that bled and then refused to be evicted.

He could see why this voice was scary, after all, this was John Smith, hardly Rambo or Arnie.

The next time he glimpsed at old faithful on the mantelpiece, it was five minutes to nine. Everything had been calm for a while, so he tried to resume normal activities. Stepping back into the kitchen, he filled the kettle and set it to boil, placing his night-time, decaffeinated tea bag into his Sagittarian mug and toasted two crumpets. With supper on his tray, he returned to the sitting room, trying to ignore the box. Flicking on the television, he tried to relax; he watched a rerun of a money program special. He thought to himself, *There should be more programs like that one,* as he retired to bed.

Lying in his bed, his mind was in overdrive. With his eyes still wide open at twenty minutes past eleven, he got out of bed, put on his dressing gown and slippers, and made his way to the medicine cabinet in the bathroom. Opening the mirrored door, he took out a packet of headache tablets and removed two extra-strength capsules, swallowing them with the help of a glass of water. Closing the door, he screamed out loud like a small child. Someone was behind him. He spun round, but there was nothing there. Very shaken, he returned to the bedroom. To his horror, an apparition was sitting on his bed. He recognized this person from an old photograph hanging on the office wall. Once again, he was rooted to the spot. He felt the top of his thigh get very warm and wet; urine was flowing freely down his leg.

By now, he was shaking; the apparition calmly looked at him. The figure was gaunt and grey and he was wearing a sacking cloak. He started to move, but his movement was displaced; his face lifted in the hood. He stood up. Because the sacking cloak took an extra second to catch up, John saw that he was wearing a tattered business suit underneath. "Mmmmister Attkiiinson..." John trembled, his breath now visible. With no apparent movement of his own, Atkinson levitated towards John Smith, right up to him and through him.

At that moment, everything inside Smith started to boil. He was wet through with sweat; everything faded to grey, and he fell, first to his knees, and then flat on his face.

When he regained consciousness, he was in bed, perfectly comfortable, perfectly safe. Looking at the alarm clock in his bedroom, he saw that it was time to get up. He walked naked into the bathroom and had his usual invigorating shower, shaved, brushed his teeth, and looked at his reflection in the mirror. He smiled and looked forward to the day ahead.

Chapter Two

histling, he ran down the stairs of his apartment building; after locking the door, he noticed a peculiar empty brown box in his lidless dustbin. Putting the lid back on, it reminded him of a dream he had had last night. Paying it no mind, he ran for the bus. The bus was a bit late, but he didn't mind — he was deep in conversation with a beautiful young woman at the bus stop. Work was the last thing on his mind. In a few short minutes, he had found out her name — Jenny. She had the deepest blue eyes, and she liked his red shirt and loud tie.

His Jenny distraction made him late for work, but he didn't care; he had a date with her in town that very evening. He arrived at his desk at 8:45 and looked at the other workers, who were all looking in his direction. He recalled his first day all those years earlier with the elderly gentlemen, and for the first time, saw their modern-day counterparts for what they were. "Any of you jerks got a problem?" he asked inquisitively. All heads went South. "Keep it that way," he said. "And a coffee would be nice, see to it, Matthews."

Phillip Matthews was the main message author — he liked to think of himself as being sharp-witted and upwardly mobile. Today, he looked like a small boy about to get his bottom spanked. He quickly made for the coffee machine and brought it straight to John Smith's desk. John took a sip and thought it was just like its maker, *wet and weak*. Today was proving to be quite different to everyone else in the office, but to John Smith it was business as usual as he announced to the workforce, "I'm back!" Braithwaite hung his head, because he knew who was now standing in front of him, but everyone else just fixed their eyes on who they knew as shy John Smith, but with different clothes on.

John Smith's telephone rang. Picking it up, he heard, "Dewhirst here, please step into my office." Picking up his coffee, he strode confidently into the office of Old Man Dewhirst, as he liked to call him. He went in, sat down, and said, "Good morning."

"How do you feel?" inquired the old man.

"I haven't felt this good in years," he replied.

"It's so good to see you again – it's been a long time."

"Twenty-two years, to be exact," he replied. "I've got a date tonight with a beautiful young woman, so I won't be staying very long."

"Not a problem," said Dewhirst. "Your office isn't quite ready yet. Will you be in tomorrow?"

"That rather depends on tonight," he replied, and left.

After leaving the office, he made his way to 'Wednesday's Wardrobe', a clothing shop that sold his kind of clothes. The proprietors looked at him as he arrived.

They were a good-looking, gothic couple; the woman had a purple Mohawk that was long at the back. She wore a corset that shaped her body like an hourglass, enhancing her already ample breasts into breath-taking beauty that this particular customer couldn't take his eyes off of. The other, her husband, he presumed, was more sedate in his apparel – long black hair, black shirt and trousers.

"It's time for a new outfit," said the customer, "Something to impress a lady," he continued. The shop proprietors smiled and came out from behind the counter to help. First, he looked through the shirts; the colour choice was easy – they only had black or white. He chose a pirate shirt in black; it had baggy sleeves with tight cuffs, and was laced up at the neck with a large, frilly collar. The second shirt was the same, only in white. Trousers were next, black of course, with lace criss-crossed up the outside of each leg; they were tight, similar to 1960s drainpipes. The coat he chose was a long, black, leather trench coat. This was magnificent – double-breasted, and fitted to his shape perfectly. It had epaulets, making it appear slightly military; it looked and felt perfect. The outfit was finished off by a size twelve pair of boots with buckled straps up the outside, a metal plate on the calf and a metal toecap. At the back, the heels stood three inches high, with a shiny chrome covering. Looking in the mirror, he saw the magnificent reflection of himself; he liked what he saw. After spending fifty minutes at Wednesday's Wardrobe and ten times that amount in cash, he left the shop and made his way to a café. Sipping his hot, creamy latte, he had a flashback to the previous night. Only it wasn't really a flashback, for he knew exactly what was happening, unlike the luckless John Smith.

As he returned to his apartment, time had moved on. It was now 16:30. He eagerly stripped off his clothes revealing a bronzed, tall, masculine body which was very well-endowed, and he was proud of it. "Welcome back," he said admiringly to his reflection. Stepping into the shower, it was warm and luxurious. His mind drifted to the coming evening...and Jenny.

Thinking of what was in store for him that night as he washed his semi-erect penis, Rod Stewart's 'Tonight's the Night' was going through his mind, and his semi-erection became a full one. It stayed with him all through his shower and took a long time to diminish. Looking in the mirror, he noticed that his hair had started to grow at quite a pace. The metamorphosis had begun. What started as a ghostly figure, a box made of skin and a boring solitary accountant was mutating into Atkinson Junior, and everything that Smith had done over the past 22 years would be wiped from his memory; tomorrow he would be starting anew on his first day at work. This had been the case ever since Atkinson Senior gave his son his own share of the work, but unlike Atkinson and Dewhirst, who could do anything at will, Atkinson Junior's needed this surrogate to exist. As for John Smith...well, John Smith was the last thing on Atkinson Juniors mind as his Administration was soon to take over Dewhirst's.

Dressed in his fine new clothes, it was time to hit the town. As he was early for his date with Jenny, he called into the Snake Pit. The Snake Pit was the absolute opposite of modern wine bars (which he personally hated). It was dark and smelled of stale beer and cigarette smoke. The place had become dirty and uncouth over the twenty-two years he had been away, so after two rounds of absinthe, he made his way to the rendezvous point, where he saw Jenny waiting. She smiled as he drew near. She wore a long velvet coat, and he was trying to imagine the pleasures that lay beneath it. He kissed her hand and strolled with her to one of his favourite bars, The Phono. Descending the stairs, she removed the coat, revealing a long black skirt that offered a glimpse of the shape of her legs when she walked. Her sheer top revealed no undergarment, so that her small breasts were slightly moving up and down with each step. She wasn't thin, but was beautifully curved. To his eye, stick-thin did not necessarily mean beautiful; he knew what beauty was, and he was looking at it. It was a shame he thought to himself that, in a few short hours, she will have slipped her mortal coil.

After paying the man in the booth at the bottom of the stairs, the couple entered the club. This dark venue heaved with the likes of people Jenny had never seen. The small dance floor was full of gyrating bodies...twisting, stomping, and smiling. Jenny gaped in awe, but Atkinson only raised an eyebrow and grinned slyly. A tall, thin figure swaggered over to her and reached out an offering hand, Atkinson immediately knocked it away. Jenny just stared as the beautiful transvestite shrunk away with trepidation and no small amount of fear...Atkinson wasn't about to let a lowly human taint the perfection that he was keeping for himself on this night.

Dancing was definitely not Atkinson's forté, so after a few drinks, he decided that they must move on. Further uptown was a night club called The Wendy House. There, the couple chatted and drank some more and made much merriment. As they were speaking, sitting in a booth, people dressed in their gothic finest looked on, as together they did make a stunning pair. Jenny had never been to this place before; it was a club for the local thriving Gothic community.

Time spun away and soon it was two in the morning, and the club was closing. They were the last to leave, arm-in-arm, just like any other couple. Making their way through town, he noticed a few of the people from the club being heckled by younger revellers. This did not affect him, but he was curious. Leaving Jenny at the taxi queue, he told her he was going to get a pizza. She was quite safely talking to some friends of hers. He crossed the road and went down the alley to the disturbance he had witnessed. It had worsened, and now punches were being thrown at the passive Goths.

"Why not pick on someone your own size?" he said to the seven hoodlums attacking them. Three of them came walking towards him. With speed difficult to detect with mortal eyes, he ran to meet them. Before they knew what was happening, two lay dead on the ground. In his left hand he held the head of one, dripping blood from its neck, and in his right the heart of the other. He turned to the third one, leaned towards his face, opened his mouth, and bit his face clean off. Everyone was completely motionless as he took a bite of the blood-oozing heart; another two mouthfuls and it was gone. His eyes now glowed red, glaring like a rabid dog. He moved to the rest of the party.

Taking two of them by the backs of their heads, he brought them together with so much force that their heads fused with a sickening crunch. Bones, brains, and a fountain of blood and gore spilled into the night, but so fast was his movement that none fell on him. His assailants fell to their knees. Grinning malevolently, he turned to the remaining two. They tried to escape, but as they started running, he was in front of them. He laughed as he lifted one of them off the ground by the eye sockets; he had already removed the orbs, as they are quite a delicacy. This one screamed like a child – only a minute ago he'd been calling all the shots. Atkinson bit his tongue off and swallowed it whole. As that one died, he turned to the last one, who screamed out as he drew near, "Who...what are you?"

This insignificant creature didn't need to know who he was, but as it seemed to heighten his fear, he told him. "I am the absolute opposite of good, the One who stalks your dreams, the very darkness you fear in the night; I ride the fourth pale horse. I am Death, and I will now deliver yours." The man soiled himself. In disgust Atkinson punched both of his hands through his victim's ribcage, and then turning his palms outward, he forced them apart, ripping the body in two. A satisfied smile came to the face of the beast, who stood there as he looked at the carnage about him; adrenaline surged through his veins like rapids in a river. Looking at the two Goths passed out on the ground, he returned to the restaurant to collect his pepperoni pizza with extra mushrooms. He paid the man, who seemed like he was trying to look Italian but clearly wasn't, and returned to the taxi queue.

"What's happened to you?" Jenny inquired. Atkinson, slightly annoyed with himself for his lack of discretion, asked her why. Moistening her fingertip she gently wiped away a smudge of blood from his face.

"I've suffered...a slight nose bleed..." he said, smiling.

"You poor thing," she sympathetically said and gave him a quizzical glance. He placed a reassuring arm around her shoulders and looked forward to the rest of the night.

The taxi ride back to her house was spent in a lover's clinch; it took just ten minutes, but what a ten minutes it was. Her kisses stirred passions in him that quickened his pulse. If the small skirmish he had just enjoyed in the alley made him feel alive, then this positively heightened him to a state of euphoria. There was no cliché of 'Are you coming in for a coffee?' – they got out of the taxi, and he paid the fare and followed her, admiring her cute bottom bobbing from side to side as she confidently strode up the path. Looking back, she asked if he was enjoying looking at her luscious rear.

"Indeed I am," he eagerly replied.

"Perhaps you can have a closer look when we get inside."

Once inside, he gathered her into his arms and pressed his lips upon hers. Their tongues intertwined, exploring each other's mouths. He picked her up into his arms and asked where the bedroom was.

"Stop talking, and let me see some action," she said.

Hmm, I like modern women, he thought as he ripped off her figure-hugging skirt. Her eyes opened wide and she drew a short intake of breath. Her legs were pale and long, and she wore a black thong, which hardly covered her modesty. Small tufts of hair were escaping from the top of her knickers. He put his fingers down the side strings of her thong – one quick pull, and the undergarment was in his hand, and her hairy but well-tended love mound was exposed. This thrilled him greatly, for nothing excited him more than a woman's pubic hair. For a few seconds, he just looked at her standing in the dim lamplight of her living room, half-naked. With no thought of her sheer top, he ripped it off; lust had taken control of him. Now she stood there completely naked, a vision to behold. Many years of want were about to be fulfilled in one short night.

She knelt down before him and unfastened his belt, then unzipped his fly. Tugging quite fiercely at his pants in her eagerness, they came down to the tops of his boots. Sliding his undershorts down until they rested in the same place, she looked up at his very erect penis. Using both of her hands, she began stroking it; gently, she drew back the foreskin at the end of his now-throbbing John Thomas. Her hands only just spanned its girth and now both of them were pulling back and forth in beautiful synchronicity. He could feel the blood surging through the swelling veins in his penis to its tip. Her mouth came tantalizingly close to its bulging head. She drew both hands down once again, taking back the foreskin, and then he felt her tongue lick its underside. Shivers went all the way through his body, and as he languished in that serenity, she slipped it into her delicate mouth and began to gently suck. She only managed the first seven inches of it, but he didn't mind, for he knew the rest of it would soon be coming into play, whether she could take it all or not.

For the next several minutes she sucked, stroked, licked and lavished all kinds of unexplainable delights upon his now huge, throbbing prick. While she busied herself on clearly the biggest cock she had ever seen, he unbuttoned his shirt, took it off, and laid it upon the floor. He now stood there, naked apart from the jumble of trousers, underpants, socks, and boots about his ankles. Withdrawing from Jenny's soft mouth, he set about removing them. Now they were both truly naked. He kissed her shoulders and then her neck; her back arched as he slid his tongue across the top of her shoulder to her nape. Moving up her long neck, kissing as he slid upwards, he came to her ear.

Her ear was tiny. He nibbled at it and she began to tremble. His hand moved onto her breasts; her nipples were large and very hard. He had never seen human nipples that stood to attention as these did, they must have been a good half-inch proud of her succulent breasts. His mouth had now discovered this phenomenon that was her erect nipple. Taking her right breast in his left hand, he suckled on her left nipple; she winced as he bit a little too hard on that firm, ample delight. Again, he lifted her off her feet and laid her on the Wilton-patterned carpet. She smiled as he parted her legs. There it was – his prize, her vagina. Placing her legs astride his broad shoulders, he moved his mouth to her glistening, welcoming pink pussy.

First, he licked the very tip of her clitoris, and then moved downwards to her open, waiting honey pot. With his eager tongue, he ravaged this delicate area to great moans of delight from Jenny. Within a few short minutes, her moans were screams of pleasure, his tongue now industrious around her clit. When his probing digits entered her most delicate area, she screamed out loud as his fingers explored the depths of her womanhood.

Her body now writhed in untold pleasure, the like of which she had never experienced, her nails scratching and clawing at his skin. "No more…" she whimpered, "No more…" but he was already moving his body into position. He lined his very long, hard cock to the mouth of her vagina; she gasped as he slotted its head into her hole. Her eyes widened, first in anticipation, then in pain, as he pushed more and more of it into her ever-widening pussy. He withdrew a little, then surged forward again, and again, and again. Now, he almost had the full ten inches of his penis inside her. She screamed in agony as he lunged deep into her over and over again.

He could hear his heart beating as his strokes got faster and faster, and deeper and deeper. Sweat now began to pour from him as her screams became less noisy; her hands had let go of him and were just lying limp on the carpet. He surged ever onward, thrusting his huge erection again and again into her now-bleeding pussy. The sight of blood just made him thrust harder; her screams had now stopped. He ejaculated with a deep, penetrating thrust and a howl of fulfilment. His hot, sticky sperm rushed from the end of his cock with the rage of a volcano; he felt it fill her cavity and make its way back down the side of his still-thrusting phallus until it came to rest on his testicles. The intensity of the moment passed. He withdrew and laid on his back in the classic 'How was it for you?' position and caught his breath.

He looked at Jenny. She was motionless, her eyes fixed. He shook her shoulder, but there was no response. He turned her face towards his to reveal a lifeless expression. He got to his knees and looked at her properly, and yes, she was lifeless. *Damn mortals, can't even fuck,* he thought. He stood up and gathered together his clothes, got dressed, and looked at her lifeless naked body, just lying there. Then he sat down and enjoyed his pepperoni pizza with extra mushrooms.

Chapter Three

The following morning, Atkinson Junior looked over the rim of his coffee cup at the headlines in the morning paper. 'Carnage in the City' was the lead front-page story. The police seemed to think a wild animal was on the loose; this could not be confirmed until two young people, who were found unconscious at the scene, could be interviewed. After another slurp of coffee, he thought, *maybe I should not have left witnesses; I must have slept too long and I'm growing sloppy in My old age.* Putting this to the back of his mind, as nobody would believe the story that the two witnesses would tell, he left for the office.

On his arrival, he noticed Mr. Braithwaite was looking older than ever as he bid him good morning. "Sad news about Mr. Dewhirst's passing last night."

"Yes, it was all quite sudden," Atkinson said. "He will be missed."

It had been a long time since he had seen his clerks – he wished them all good morning. Observing the timid-looking new man sitting at his desk, he asked him his name. "Smith," was the nervous reply.

"Yes, that's right, John Smith. Work well and you will have a long future at Atkinson, Atkinson & Dewhirst. With this in mind, the next three days are going to be hectic, and I will need you here with me, so you will sleep upstairs in the Apartment above this office and not go home – is that understood?" With a smile on Atkinson's face, he said, "Braithwaite, give him the new account". The old gentleman nodded. Atkinson then strode confidently into his refurbished office. Although still confused, this was the best thing that had happened to John Smith all day, because for the life of him, he couldn't remember were home actually was.

Sitting at the secretary's desk was a familiar old friend; Tamara had been with him as far back as he could remember. With her long blonde hair and legs to match, and a smile as devilishly naughty as if he was seeing her for the first time, Tamara was not just a secretary, she was the Listmaker...and she loved her job.

"Good morning, my dear," he said with a grin. She leapt from her chair, wrapped her arms around him, and planted a loving kiss on his lips. Her perfume was intoxicating as it hung in the air. Their clinch lasted a couple of minutes as he re-familiarised himself with her firm, tight bottom with his eager hands.

"I think the day should start with a coffee. Do you remember how I like it?" he asked.

"Strong, milky and sweet," she replied.

It was definitely good to be back, he thought.

Atkinson Junior was now fully awake, his senses sharp, and he was ready for work. Out of the Unholy Trinity, he was by far the worst, which meant he was the best. He loved his work with a passion, and did it well. He took great delight in delivering death, whereas his father and his father's original business partner Dewhirst just did the job. It was time to clock in.

After his coffee, he asked Tamara for his first list.

"Here it is, Mr. Atkinson."

"Thank you, my dear," he said.

He perused his first list.

"It's dated for three days hence, to give you time to adjust," explained Tamara.

This is how the list works – if a name is on his list, that person is destined for his domain, and he would pay them a call.

It takes place in his eternal night-time, which is the target's last day on Earth. This gives him time to visit everybody, a bit like Father Christmas on Christmas Eve. Of course, the present he delivers isn't as nice.

The countdown to the end of the 20th century was now into its final stages. Some people were organizing millennium parties; Prince and Robbie Williams were battling for the number one song with '1999' and 'Millennium', respectively. A number of people were predicting the world's computers would crash at midnight...and of course, there was the usual 'Woe is me' crowd, believing the end was nigh. As for young John Smith, groundhog twenty-five-year day was starting all over again with his first day at Atkinson, Atkinson & Dewhirst, and he looked very confused as he was escorted to his desk. Atkinson Junior understood his confusion, because in a few days' time, he would enter Smith's body and use it on the plane of existence, so Smith would have to get used to that feeling.

During Atkinson Junior's Administration, Smith would be a lot busier than he was during Dewhirst's. He called Smith into his office and explained his way of doing business; Smith would be in charge of a special account, which only he would work on.
This would keep him busy until Dewhirst was ready. Old Dewhirst always took the full twenty-five years back at the main office with Atkinson Junior's father. They had been together for many millennia, so he milked the time he had off; Atkinson Junior, of course, didn't mind – he loved his job.

Atkinson's first list was long. The edges of his mouth turned upward into a small grin as his perusal continued. It was annoying to him that he had to wait so long, but he understood what she meant. "I will enter the domain to acclimatize myself," he said, slightly dejected. He put the list down on the desk, bid good evening to Tamara, and opened the old door behind it; with a familiar creak, it widened slowly into the shrouded, cold arena of death, where he was the only gladiator and victims awaited their end. This was that scary night-time between here and there...that dark place at the back of your mind that you hope doesn't exist. But it does.

Lawyers, priests, judges, doctors, politicians, rich or poor — there is no discrimination, they will be dispatched with callous eagerness. He walks amongst the population, and will scratch each name off his list with his long fingernails, then a victim's journey to the golden staircase or the fiery depths begins, and he will move on to his next. One by one, he will scratch names off of his list as he trolls the depths of despair. That gripping feeling as a human clutches his or her chest and falls to their knees is Atkinson's long, skinless fingers squeezing the heart until it bursts. 'War, pestilence, and famine — your storybooks describe these as my brothers, but they all reside in me and are at my disposal'. It would be a 'revelation' to call him the Grim Reaper. Call him what one will, but one will feel his icy cold breath on the back of one's neck. This is how story books describe the reaper, the truth however is somewhat different.

Atkinson enjoyed his first night back, and was very eager to start work properly. He emerged from the Realm of Death through the old door behind his desk and looked at the clock on the wall; it was only ten o'clock. This brought another smile to his contented face.

On leaving the office, he checked his reflection in the mirrored chrome work of a parked car. He was as well-groomed as ever, and ready to go clubbing. He called Tamara on her cell phone and arranged to meet her.

Tamara put her phone down and continued to dry herself, as his phone call had persuaded her out of the shower. She looked at her naked body in the mirror and liked what she saw. Her hair was hanging down, dripping wet and straight. Her pert breasts, with nipples that had gone hard during her conversation, were pointing straight outward. Her eyes continued downwards, looking at her fluffy hair making a perfect 'v'. She felt a tingle inside her vagina, and unusually an arousal that only males have. Her thoughts drifted to when she would return to her house with her long-time lover. She knew she was the only one who could truly satisfy him. Tonight was the first time in nearly a quarter of a century that she would feel his intense love deep inside her.

After drying herself, she went to the dressing table and started to apply her makeup. She was of pale complexion, and highlighted this by adding a touch of ivory foundation to her cheekbones and forehead. Dark lashes and eyeliner were her favourite, with very dark red-to-purple lids; the last and finishing touch was very deep red lipstick. After drying her hair, she picked out her underwear – first a pair of small, lace, black thong knickers. She watched herself slowly pull them gracefully past her knees and all the way up until they fitted effortlessly just over her mound of tight little curls and slotted into position on her bum.

Her knickers now perfectly placed, she took a lace suspender belt from her drawer. Black in colour, she placed it around her waist. The fastener was at the back, so she had it on back to front so she could fasten it. When the fastener was secured, she twisted it one hundred and eighty degrees until the four hanging straps were centralised down the front and back of each leg and the fastener was aligned with the very elegant line of her bum.

Taking a pair of seamed black stockings as fine as gossamer, she gently ran her fingers through both of them, checking for imperfections. When she was completely satisfied that they were flawless, she rolled one to its toe and very precisely placed her delicate foot in the very tip of the stocking. Unravelling the stocking, she gracefully pulled it first over her heel and then her calf, then over her knee and all the way to just past her mid-thigh.

Using the very tip of her right index finger, she shaped the seam of the stocking into a perfectly straight line from her ankle to the very top. Very gently, she put the rubber bottom of her suspender clip behind the front of the lace top, and then snapped the metal clip over it; she twisted her upper body around to do the same manoeuvre on the back of her stocking. After repeating the same operation to her other leg, she checked once again in the mirror at her now semi-naked body, and smiled with approval.

Having no need of a bra due to the small pertness of her breasts, she took a perfume atomiser from the dressing table. Sending three blasts of it into the air just in front of her, she walked through it and adorned herself with Chanel Number Five, a perfume she had used since its introduction earlier that century.

Last, but by no means least, she took out tonight's gown of choice. A long black dress of velvet and lace, it was hand-sewn in Victorian times by a large-busted, frumpy lady who spoke very little and boasted that she made a gown for Queen Victoria herself when she was a princess. The quality of this dress certainly stood up to the seamstress' boast. It had a high lace collar that fastened with three small black pearl buttons. The bodice was lace – very daring for the time it was made, but there were no other women like Tamara in those days. The sleeves, fashioned from velvet, puffed out at the top and were skin tight as they came down to the wrist. Fastened with six black pearl buttons, the bodice was shaped to Tamara's figure. The skirt of the dress fishtailed at the bottom, but slinked around her bum and legs. Once again, black velvet with an overlay of fine lace finished the dress off.

Tamara stepped into a pair of small, ankle-length, black side-button boots with lace around the top to soften their image. Looking at the finished result in the mirror, she smiled at the beautiful creature looking back at her. Picking up a black shawl and throwing around her shoulders, she took hold of her purse from the dresser and placed it under her arm, left the house, and stepped into the waiting taxi cab.

As she opened the door, the waft of expensive perfume preceded her. Her beauty took the breath of the unshaven taxi driver, who was having a bad day due to no fares, runners, and drunks – bad day that was, until this vision of a Goddess entered his taxi. All the day's trials and tribulations melted away into his rear view mirror. Who was she? He had worked this patch for years, but had never picked up this sophisticated lady. His passion was aroused; Tamara was well aware what he was thinking, so she leant forward a little, revealing part of her breasts. The driver could not believe what was happening to him; he pulled over and stopped the car.

"Why have you stopped?" enquired Tamara with a grin.

"You want a bit of rough," the taxi driver replied.

"Do you think you are man enough for me?" asked Tamara.

"I will show you," said the driver. As he exited through the driver's door and entered the back, putting his hand on Tamara's right breast, he began to breathe faster, almost panting. He got no response, so he let his hand wander down the front of her Victorian dress to her crotch. This turned out to be not as much fun as she thought it would be, so she asked him to stop. He kept on trying to pull her dress up.

"I asked you nicely to stop, now I'm telling you – if you don't stop, I will rip your fucking head off, darling."

Amused by this, the two-hundred-fifty pound part-time body builder said, with a laugh in his voice, "Be my guest."

"Fine," said Tamara in a much gentler voice. With her left hand, she grasped the back of his head, and with her right hand, she grabbed the front of his face, carefully placing a finger in both of his now-startled eyes, and simply ripped it off. She did this at such speed that his blood did not spoil her make-up or clothes. She vacated the taxi, straightened her dress, and continued the last quarter of a mile on foot.

She walked serenely towards Atkinson, who was waiting at the entrance to the club. With the corner of a silk handkerchief, he wiped a spot of blood from her otherwise blemish less face and enquired after the incriminating little spot. "Some poor man lost his head over me," she answered with a grin. Atkinson raised an eyebrow, smirked, and escorted his lady inside the club.

JOHN PAUL BERNETT

Chapter Four

The club was heaving with all kinds of alternative people. The very elegant couple entered the main dance room, their presence making everybody take notice of their arrival. The man looked to be in his mid-forties, the woman in her mid-thirties. They made their way to the bar and ordered two double absinthes, picked up their drinks, turned, and surveyed their prey.

The couple split. Tamara made her way to the dance floor, while Atkinson sat near a group of young women. As he sat, two of the girls were clearly interested in the elegant figure that was sitting near them. One girl, who looked about nineteen years old, smiled quite sweetly at him – while the other, more forthright, scooted over and sat opposite him. In a voice more befitting the fish docks rather than an upmarket club, she enquired, "You buying me a drink, then?"

"I may do…" said Atkinson, "If you give me the name of your friend over there," he continued.

Tamara was dancing with a rather girlishly-handsome boy and two delightful girls; all three were totally besotted with her.

"Let me introduce you to my friend," she said to her three followers. Willingly, they came to the table where he was sitting with the two girls. Everyone smiled at each other as the introductions took place. Atkinson ordered seven more drinks. The usual chit-chat occurred, like…'Do you come here often?' and 'I haven't seen you here before…'yes, all the things that get you by those first embarrassing five minutes. As a group, they all got on well; some of the conversation was stimulating, some was funny. One of the topics, however, was that one of the girls' two friends 'witnessed a murder the other night.' They did not have to delve too deeply into this before Atkinson changed the subject, once again wishing he had not left witnesses.

The night was getting on. Atkinson glanced over at Tamara, and then at the rest of their newfound friends, and knew that at least two of these people would not be alive in a few hours' time. Tamara caught Atkinson's eye and grinned; she stood up and announced, "We're having a party back at our place and you're all invited."

Quickly, everyone gathered their coats, cloaks, and hats and followed Atkinson out of the club like he was the pied piper taking them from Hamlin town.

The journey from the club to the nearby taxi queue evoked the usual Neanderthal taunts from the city sheep…'Morticia! Ozzy! Goths!' They had no idea why they shouted these things, it was just something that insecure young people felt they had to do. As always, this caused amusement to the bystanders waiting in the taxi queue, but as ever, they did not really know what they were laughing at. The Goths did what they always do – pity the fools and laugh at them (inwardly, of course).

As Atkinson and his entourage climbed the stairs to 3 Lindale Mews, Chief Inspector Jack Thompson was burning the midnight oil at police HQ. He had received the autopsy reports from the coroner earlier that day and it made very disturbing reading. Somewhere in his jurisdiction was a psychopath, ripping people's heads off – and if the autopsy report was right, he was doing it with his bare hands. This was the worst crime that had happened there for nearly twenty-five years, and he placed every available officer on the case. The two people found on the scene either could not, or would not, say what they had seen. One thing was clear, though, and that was they did not possess the strength to have committed the crime. Chief Inspector Thompson had made it quite clear to everybody working on the case that he wanted it sewn up quickly before the papers blew it totally out of proportion, if that was indeed possible.

Jeff Clarke was one of the reporters standing downstairs at the police station's front desk; he, along with thirty other reporters from all over the country, was waiting for the first statement to be made by the police. They had indeed been waiting there since mid-day and there was still no statement. Detective Inspector Paul Johnson relayed a message to the chief from the front desk that if he did not come up with something soon, they were going to print the head-wrenching maniac story, which the police definitely did not want. So reluctantly, Chief Inspector Jack Thompson put on his tweed jacket, fastened up his tie, and walked down the twenty-four steps that led to the ground floor and the waiting media.

Chief Inspector Thompson and Detective Inspector Johnson entered the lion's den. The first question came before they could sit down. "Do we have a copycat killer?" asked veteran newsman, Sidney Jones. The room hushed; everyone looked at Sidney, who had a worried look on his face, then everyone waited for the police response. D.I. Johnson looked puzzled, but Chief Inspector Thompson, who had been on the beat when Sidney Jones first started at the Herald, clearly was disturbed by the question. He knew exactly what was being referred to. The normally flamboyant Chief Inspector was looking troubled, as he tried in vain to stop his necktie from strangling him.

"There is…no evidence…to support that particular question," he stuttered.

D.I. Johnson looked at his superior as lawyers would when they find out their clients haven't told them everything. Jeff Clarke listened and watched the Chief Inspector and the most respected newspaper man looking at each other, and knew there and then that he must find out more.

Three miles down the road, Atkinson led his friends into his lair, unaware of what was happening at the police station, unaware also that certain people were still around who knew him when he was last here. These people were due to die before he returned, but he did not wait the full 25 years back in his father's domain which was the full term, he was early – three years early, to be exact.

At the party, the drink flowed and laughter rang out. Anna and Julie had started undressing each other, much to the pleasure of Tamara, who had already helped her lady boy, Peter, out of most of his clothes. When undressed fully, he was quite a large young man, and Tamara made him larger and harder. Angela and Zoe were working on Atkinson, taking off his shirt and scratching at his chest. The more common of the two girls – Angela – undid his trousers, pulled them down, and drew down his undershorts, revealing his semi-hard penis. She gasped when she saw the size of his manhood. Peter also looked on with a gleam in his eye. Tamara kissed her little boy and asked if he wanted to go to where they were; he nodded excitedly and joined the now completely naked threesome. Tamara went to Anna and Julie, who were also naked. "May I join in?" she enquired. Both girls smiled invitingly and began to undress her slowly.

Angela caressed Atkinson's large erect cock while Zoe offered her moist pussy to his mouth. Peter was playing with himself while watching, but Atkinson was watching Tamara and her two lovelies exploring each other. By now, Anna was pulling down Tamara's knickers and licking at her clit; Julie sucked her nipple, which was very erect. Atkinson placed his ever-hardening penis at the mouth of Angela's vagina. It went in slowly, Angela's face showing the strain. He kept on driving forward. Angela screamed with delight and pain. Peter was now being fondled by Zoe. he was very erect and was enjoying what Zoe was doing, but he was concentrating on the largest penis he had ever seen. He could not believe his luck! He couldn't help but wonder if this naked man in front of him was bi, and if he was, did he dare ask?

Zoe slowly opened her legs, revealing her glistening pussy to Peter. At last, Peter took his eyes off Atkinson and placed his inferior, but still large, penis into Zoe's waiting vagina.

Angela's last scream echoed around the house as Atkinson thrust the last cock she would ever feel inside her torn pussy. She slipped her mortal coil, and slumped in a heap on the ground. Thinking she had merely passed out, Peter kept making love to Zoe. Tamara took her two girls by the hand and led them to the bedroom. After the bedroom door closed, Atkinson turned to Peter and Zoe. Peter withdrew his hard cock from Zoe and excitedly said, "Take me next," as he tried to fondle Atkinson's still-firm cock.

Atkinson's eyes changed to a piercing stare; his talons curved out of the ends of his fingers.

"It will be my pleasure," said Atkinson, and like an animal, he grasped the back of Peter's head. With a snarl, he sunk his teeth deep into Peter's throat, ripping out the petrified boy's oesophagus and spitting it on the ground. "In answer to your question, Peter – no, I am not bisexual."

The boy fell to the ground into a pool of his own blood. Atkinson looked at Zoe, who was now trembling, huddled up in a corner.

"Take my hand," said Atkinson. Zoe was too scared to do anything, her trembling had worsened.

"Be a good little girl, and you might survive this night," he added.

She took his hand in the knowledge he would kill her there and then if she didn't comply. Atkinson led her to the bedroom, where Tamara's little party was waiting for them, and after Tamara worked her own kind of magic on Zoe, party they did.

At the police station, the front door opened and members of the press spilled out, most of them still blissfully unaware of what was going on. Most of the police inside were in the same state of ignorance. As Chief Inspector Thompson made his way back to the solitude and safety of his office, like a prize fighter making his way back to the locker room after a bruising bout, D.I. Johnson pulled on his arm. "Copycat killing?" he said.

"You had better step into my office – what that confused old man had to say has nothing to do with this case." said the Chief Inspector

"Why did he call it a copycat killing, then?" asked Johnson.

"Slight similarities, that's all," said Thompson, with his voice raised.

Johnson's voice, now also raised, said, "What similarities?"

"Who do you think you are, questioning me like this? Don't you think I'm under enough stress?" shouted Chief Inspector Thompson.

"This is nothing compared to what it will be like after the press print their angle of what's happening."

"It's not the same man as before. He wouldn't wait for over twenty years and then start up again. I refuse to believe it," panted the chief, now sweating profusely and clutching his chest.

"Sit down and put one of your pills under your tongue," said Johnson in a more comforting voice. "Calm down. You know what your doctor said. Just tell me what happened. It will be easy for me to dig out the records."

The Chief inspector sat back in his swivel chair, which had long since lost its ability to swivel. Opening the third drawer down, he said, "You won't find it in the record cabinet. I keep it here."

"Why?" asked a puzzled D.I. Johnson.

"Read it and see. I'm going home to get my head down. I need to think. I have to get out of here."

D.I. Johnson opened the file and began to read, and within a few short pages, he could see what was meant by 'copycat killer'.

He thought about paying a visit to the newspaper the next morning, not knowing that when the morning came, he would have much more pressing business to deal with. The D.I. glanced over the document. As he looked out of the window at the newsmen leaving, he concentrated on one in particular.

As the Chief Inspector left the police station, it was raining and all the newsmen had driven off in their respective vehicles. All, that is, except one very old newsman, and one young gun following him. The two old men looked at each other. "It's not the same man, Sid," said Thompson.

"I think it is, Jack," said the reporter.

With that, the chief gave him an acknowledging smile and said, "Can I give you a lift?"

"No, thanks, I need the fresh air," the old reporter replied. Chief Inspector Thompson drove out of the now-empty parking lot, turned right, and made his way up Park Road and the short journey home.

Sidney Jones turned left from the police station and walked down Park Road, realising he was being followed he stopped at the Happy Cuppa, an all-night café. He ordered a cup of tea and an egg sandwich; he preferred his egg boiled, not fried. Sitting down he stared out of the window, and saw the reflection of an old man looking back at him. He wondered where all the years had gone, reflecting on never getting the 'big story' that would have elevated him to the broadsheets. He was brought out of this dreamy state by a young man putting his egg sandwich on the table and asking if he could join him.

"It's still a free country," Sid grimaced. "Sit if you must."

"Hello, my name is..."

"I know what your name is," said the old man. "Do you know who I am, boy?" the old man enquired. "I thought not. So, you're the newsman of tomorrow?" said Jones slowly, shaking his head.

"I'm sorry that I don't know your name. Please forgive me for that, but I am interested in what you had to say in the police station," stuttered Jeff Clarke. "I was only sent there to observe what goes on at a police press conference, but I'm more interested in what wasn't said there – and you seem to know more than anybody, apart from the rather ill-looking Chief of Police."

Jones looked at the young man over the rim of his chipped tea cup, and remembered a time when he had that same fire in his belly. He smiled, revealing teeth that had needed the attention of a dentist long before the young man was born.

"If you really want to know, come and see me at my newspaper tomorrow. And, incidentally, it's the same one that you work for. Just ask for Sid."

Atkinson looked out of the bedroom window at the sunrise, then turned and looked at the staggering beauty of the four naked girls on the bed, and then at the devastation in the living room where the bodies of two lovely young people lay. He wasn't particularly bothered, as he knew he would soon be changing into his work mode. Once in that state, he was untouchable and untraceable.

Tamara wafted over to him and asked, "How long do I have you this time?"

Atkinson smiled. "Two more days, and then my Administration begins. I am longing to start."

"Two more days? That's a long time for you to stay in human form – will you be all right?"

Again, Atkinson grinned. "There are a few people that are here who shouldn't be, but they have no idea I'm back, so they won't be a threat to me."

Tamara looked concerned. "Be careful, my love, for while you are like this, you are vulnerable."

"My sweet one, you worry too much." Atkinson placed a kiss on her cheek.

The tender moment was shattered by the wailing of a police siren outside of the building.

The police were answering a call that had come in during the night about a domestic argument, and noise coming from the flat upstairs, but the wrong address had been given. Only because the woman who called rang back to see why nobody had come, did they manage to get the right address. Atkinson knew that he and Tamara could not be caught, nor could they leave witnesses – so, albeit reluctantly, Tamara went back with Atkinson and helped snap the necks of the three young girls lying there.

As the two police officers came up the steps, Atkinson and Tamara exited down the rickety fire escape, and left the scene, never to return to Lindale Mews.

When the police could not gain entry, they broke down the door; all their training could not prepare them for what they saw. By the time full daylight arrived, Lindale Mews had been cordoned off as a crime scene. The chief and his second in command started work very early.

The coroner's team arrived; the usual two guys known to everyone but themselves as Burke and Hare got out of their black van with the word 'Coroner' on the side. They had with them the customary black body bag.

"You are going to need a few more of them," informed D.I. Johnson.

"Don't worry, Detective Inspector. We have a van-full, the more the merrier," the taller of the two pathology department men said.

These are strange guys, thought D.I. Johnson, and he made his way back to his Chief Inspector. The S.O.C.O also arrived in force. Chief Inspector Thompson had made it very clear to everybody that nothing was to be touched until the coroner arrived.

A vintage Jaguar pulled up behind Burke and Hare's van, and out stepped a very confident-looking young man.

"Who the hell is this?" Thompson snarled to Johnson.

"Did you not read the memo from the coroner's office last week?" Johnson replied.

The Chief Inspector, not listening to his younger counterpart, marched over to where Gavin Jackson stood at the side of his gleaming Jaguar. "Can't you see this is a police incident area and members of the public are not allowed in it?" said the Chief Inspector, with a measure of self-importance in his voice.

Gavin Jackson slowly removed his sunglasses and calmly enquired, "You were expecting the now-retired Dr. James Grayson, I presume?" said the new coroner, with a measure of superiority in his voice.

"The worst murders in years, and they send me a kid..." said a now old-feeling police chief.

"I think it should be up to me to define if there has or has not been a murder, Chief Inspector. Perhaps you could show me the bodies. I trust they haven't been touched," said the young coroner, having won his first stand-off with the old school that he was expecting.

"Everything is how we found it. Just let my D.I. know when you're done, so he can report your findings to me," shouted Thompson as he walked towards his car. The new coroner made his way up the steps of 3 Lindale Mews, and to his eighth suspicious death since he replaced his predecessor the previous week.

"Good morning, Sid," greeted the door commissionaire at the Daily Herald building. "You haven't been in this early for years. Got yourself a good story, have you?" he continued.

The old man barely noticed the immaculate uniformed ex-soldier greeting him. He scurried past, with folders and papers under both of his arms. When he got to his office, he saw young Jeff Clarke already there.

"Good morning, Mr. Jones," enthused Jeff Clarke.

"Sid! I told you to call me Sid," the older man said excitedly. They made their way into his old-fashioned office; he threw his papers and files on the already-cluttered desk, unleashing a large dust cloud around the two men.

"The place could maybe do with an odd dusting here and there," smirked Sid.

Young Jeff acknowledged with a cough.

"Go and get us both a cup of tea, and we will begin."

Jeff Clarke ran out of the office and down the staircase to the canteen, where he ordered the two beverages and talked to Cindy, the canteen assistant.

"You're in a hurry this morning, Jeff," Cindy said.

"I'm on a big story!" Jeff boasted.

"Don't let me get in the way of your scoop," smiled Cindy. As he turned to go, she said, "Don't forget our date tonight!"

"I will be there," came the faint reply from halfway down the hall.

Donald Steele, the paper's editor, was listening from his table in the canteen; he had escaped from his office and was having a quick coffee before going back to the daily shouting match with everyone. He didn't know why he shouted all the time, it just felt good, and let everyone know he was the boss. He strolled over to Cindy and said, "He's a smart kid. What scoop is he on?"

Cindy just shrugged her shoulders and said, "Don't know."

"Good vocabulary you got there, girl. Ever thought of being a reporter?" he snapped sarcastically and made his way out, shouting at one of the secretaries who was in his way.

Jeff arrived back at Sid's office, and the old man began to show him all the evidence he had to promote his theory that a murderer had returned to this neck of the woods, or that a copycat had taken his place. Jeff started reading, with excitement in his eyes.

Back at 3 Lindale Mews, Burke and Hare had now been joined by Gavin Jackson. He quickly looked around the room where most of the devastation was, and then knelt down beside the first body. He took a small Dictaphone from his pocket and began describing the young man's horrific injuries; he then moved to the girl by his side and noticed that the only apparent injuries were vaginal.

He noted that whatever had caused her injuries was not consistent with anything the boy had about his anatomy. It was almost as if the boy had been attacked and the girl raped by a large bear; he, of course, did not utter this into his Dictaphone. Moving into the bedroom, he saw the three young girls laid to waste. After examining them, he reported to his faithful little tape machine that all three had sustained broken necks, and that there were two assailants. Two of the girls' necks were snapped by someone or something much stronger than the other one. The coroner, on his first case alone since he took up the post, passed the message to D.I. Johnson that he had all he needed for now and he would have the report as soon as he had finished the autopsies.

Paul Johnson said, "I have never seen anything like what has been going on over the last day or two – that is, until last night."

"How so?" asked Gavin Jackson.

"I was reading about a case last night, and the incidents from the last two days have remarkable similarities to a case twenty-two years ago."

"I would like to hear about that when I'm done with these guys, please tell the Chief Inspector I will have a full report on his desk by tomorrow morning." With that, Gavin Jackson put his sunglasses back on, got into his Jaguar, and drove back to his pathology lab. Burke and Hare started loading the corpses into their van, and the D.I. went back to the police station to report to his Chief Inspector.

By the time two o'clock in the afternoon rolled around, several conferences were underway. Chief Inspector Thompson and D.I. Johnson had set up an incident room, and all their available police officers were in attendance. Donald Steele was shouting out headlines to Sidney Jones and Jeff Clarke, and Gavin Jackson was reading through a mountain of paperwork at the home of his predecessor, James Grayson. Atkinson, however, was at the offices of Atkinson, Atkinson & Dewhirst, talking to Tamara about a possible new residence they might go look at, when he was returned to a different plane of existence.

"Why am I back here, father?" Atkinson Junior snarled.

"Why do you think?" retorted Atkinson Senior, the most powerful entity in existence. "You left here too early, and there is unfinished business from your last visit there. It must be put right before your Administration starts. If you are shown to the world to be who you are, the results would be catastrophic. Now go, remove anyone in your path, and stop drawing attention to yourself! Dewhirst grows weak – soon, all of existence will be ours and ours alone. Remove those who need removing, and leave the rest to their pointless existence."

The grand cave-like dwelling of his father changed back to his office, and in that office stood a worried-looking Tamara.

"I feared the worst. What did he say?" said Tamara, with trepidation in her voice.

"We have a slight problem – there are people here who could know of my existence, this obviously must be put right. We must find them before they find me," said Atkinson, not knowing who they were.

Back at the pathology lab, the day crew had finished their shift. The graveyard shift was in attendance when Gavin Jackson got back from his afternoon visit with Dr. James Grayson.

"Good evening, boys and girls," said Gavin to Tom Harper and Sarah Louise Mitchell, the mortician and assistant, respectively. Tom greeted him in return, but Sarah just gave him a little smile, even though smiling didn't seem to come easy to the heavily-pierced and tattooed mortuary assistant. Tom was a twenty-eight year-old university graduate, clean cut, and didn't say boo to a goose, but Sarah was a spitfire. The only thing she loved more than her job was telling people about its gory details over a beer, or better yet, a meal.

In the week that Gavin had known Sarah, he had found her to be quite funny and charming, as well as being the strangest girl he had ever seen in his life. He was attracted to her in some strange way. Not in a 'Let's go to the country home and meet Mummy and Daddy way', but there was an attraction.

Gavin asked Tom if he could hold the fort for a couple of hours while he and Sarah went out to collect more evidence from the crime scene. "No problem! She's having one of her gore attacks on me, and it will give me time to get some work done," he said jokingly.

Sarah ran to her locker, took off her white coat, and replaced it with her fluffy bunny coat and spiked dog collar and ran out of the door.

"Does she always get this exited?" asked Gavin, with a smile on his face.

"She is the most excitable young thing I have ever known, but she really is a good assistant," was Tom's reply.

Gavin left and joined Sarah at his car.

"I love crime scenes!" enthused Sarah.

"We're not exactly going to the crime scene. If you don't mind, we're going for something to eat. I haven't eaten all day and I am starving, and I hate dining alone."

"Wow! You're taking me out to dinner! Nobody takes me out for dinner...come to think of it, nobody takes me out," exclaimed a very excited Sarah.

"I take it you have no objection, then," enquired the now-happy coroner. "I know a nice little public house that serves wonderful meals, we shall go there."

"Cool as fuck!" said Sarah, instantly blushing when she realised she had just swore in front of her rather posh boss.

Gavin just laughed, saying, "What a wonderfully uncomplicated girl you are." The Jaguar pulled into the car park of the Unicorn public house, and the couple made their way indoors.

Inside the Unicorn, a young couple was sitting at one of the tables, holding hands. Obviously two people in love, thought Gavin Jackson, when he and his dinner date sat at the table next to them. "One thing, Sarah..." said Gavin, "no talk of body parts during the meal."

Sarah just laughed. Gavin ordered the house white and Sarah asked for a pint of cider. "I think a glass of wine would be better, considering we have a lot of work to do on our return."

Sarah shrugged her shoulders and said, "Ok, then."

Gavin ordered a steak with side salad, and Sarah ordered a cheeseburger and chips with loads of tomato sauce. Gavin smiled once again.

During the meal, Gavin could not help overhearing parts of the conversation from the next table. "It's a beast of some kind, and it's come back to kill again...well, Sid is writing about it in tomorrow's paper," said the young man excitedly. "I'm helping to get more evidence with him. Sid has said he has more information than the police have, but they refuse to listen, so this time, he is going public."

The young woman asked, "What did the editor say?"

"He just started shouting about making sure we had our facts straight before printing it, and just because I was involved, it didn't mean I would get any more pay than I was already getting."

This worried the coroner; he wanted to know what the papers thought they knew. He introduced himself to the young man and said, "We both appear to be working on the same case. What's your name?"

"Jeff Clarke – and this is my girlfriend, Cindy."

"I am very pleased to meet you. I am the new coroner, and this is Sarah, my dinner guest. What paper do you work for, if you don't mind me asking?"

"The Daily Herald," said Jeff Clarke, with pride in his voice. "Perhaps you would be good enough to show me. I would certainly be interested in the information you might have," asked Gavin.

With that, Gavin and Sarah, complete with tomato sauce on her top lip, said goodbye and made their way first to the bar to pay the bill, and then out to the car. Once in the car, Sarah said, "That was great! Now let's go cut up some corpses!" Again, all Gavin could do was smile.

JOHN PAUL BERNETT

Chapter Five

The next day, Donald Steele shouted for Sidney Jones and Jeff Clarke to get into his office; anybody else would have used the internal phone. He wanted to know why the coroner's office had asked him not to print this morning's headline.

"Have you not printed it, sir?" Jeff asked meekly.

"Are you insane, boy?" shrieked the overheating editor. "If they want it stopped, we must be onto something! Now get out there and bring me more!"

On leaving the office, both men were suffering mild tinnitus, Sid wondered how the coroner's office had got on to their story so fast. The red-faced young reporter owned up to talking about the story in the pub the previous night, while he was trying to impress Cindy.

"It's a good job you didn't confess that little gem a couple of minutes before, the response would have measured on the Richter Scale," said the older reporter.

Sid went to his office and Jeff went to the canteen for two cups of tea and a boiled egg sandwich for Sid.

"Last night was great!" said Cindy.

"I know, but it nearly cost me my job," said Jeff.

"Yes, we could hear the conversation in here," laughed Cindy.

"I think they heard it in Fleet Street," replied Jeff.

As Jeff left the canteen, the coroner and D.I. Johnson were standing in the lobby.

"Can I help you?" inquired Jeff.

"Remember me from last night?" said Gavin Jackson. "This is D.I. Johnson. Can we look at what you have on the story, which I noticed, you went ahead with?"

"You better come with me," said Jeff. They went up to Sid's office. Once inside, both men introduced themselves to the old newsman.

"Does your boss know you're here?" Sid asked DI Johnson.

"I think we both know the answer to that," replied Johnson.

"I thought not," muttered Sidney Jones in a school-master way. "You must be Gavin Jackson, the new coroner. Pleased to meet you," said Sid, shaking his hand.

"What did old Thompson make of you, I wonder?" inquired Jones. Both Jackson and Johnson smiled simultaneously. At that point, the still rather red-looking editor burst into the room.

"What the hell is this? Wild animals eating people! What the hell do you think you are doing writing this shit? And who the hell are these two? I'm paying for lame ducks! Buck your ideas up, or you're fired, all four of you!"

The door slammed, and a picture of Sid Receiving the 1978 March Employee of the Month award fell off the wall. The four dazed men all looked at each other.

"Don't mind him," explained Sidney. "He is the only man in existence ever to be asked to leave a Tourette's syndrome meeting for being too loud. He is our editor. Now if I show you what I've got, what's in it for me?" asked Jones.

"We don't even know what you have, and you're already wanting something from us," said a defensive D.I. Johnson.

"He's training you well," the newspaperman said, while closing his folders and putting them out of sight.

"Now, now..." the coroner said, changing his cap to one of an arbitrator. "I'm sure that if we all get together on this, the quicker the case will be solved, and we all will be able to sleep easier at night."

"We will bring what we have to the police station when you have your pathology report, but I want exclusive rights to the story if I hold it back for now," said Sidney Jones. The two other men agreed.

The editor came back in the room and promptly fired all four men.

"What will we do now?" a worried Jeff Clarke said to his ex-workmate.
"What do you mean?" inquired Sidney Jones.
"We've lost our jobs!" said a distraught Jeff.
"Don't be silly. He fires me on average three times a week and has done so for the past twenty years. It's the first time he has fired people who don't work for him, though," said Sid, laughing.
"I will be much calmer when I'm the editor," said Jeff.
"You're very sure of yourself, I will give you that," said Sid, still laughing.

At 2:00 p.m. Gavin Jackson knocked on the door of Chief Inspector Thompson. He stepped inside, where the chief was sitting at his desk. He put a bottle of Malt whisky on the chief's desk and said, "Shall we start again?"
The Chief Inspector picked up the bottle and pulled out a couple of glasses from his desk. "Ok," replied the chief, pouring out two large measures. "What do you have for me?"
"Only part of the story..." said the coroner, "but with what you have and what that old news guy says he has, I think things will be clearer."

Thompson started reading the pathology report, his eyes widening. "You can't put this in a report," said Thompson, feeling his chest tightening.
"I have cross-checked everything in that report. I even had it checked out by James Grayson, and he added his signature to it," Gavin said calmly. "Your D.I. is bringing Sidney Jones in with his

files on the subject. It's time to get our heads together and be a team. This could be all over by the weekend," pleaded the new coroner.

A knock came on the door. D.I. Johnson and the two newsmen walked in. The younger of the two men put a large box on the chief's desk.

The coroner said, "Shall we begin? I have shown you my findings, now let's see what we have communally."

At Atkinson, Atkinson & Dewhirst, Atkinson Junior stormed out of his office, barging past John Smith sitting at his desk. They both looked at each other. "Get on with your work!" Atkinson snapped. Smith just gaped at him as he marched out of the reception area. Something felt strange, but Atkinson didn't know what it was.

Forty-five minutes later, the police arrived at the front desk of the accountancy firm. The elderly gentleman sat there pointed to where John Smith was sitting. One of the two rather stocky police officers came over to Smith's desk, and with a very gruff but official-sounding voice, said, "John Smith of 3 Lindale Mews, I am arresting you on several counts of murder. You need not say anything, but anything you do say will be taken down and may be used against you in a court of law."

A bewildered John Smith was taken from his desk and escorted to the awaiting patrol car outside, and then down to the police station.

At the police station, an excited constable burst into the room where the chief was in conference with the coroner and the reporters, and exclaimed, "We've got him, sir! We've got him!"

"Got who?" said Chief Inspector Thompson calmly.

"The murderer, the guy who lives at 3 Lindale Mews! He's downstairs, sir!"

Thompson looked at Johnson and said, "Come with me." Then he turned to the coroner and the newsmen and said, "Wait here. We will check this out." The two ranking police officers ran out of the room, leaving the files still on the table.

Sidney Jones instantly sat in Thompson's chair and started reading as fast as he could, while the coroner went and looked out of the window, saying, "If I can't see you looking through that document, I don't have to lie about anything."

"You deal with it how you want, young Gavin, but we need to know what's going on."

Then Jeff Clarke said, "Will this help, Sid?" and he pulled from his inside pocket a small hand scanner.

"I must protest strongly about this..." said the coroner.

"I thought you couldn't see anything!" snarled Sid. "And what use is a transistor radio to us?"

"It's not a radio. It's a device for copying everything in that file before they get back," Jeff quickly answered.

"Get on with it then, lad," Sid enthused.

"I'm going," said the coroner. "I can't be a party to this, not here in the police station anyway. I will see you both later."

With that, Gavin left. Jeff finished the last of the pages, closed the folder back up, and put away his scanner. Jeff and Sid sat back in the chair and waited for the chief's return.

In the interview room, things were not as clear-cut as the Police Officer had thought. The police had discovered that John Smith had occupied that building for as long as records for that building existed, which was odd, since the first records for the building dated back to 1666 – which made Mr. Smith around three hundred and thirty-four years old. Also, the coroner's reports said the wounds were caused by something with the strength of a large animal, and, at around one-fifty-four pounds Smith was no grizzly. Could he have been the accomplice? The coroner would know the answer to that, and he was in the chief's office, so the chief made his way back to his office. Much to his disappointment, the coroner had gone and all that were left were the two newsmen.

"Is it the man?" Sid asked.

"You know better than to ask me that," replied the Chief Inspector

"I thought not," smirked the old man.

After seeing the information that Sid possessed in his files, Thompson said, "It's getting late, and if you hang on to the story, you will get the rights to it."

As Sid and Jeff were leaving, Atkinson and Tamara, posing as John Smith's lawyers, passed them at the front desk. Sidney Jones felt a shiver run up the back of his neck as he made eye contact with Atkinson. Atkinson stared at him for an instant, and then moved on to the front desk.

"Are you alright?" asked Jeff.

"Yes, let's get back to see what we have on that contraption of yours."

Atkinson asked to see the prisoner that they were holding, along with the officer in charge.

"I am here," said Thompson, as he walked from the other side of the reception area.

Once again, Atkinson saw another face he recognized. "P.C. Thompson," said Atkinson.

Thompson could feel his heart pounding in his chest cavity.

"I am at a loss for your name, sir... and it's Chief Inspector Thompson. I haven't been a police constable for over twenty years. Your man is free to go, Mr., err..."

"Atkinson is my name and I have been working abroad for a long time. Do accept my apologies."

"No need for apologies," said Thompson in a rather shaky voice.

"What are you charging Mr. Smith with?" inquired Atkinson.

"No charges yet, he has been helping us with our enquiries. Should we need him again, we will contact you. Do you have a card?" asked the chief.

Tamara reached into her briefcase, and pulled out a card that simply had 'Atkinson' printed on one side, and a mobile phone number on the reverse. Atkinson and Thompson just looked at each other in an uneasy silence.

The silence was broken by Tamara saying, "Let's go, then." The two men parted their gaze, and John Smith and his two lawyers left the police station.

"Are you ok, Chief Inspector?" enquired Desk Sergeant, Glenn Simpson. Thompson turned and went back to his office, saying in a slightly raised voice, "Get me Johnson in my office as quickly as possible."

D.I. Johnson knocked on the chief's door and entered.

"I want John Smith watched, and find out all you can about his team of lawyers," demanded Thompson.

"Consider it done, sir," said Johnson as he left the office.

The Chief Inspector walked down the steps with his coat over his arm and said, "Goodnight Glenn," to the desk sergeant as he left for home.

Sidney Jones accompanied Jeff Clarke back to the young man's house. Once inside, the two men made for Jeff's computer and started downloading the file that Jeff had scanned.

"It will take a long time to download all this information, so we could go and have a cup of tea," offered Jeff.

"No, just print out what you have, and bring it into work tomorrow. I'm getting tired, and I don't feel too good. There was something strange about that man at the police station, almost like we knew each other. He certainly reminded me of a man I met a long time ago...but no...he would look much older now...this man looks exactly like he did all those years ago," said a weary Sidney Jones as he added, "You have done well today, Jeff. I'm enjoying working with you."

Jeff helped his new friend Sid to the door and said, "I will be in extra early tomorrow. Good night, Sid."

The door closed. The old man walked slowly down the path, opened the gate, and made his way down York Road, which took him past York Park, a beautiful spot only five minutes away from where Jeff lived. He stopped for a moment to catch his breath, raising his glance forward he noticed a man standing in the path in front of him.

"We meet again," growled Atkinson.

"Who are you?" Sid trembled. He fumbled in his pocket for his trusty Dictaphone, and depressed the 'record' button.

"Come on, Sidney, you know me! How many times over the past twenty-two years have you tried to write about me and your editor always stopped you? I am the story that would have made the headlines, but nobody believed you."

"I'm not afraid of you," said a defiant Sidney.

Atkinson smiled. "Tonight you rest, old man".

"Who are you?" asked Sidney hopefully.

"I am Death. I know that sounds theatrical, so does Atkinson jog your sad old memory?" He raised his right arm, bringing his mighty fist crashing down on top of the journalist's head.

As Sidney hit the ground, Atkinson calmly left the scene. The tape recorder in the old man's pocket clicked off. After a short time, a passing couple stumbled across the body, lying in a pool of blood. The police arrived, quickly followed by an ambulance. The sad and lonely old man, who never got his big break, was taken first to the hospital, and then to the morgue – where he met up again with his newly acquired acquaintance, Gavin Jackson.

Gavin was stunned when he pulled back the sheet, revealing the man with whom he had been talking only a few hours earlier. He put the sheet back and drew away from the corpse. Sarah put down the jar of formaldehyde containing a brain, which she had been staring at for the past few minutes, and came over to him. "What's the matter, Gavin?" she asked.

"Nothing – I just got a bit of a shock," replied a pale-looking coroner. "This is the man that had quite a dossier on the case we're working on, and looking at the blow he has sustained to his head, this could have been done by the same assailant."

Sarah looked shocked and said, "I hope they aren't killing people off who are connected to the case!"

"Now, now, we cannot make wild assumptions like that in our line of work. I was wrong to say that; he may have been hit by a car. I'm sorry for frightening you, dear. We won't know anything until I have performed an autopsy. Now, you go put the kettle on, while Tom and I prepare the table."

As the assistant began to make the tea, her words were ringing in a worried coroner's head. What if she was right? Was there going to be a procession of corpses, all to do with this case? He rinsed his hands and face, cleared his troubled mind, and began to speak into the microphone above the body, "Male, Caucasian, about sixty years old."

Chief Inspector Thompson woke up from a troubled sleep to the ringing of his phone. "Sorry to trouble you at this hour, sir, but there has been another death," informed his desk sergeant.

"Not again, tell me it's not happening again Glenn..." said a drowsy Chief Inspector.

"It's not for me to comment Sir – but I hope not too."

"Tell Inspector Johnson to meet me at the morgue in forty-five minutes," a quickly-awakened Chief Inspector said.

"It's D.I. Johnson's night off, Sir," the desk sergeant tried to explain.

"I don't care whose night off it is! Get Johnson, and do it now!" shouted a very worried Thompson.

"I'm on it, Sir...and by the way, the dead man is, err..." the desk sergeant sputtered.

"Spit it out, man," snapped the Chief Inspector.

"It's Sidney Jones, Sir," was the reply.

Chief Inspector Thompson sat back on the bed and felt very cold all of a sudden. He hung up the phone and cupped his head in his hands. After getting dressed, he left the house, got in his car, and drove to the morgue. On his arrival, he noticed D.I. Johnson leaning on his car hood.

"What's so important that my only time off in days is ruined?" moaned D.I. Johnson.

"Follow me, I will enlighten you," snapped Thompson.

The chief pressed the doorbell and the little assistant answered.

Thompson looked at her and asked, "Are there no normal people working for this department?"

"Don't know what you mean, Chief Inspector. Do come in. Care for some tea?" said an impish Sarah.

Thompson barged past her, shaking his head. Once inside, he made his way to where Gavin Jackson was performing his autopsy. He knocked on the glass window to the lab; the coroner bid him to enter. Both Thompson and Johnson entered the pathology lab where the body of Sidney Jones lay partially dissected.

"Chief Inspector, we have a problem..." a gloomy Gavin reported. "I'm pretty sure this man was killed by the same man who killed the unfortunate individuals two days ago and some of the people at Lindale Mews, but not the taxi driver."

"How sure are you?" replied the Chief Inspector.

"Ninety-nine point nine percent," said Gavin Jackson confidently.

"What is the connection?" asked a puzzled Chief to his understudy.

D.I. Johnson quickly replied, "Maybe the connection between the young ones and Sidney was that Sidney was on to it, and because of that, he was killed."

"You could be on to something. Go and see his editor, and that young kid he had with him, and bring back those files he has on this case! Get a warrant just in case they don't want to cooperate. I want to see action on this! I want results!" ordered Thompson.

D.I. Johnson left the mortuary and made his way back to the police station. Chief Inspector Thompson followed Gavin Jackson into the pathologist's office, and they both sat on either side of the desk. There was a shuffling outside the office, and the door was slowly opened by Sarah's bum as she came in backwards, holding a tray with tea and biscuits in her hands. Both men noticed at the same time what she was wearing – the smallest tartan mini-skirt in existence with a sheer top and lacy bra underneath.

"What has happened to your white coat, Sarah?" Gavin enquired.

"I spilled tea on it," she replied.

"Go put another one on instantly. You can't work in those clothes."

Sarah turned rather quickly so the pleated tartan would rise up, showing her bum, which was barely covered – and stormed out like a scolded school girl, giggling to herself.

"Sorry about that, Chief Inspector," said a red-faced Gavin.

"Call me Jack. It's a long time since I've seen anything like that, so don't apologise. I will have to see her before I go. I was rather rude to her when I arrived," said Jack Thompson, smiling for what seemed like the first time in weeks. "Now, who or what are we looking for?" he asked after he sipped his tea.

"Science would tell me that we are looking for a man, but if this was a man, he would be at least eight feet tall and have arms like a silverback gorilla," replied the coroner.

Thompson spit his tea back into his cup. "An eight-foot-tall man with gorilla arms? Let's try and keep it this side of farcical," gasped Thompson.

"Or…we could be looking for a lawyer with super-human strength. Listen to this tape that was found in the deceased's pocket," Gavin continued as he depressed the play button on Sid Jenkins' Dictaphone.

'Come on Sidney, you know me. How many times over the past twenty-two years………I'm not afraid of you………Tonight you rest, old man………Who are you?…………I Am death………Does Atkinson………'

Thompson could not believe his own ears. As the tape abruptly stopped, his astonished stare stayed with him as he placed the Dictaphone in his pocket, picked up the rest of Sidney's personal effects, and rushed out of the coroner's office.

It was almost daybreak when Jeff Clarke rose from his bed and rushed over to his computer. There, in a neat pile of A4 paper, was all the information that he had scanned. He began reading.

There were different files for each of the sixty-seven unsolved murders that had taken place between 1953 and 1978. Each file had gruesome pictures of mutilated bodies, heads missing and arms ripped from their sockets. All of the victims had one thing in common: they were all aged between seventeen and twenty. No charges were brought against anyone; no motive could be found other than it was a wild animal that was loose and caused havoc without detection. He placed all of the printed material along with all of Sid's files into his backpack, grabbed an apple from the fruit bowl on the kitchen table, and raced out of the front door.

Jeff arrived at work to find D.I. Johnson waiting for him in the editor's office. "Come in, lad, and sit down," said an unusually quiet editor. "Do you know where Sid left his case files you were working on?" he continued.

"No," was Jeff's untruthful answer. "Why do you ask"?

D.I. Johnson replied, "Unfortunately, Mr. Jones was murdered last night."

Jeff was stunned, and there was an uncomfortable silence for what seemed like an eternity. The editor broke the silence. "You had it with you when you went to the police station yesterday."

Jeff was confused, and he was trying to think like a journalist and trying to keep the story he was on to himself, at least for now.

"He had it with him when he left my house," Jeff replied, with confidence far beyond his years.

"Then the attacker must have it. If we find the man with the evidence, then we have our murderer," stated D.I. Johnson.

Jeff gulped and said, "Do you mind if I go home, sir? All this has been a bit much for me to take in."

"Nonsense, you hardly knew the man. Journalists don't go home because there is a little upset!" shouted a more normal-sounding editor. "They're demonstrating outside the nuclear plant again. Go and find out what's up their ass this time," he continued.

Jeff quickly replied, "I'm already on this story, sir."

"Was on this story – this story no longer exists. The evidence we had has been lost, or have you forgotten already? I'm getting another experienced man to start it again. Now get down to the power plant...or to the job centre...the choice is yours," growled Don Steele.

Jeff left the editor's office, sad, dazed, and confused. He wondered who he could talk to now that Sid was gone. He was sitting on the story of a lifetime, but how could he take it further? He now thought the police would see him as being involved if he went to them with Sid's evidence, because of what D.I. Johnson had said about the man with the evidence being the murderer. Despite what his editor had told him, he didn't go to the power plant, he went to a café to try and work out what to do next.

Atkinson met with Tamara. "The journalist is out of the picture, which only leaves the Chief Inspector and the coroner, who by tonight will be under his replacement's knife. Tomorrow will see the end of the meddling Thompson," announced Atkinson in a smug way.

"Will everything be alright then?" asked Tamara.

"Everything will be fine. I will be able to start properly, and this time, I will not let Dewhirst back. This is how I always wanted it, so shall it be."

At the small Tudor-styled, old English café in the town centre, Jeff drank from a large mug of frothy coffee, the type that leaves part of your drink on the end of your nose. The café was quite full, so he had to join someone already sitting at one of the tables.

He had been polite and asked if anyone was sitting there, but the rather sad-looking man said that nobody ever sat there and he was quite welcome to the seat. After a few minutes, Jeff asked him if everything was ok; the man was looking very dejected and sad. "Yes," said the man. "I've just had a bad few days."

"I know how you feel," replied Jeff. "A problem shared and all that," said Jeff, trying to lighten the moment.

"Well, if you really want to know, I'm having problems with both work and it seems my home life...but you don't want to hear it..." started the young man.

"I have nothing else to do right now," replied Jeff.

"Ok then, I am employed by a team of accountants called Atkinson, Atkinson & Dewhirst, and my name is John Smith."

Jeff instantly knew the names 'Atkinson and Dewhirst' and 'John Smith' from Sid's files, but this John Smith was far too young to be the same man. He didn't let on that either name meant anything to him, and he let Mr. Smith carry on.

"I was arrested yesterday for murder, and I have no idea why. The police let me go when my employer came and said he was my lawyer. I live such a boring but steadfast life. Nothing like this has ever happened before; at least, I don't think so. I can't remember. I don't know anything other than I work for Atkinson, Atkinson & Dewhirst, and I always have."

"Wow – arrested for murder!" Jeff grew more interested by the second.

"Do you believe in coincidence, Mr. – sorry, I don't know your name?" enquired John Smith.

"Jeff – my name is Jeff – and no, I do not believe in coincidence. I believe everything happens for a reason; even meeting you I believe has happened for a reason. I don't know what the reason is yet, but I'm sure going to find out!" was Jeff's eager answer.

Jeff drank his coffee and said 'goodbye' to his new acquaintance. He left the old English coffee house and made straight for home and Sidney Jones' files, and at that point, the young boy felt like a real newsman who was onto something very, very big.

The home of Dr. James P. Grayson, the retired coroner, was in darkness when Atkinson strode up the Yorkshire stone path and entered the building with consummate ease. Climbing the steps, he noticed an office at one end of an upstairs corridor. He could tell it was an office, because the door was ajar – and he could see a desk and filing cabinet within. Past the office were three other doors, two closed and one open...with the sound of snoring escaping from within. Silently entering one of the rooms, he saw James Grayson, fast asleep. Carefully standing at the side of the bed, he put his right hand around the old man's neck. The old man's eyes opened wide with fright as he felt Atkinson's grip tighten around his throat. The poor man's neck quickly snapped. As blood started to squeeze through Atkinson's fingers, he released his grip on the retired coroner's throat; his head fell to one side as he lay slain in his own bed. Atkinson left the bedroom and made his way to the office, where he set it on fire, burning any incriminating evidence that Grayson might have lying around.

Atkinson smiled as he exited the front door. The top of the house was ablaze, and he knew that evidence against him, and people who knew him from the past, were disappearing fast. *Only one to get rid of now, and then it will be sorted*. Atkinson grinned as he patted himself on the back for a job well done.

Jeff, however, was reading the very last page of Sid's notes and was thinking of the job in hand.

The night-time calm was shattered by sirens. The fire brigade, ambulance, and police were all en route to The Meadows, an upmarket part of town where the rich people of the area resided. One such residence was well and truly ablaze when the emergency services arrived. All efforts to save the property were in vain. Within forty minutes of arriving at the scene, the once-beautiful mansion was left a smouldering shell. Everything inside, including the occupant, had been destroyed. Everything was going exactly how Atkinson had planned...or so it seemed.

The following morning, Gavin Jackson had the unhappy task of matching Dr. James Grayson's dental records to check if this burned skeleton was that of his predecessor. It didn't take very long to match, and until the fire department could tell what started the fire, Jackson had the uneasy feeling that this was the second execution in as many days.

At the same time that Gavin Jackson was doing what seemed like his daily autopsy, Jeff Clarke was reading the morning headlines in the papers. One headline stated that the fire was at the retired coroner's house, and that there was at least one fatality. Jeff knew that the retired coroner's name featured prominently in both Sid's and the police reports.

With his knowledge of both reports, he had concluded that the third slaying would be none other than the Chief Inspector. He had to come clean. He needed to talk to somebody about this, so he went back to his editor. Very sheepishly, he knocked on Donald Steele's door.

"Go away!" came a booming scream from within, but Jeff went inside anyway.

"You're fired!" screamed the editor, with his mouth full of bacon sandwich, some of which ended up on his desk.

"Yes sir – but before I go, I must tell you something..." stuttered Jeff.

"Make it fast, boy, and don't think you will change my mind!" snarled the editor.

"I still have Sid's file."

The editor's mouth opened slightly.

"Not only do I have Sid's file, I scanned all the police evidence while I was there with Sid, and I think I'm in big trouble with the police as well as losing my job," sighed a despondent Jeff. The editor's mouth opened so wide that what was left of his bacon sandwich fell out of his mouth and onto his desk. There was a silence while Donald Steele regrouped himself.

"Fired?" shouted the editor. "More like promoted!" he continued. "Bring it in, boy! We can say an anonymous citizen delivered it here. Now quickly, go and get it!" the editor roared.

Jeff felt like a ton of weight had been lifted from his shoulders as he sped home to collect his evidence.

The news that everybody was expecting arrived at the police station. The charred remains at the fire were indeed the remains of Dr. James Grayson. Also, the fire brigade had found evidence of arson. Chief Inspector Thompson, with D.I. Johnson at his side, began a briefing at the police station about an unsolved set of crimes that spanned about twenty-five years – half a century ago – and the likelihood was that the current wave of murders was somehow connected.

"Are we looking for the same man?" asked Police Officer Linda Harper much to the amusement of the others.

"I really don't know," was the truthful answer from the Chief Inspector.

The room hushed as the Chief went on to brief them on the case that was left open twenty-two years ago and to the exact execution of the present murders.

"Nobody could repeat these murders exactly like they were committed, so it leaves us saying, however improbable, that we are looking for the same man, or..." The chief stopped short of saying 'beast.'

D.I. Johnson brought the briefing to a close, leaving only himself and his superior. When the room was clear, he pointed out a finding that he had seen in the file during the briefing.

"Apart from the assailant, the three main players in this case seemed to be the enquiring journalist, the coroner, and the then PC Thompson. Need I point out, Sir, the former two are now dead under suspicious circumstances?"

Jack Thompson was painfully aware of this fact; he was also aware of the cocky remarks that John Smith's solicitor made, especially the one about being abroad for a long time. He wondered how long, and why some of these murders were in Smith's house, and how did his lawyer know he had been arrested? Thompson told Johnson to bring Smith back for questioning.

"I'm on it," replied the young D.I.

Jeff Clarke arrived back at the editor's office and knocked on the door. The words, "Go away!" bellowed from inside and Jeff, complete with boxes and computer discs, walked in. Laying all the information on the editor's desk, he said, "Apart from all this, there is a new lead. John Smith has already been interviewed by the police. He clearly didn't do the murders...but I'm sure he is implicated in some way."

"Who is John Smith?" enquired the editor.

"A man I had a chance meeting with in a café. I talked to him over a coffee. He said he seems to have some kind of amnesia, and that there are a lot of blank patches in his life. I'm going to gain his confidence and find out what he knows."

"How will you do that?" queried an eager editor.

"I have a good friend who knows hypnosis, and he has regressed people in the past. Who knows what we might find?"

"He won't want paying, will he – him being a friend and all?" asked the editor.

"Don't worry too much about that. A couple of drinks in a bar will be plenty."

The editor sat back in his chair and started reading the files. "Get on with it, lad, and send Jefferson in. He is off the case and you're back on it. Make me proud, lad, make me proud!" the editor said with a smile.

D.I. Johnson asked his chief if he wanted a lift home.

"Would that be an escort home for the rest of my life?" replied a despondent Chief Inspector Thompson. "I don't think so. If something's coming after me with the strength that this thing has got, well, I don't see the point in wasting two perfectly good

police officers. I don't think we can stop this thing, I really don't –
so I will bid you good night and hope to see you in the morning,"
he said dejectedly.

"Good night, Sir."

As D.I. Johnson said those words, he didn't realize they were
the last words he would ever speak to his boss. The two men
parted, and Chief Inspector Thompson left the police station for
the last time.

Thompson's journey home was uneventful. He pulled into his
driveway, got out of the car, locked the door and made his way
over the shale path to his front door. He performed a quick walk
around the premises. The front door was still locked and all the
windows were intact. Thompson quickly shuffled inside and
started to feel better. Putting the kettle on for his night-time
drink, he began to think about all that had transpired in the last
few days, and how it had turned his usually quiet world upside
down.

His mind slipped back a quarter of a century to a dark side
street, where he witnessed the last killing that ended twenty-five
years of gruesome murder. He had run to the aid of three young
men, who were desperately trying to get away from what could
only be described as a sadistic monster of a man about six feet
seven inches tall in dark clothing with long hair. Two of them
broke free from his grip and ran; the third man was left
screaming. P.C. Thompson was only thirty yards from where they
stood when he saw the young man ripped in two by this man's
bare hands. At the sight of the police, the murderer dropped both
halves of the dead man and began to run; instinctively, P.C.
Thompson gave chase. Thompson kept up the chase for about a
quarter of a mile, and then the man disappeared up the side
passage that separated Slater's butchers and Atkinson, Atkinson &
Dewhirst, the local accountants. On remembering that last chase
and where he ended up, Jack Thompson discovered the link he
had so desperately sought.

"Atkinson, Atkinson & Dewhirst!" he said out loud. With beads of perspiration upon his face, he fumbled to find his phone in his pocket. Trembling with excitement, he quickly started to press the buttons on his phone, trying to connect to his D.I., but he was misdialling, his hands now shaking and his chest tightening. He felt agonizing pains running up his left arm. Deep in his armpit was the most excruciating pain – like a knife piercing his muscles. His chest felt as if it was in a vice, and all the time, he was trying to dial D.I. Johnson's phone. Just as Johnson answered his phone, Chief Inspector Jack Thompson fell to his knees, dropping his phone to the floor, gasping for breath and clutching at his chest.

By the time he had fallen full-faced to the floor, he was dead, and with him went the best clue to the murders. At the side of the Chief Inspector's lifeless body, a tiny voice could be heard, saying, "Hello, Chief, is that you?" The voice stopped and all was quiet.

Chapter Six

etective Inspector Paul Johnson's car screeched to a halt outside Chief Inspector Thompson's house seconds before the marked police cars arrived. With his car's engine still running, D.I. Johnson sped up Thompson's garden path, closely followed by the uniformed police. Without knocking, he tried unsuccessfully to barge down the door. Through a window, one of the other police officers could see the Chief Inspector lying motionless on the floor.

"He's on the floor, Sir!" shouted police officer Phillip Squires. D.I. Johnson moved aside to let the uniformed guys batter down the door.

With a crash and splintered wood dispersing in all directions, they were in, running to the assistance of their fallen chief. An ambulance was called, but it was too late; the chief and the most damning piece of evidence so far were gone. It was confirmed that no entry had been made, and there were no signs of a struggle; there was just his phone on the floor with D.I. Johnson's number showing on the now-dimmed screen. From a vantage point across the road, just out of the view of the police, a tall, smug-looking man thought to himself that he had been saved from finishing a job tonight and could now fully relax, knowing nobody knew of his existence. He called Tamara on his mobile phone. "Hi, babe – we are in the clear! There is nothing that can stop me now!"

Gavin Jackson was saved the shock that he had experienced with the late newspaper man by a telephone call from D.I. Johnson. The coroner asked for the body to be left until he arrived.

"That's been taken care of. I will be here when you arrive," replied a sombre Detective Inspector.

The next day brought the news that the Chief had died of a massive heart attack, and this had left the new Chief Inspector Paul Johnson, the new coroner Gavin Jackson, and the new newsman Jeff Clarke wondering if this was really a coincidence. All three were unconvinced.

Gavin Jackson was sitting at his desk, watching Sarah cleaning her new nose piercing. It reminded him of his dinner date and brought a much-needed spark of light to the very dark past couple of days. He smiled, and thought that maybe he had let all of what had happened cloud his thoughts. Fires happen all the time, as do heart attacks...but then he remembered the voice, "I am Death," on Sid's Dictaphone and this brought him right back. He phoned the new chief and Jeff Clarke and asked if they could all meet off the record. All agreed to meet at the Unicorn public house.

The three men went inside. Gavin bought a round of drinks. They sat at a table in a nook that offered some privacy. There followed an uneasy silence that was broken by Chief Inspector Johnson, saying, "Why is the boy here? He has nothing to offer the investigation. His predecessor's files are now missing...and is he even old enough to drink?"

Gavin immediately snapped back, "I said, 'off the record'! What the hell does it matter if he is old enough or not?"

Paul Johnson stood up and began to leave.

"I do have his files..." said Jeff in an unconvincing voice. "And I'm eighteen, Sir."

The new Chief Inspector sat back down.

"Atkinson, Dewhirst and John Smith appear in it – as do the deceased coroner and the Chief Inspector," informed Jeff.

"We need to see this file," said Gavin Jackson.

"It's at my house," enthused Jeff.

"Will you show us?" a calmer Chief Inspector asked.

Jeff agreed and as they were leaving, he said, "I've met John Smith."

"How?" enquired Paul Johnson.

"A chance meeting in a coffee house," Jeff added.

"Rather like how you and I met..." mused Gavin.

"A coincidence, but a fruitful one. We got on quite well," said Jeff, excitedly.

"Too many coincidences for me..." said the policeman.

"It's almost like some force is trying to tell us something!" exclaimed the coroner.

"Let's try to keep it this side of the rainbow," scorned D.I. Johnson. At that point, the quiet of the pub was crushed when twelve of the nuclear protesters came in from the power plant, shouting their drink orders. The new Chief asked the newsman if he could befriend this John Smith, "Off the record, of course." Jeff smiled and nodded his head. The coroner thought it was a good meeting and wondered what his pierced, tattooed workmate was doing that evening, and what his mother would think if he ever took her home.

The coroner and the policeman bid Jeff goodbye again. As they did, Jeff asked them both not to let his editor know he was passing on this information to them. Both agreed and asked Jeff if he could not print anything yet. Chief Inspector Johnson said, "There is a murderer out there, and we need him behind bars as soon as possible. While you are getting to know John Smith, I will find out more about this Mr. Atkinson."

"John Smith's boss," said Jeff, in a knowing fashion.

"No," retorted Johnson, "his lawyer."

"John Smith told me in the café that he was his boss pretending to be his lawyer, and he didn't know why," said the eager young gun.

With that, Gavin Jackson and Chief Inspector Paul Johnson got into their respective cars and drove off. Chief Inspector Johnson was intrigued with what young Jeff had said, and was already planning on seeing Mr. Atkinson again very soon.

Jeff had refused a lift from both of them in the style of his late friend Sid, and walked off for his rendezvous with Cindy. Jeff tapped on his phone keypad, put the phone to his ear, and heard Cindy say, "Hello?". They had arranged to meet behind the newspaper building, but his just-concluded meeting had made him slightly late. "I will be there in ten minutes!" said Jeff, eagerly.

"Be careful, sweetheart. Mr. Steele said he is going to sack you, then reinstate you just so he can sack you again for not coming in today," said a worried Cindy.

"Just leave Donald Steele to me," assured Jeff

Gavin pulled up outside the coroner's office. He strolled inside and said to Sarah, "Fancy a drink?"

She yelled, "Yes!" Sarah threw her white coat on the table and ran straight past him to the car. Gavin placed the white coat in her locker, waved at his understudy, who gave him a knowing wink, and joined the rather-excitable young lady waiting outside with a rather red sore nose.

Atkinson was now back in his office, clinched in a loving embrace with Tamara, planning his long-term future, while the luckless John Smith was allowed back into his dwelling at Number 3 Lindale Mews. He climbed the steps to his flat, unlocked the door, and with no knowledge of what had happened there, he went on about his night-time routine of tea, television, and sleep.

Across town, a smart Jaguar pulled into an underground car park of a tower block of luxury apartments. Gavin exited the car first, and walked around the front of the car to open Sarah's door. She sprang out of the car, looked around at all the different types of high-performance vehicle, and exclaimed, "Wow! Cool cars!"

Gavin raised an eyebrow and said, "Follow me." The strange-looking couple got in the elevator. He turned his security key and pressed the button marked 'penthouse', and very smoothly, they journeyed up an external elevator to the top of the tallest building in town. The scene was breath-taking for the young, excited girl. As the elevator reached its destination, the doors majestically swished open, and the lavish layout of Gavin Jackson's penthouse suite lay in front of them.

Behind the newspaper building, Cindy was waiting with a cardboard cup full to the brim with coffee, just how Jeff liked it. Jeff took the beverage and gave Cindy a kiss on the cheek.

"I am on to something big!" said Jeff. "But I'm sworn to secrecy," he added.

"You're sworn to a life on the dole! You're fired!!" boomed a voice from the editor's open window. "Get up here now!" the rant continued.

"Oh, no..." sobbed Cindy. "You're fired! What about our plans?" she sobbed further.

"It's ok. He sacks me two or three times a week," said the confident newsman. "I will go and give him a snippet of what's going on to calm him down and we will go out for the evening," said Jeff.

Meanwhile, Chief Inspector Paul Johnson was at the house of the man who had taught him everything he knew about being a detective. He had been with Chief Inspector Thompson ever since he was promoted to Detective Inspector some eight years before. The thing that Johnson could not understand was why his ex-boss was phoning him, instead of the doctor. If the man was in the middle of what turned out to be a fatal heart attack, he would phone an ambulance. *Was he going to tell him something about the case?* thought a rather sad Paul Johnson.

He moved to Jack Thompson's home office and started looking through the manila folders in the drawers. Fingering through file after file, all duplicates of the ones in his office at work, he came upon an old one: "For the attention of Detective Inspector Johnson," was written on a post-it note and stuck to the flap. He quickly opened it.

This document was about one and a half inches thick; in it were photographs of dead bodies that looked like animals had fed on them, as well as statements from people describing grown men ripped in two.

There were a couple of photos that the chief must have just put in recently, because they were of Mr. Atkinson, and another of John Smith. On closer inspection, the date on the back of the photographs was 10/3/72. The new chief sat down. *How the hell could they still look the same?* Johnson thought to himself. He gathered up all the files and sped out to his car. With wheels screeching, he made his way back to Jeff Clarke's house.

Beverly Clarke answered the door.

"Hello, I'm Chief Inspector Johnson," he said, holding up his ID.

"Your ID says 'Detective Inspector'," replied Jeff Clarke's mum.

"Yes, sorry about that. Is Jeff at home, please?" said Johnson through his teeth.

"Chief Inspector," said a voice from behind.

When Johnson looked behind him, Jeff and Cindy came through the gate.

"I need your file," said the chief.

"It's inside," said Jeff. "Follow me."

"Will your friend be stopping for tea, Jeff?" said Jeff's mum sarcastically.

"What is your mother's problem?" inquired Paul Johnson, quickly running out of patience.

"She hates cops," laughed Jeff.

Johnson took Sid Jones' files, added them to the one he acquired earlier, and left for his office. On leaving, he told Jeff to report to his office at ten the next morning.

"Do you have a warrant?" enquired a grimacing Beverly Clarke.

"Cute, Ma Baker," was the chief's witty reply.

"The stars look beautiful..." said Sarah, leaning on the handrail of Gavin Jackson's twentieth-floor balcony. "You can see the Wendy House – look over there." Sarah was pointing at the university building where her favourite club was.

"What's the Wendy House?" Gavin enquired.

"It's only the best club on the planet," enthused Sarah in the manner that Gavin was growing accustomed to. "Will you come with me next time?" asked Sarah.

"Of course, Sarah, it would be a pleasure," replied Gavin. "It's starting to get cold out here. Let's go inside," he continued.

"Will I be safe?" Sarah asked, with a wistful smile.

"Of course," said Gavin.

"I'm staying out here, then," said an impish Sarah.

"What if I had said no?" was Gavin's quick reply.

Sarah grinned broadly and ran indoors. Gavin smiled and followed her through the open balcony doors. He walked up to her and put his hand on her shoulder. Sarah was much shorter than Gavin, so she stood on her tippy toes and gave Gavin a little kiss on his lips. She stepped back and began to undo her baggy Skid Row shirt. Taking it off and throwing it on the chair, revealing her lace black bra, which held her rather impressive breasts. Gavin began undoing his tie and laid it neatly on the coffee table; he then unbuttoned his shirt methodically from the neck to the bottom button, folded it and put it at the side of his tie. They both stood there, just looking at each other. Sarah slipped off her little mini-skirt, revealing a matching pair of lace knickers. He thought her tattoos were magnificent as she stood there, looking down in a shy manner with her hands clenched together in front of her knickers.

"Have you not done this before?" said Gavin in a soft voice.

"Of course, millions of times!" snapped Sarah.

"Sarah," said Gavin, lifting her chin so he could look in her pale blue eyes.

"Err, well, I came close once, but the boy was just going to do it with me for a bet with his friends. He just undressed me and then he took a photo of me and ran out laughing," sobbed Sarah.

"You poor thing," whispered Gavin as he held her close. He caressed her tiny ear and whispered, "If I'm going to have the privilege of being your first, it's not going to be like this." He slipped her shirt back on and kissed her on the forehead. He wiped the tears from her cheek and smiled.

"I don't understand..." said Sarah, with a quivering voice.

"Sarah, would you be my girlfriend?" enquired Gavin.

Sarah's mouth fell open and she just nodded her head and burst into tears again.

"I want it to be right, and above all, I want it to be romantic," Gavin said softly. "Let me take you home," he continued.

As Gavin dropped Sarah off at a rundown, terraced house in the worst part of town, he heard her father shouting, "Where the fuck have you been, you little tart?" Gavin shook his head in disgust.

On the way back to his apartment, he phoned his mother. On hearing it was her son, she asked in a very sophisticated but angry voice, "Who is this common female you have been seen out with?"

"It's the girl I will marry, Mother," replied her defiant son. Gavin heard the thud of his mother falling to the ground; he smiled, hung up the phone, and drove off into the night with no thought of dead police chiefs, reporters, or killers. Only one wonderful thought filled his mind: 'Sarah'.

Chapter Seven

Jeff Clarke woke early, quickly showered and dressed. He phoned a taxi, and made his way to Lindale Mews – the bus stop on the main road, to be exact – to wait for John Smith. Although Smith's address wasn't publicly known, Jeff had procured it from Sid's files.

Several buses had passed before he saw a very plain man in a grey two-piece suit and a grey tie crossing the road towards the bus stop.

"Hello again," said Jeff, in a friendly manner.

"Oh, err – hello. I'm sorry, do I know you?" enquired John Smith.

"We met yesterday in the café, remember?"

"I'm sorry, I don't have a good memory," stuttered John Smith.

"You were telling me about your boss getting you from the police station, saying he was your lawyer," explained Jeff.

"I don't understand. This is my first day at work, and I have to report to Mr. Braithwaite. I don't know anything about the police station," said John Smith, looking totally confused.

"Ok, I'm sorry. I must have you mistaken for someone else," answered an even more confused reporter.

Jeff knew he had to be at the police station at 10:00, so he rode the bus in the seat behind the befuddled John Smith. Jeff exited before John and made his way up Park Road to the police station. The desk sergeant told him to take a seat, as the new

Chief Inspector had just arrived moments earlier, having been working deep into the night. It wasn't long before Chief Inspector Paul Johnson came down the stairs and motioned him up. Once in the office, Jeff told of his strange meeting with John Smith.

"It does not seem so strange, when you put all the information together, believe me," said Paul Johnson.

"How so?" asked Jeff eagerly.

"All in good time; let's wait until Dr. Jackson gets here," announced Johnson. The phone rang and Sergeant Glenn Simpson said that the coroner was downstairs.

As the three men met, another meeting was taking place at Atkinson, Atkinson & Dewhirst. Tamara had just made a coffee for Atkinson Junior. "Just how you like it, darling," pouted Tamara.

Atkinson's lips curled into a small grin. "So much for arriving back three years early," he smirked. "You are looking at the most powerful force on the planet," Atkinson added.

"May I remind you that you are still in human form and are vulnerable, my love?" said Tamara.

"As a human, I can tear the other humans apart. Who can stop me?" inquired a resolute Atkinson.

"Anything that can kill a human can kill you at the moment," she added.

"Do you think my father would let anything happen to me?" he said defiantly.

On this morning of meetings, one more was taking place in another realm on another plane. Two old friends who had not seen each other for twenty-two years had a lot to talk about.

Atkinson and Dewhirst had walked between the Plane of Existence and the Realm of Death since time began and always did the job perfectly; one did the Reaping, the other did the eternal paperwork. Both had to be done if the Life Circle was to continue. Life and Death need each other. Many people believe in different meanings of this. Be it religion or fate, it does not matter what one believes in; the only sure thing is, if it lives, then it must die, and Atkinson and Dewhirst are the dispatchers of the latter.

"Why did he come back so soon?" asked Dewhirst.

"He grew impatient," replied Atkinson Senior.

"This will not do. There is a way of things, and this isn't it; it was more straightforward when it was just the two of us."

"Things change, times change, and I grow weary, old friend," was Atkinson's slow and deliberate reply.

"You were wrong to let him return. He is not like us – he needs to use this ridiculous surrogate John Smith, who, I might add, the authorities are getting suspicious of. He thinks he can reap on the Plane of Existence. He is drawing attention to himself. It's wrong," explained Dewhirst.

"The discrepancies have been taken care of," retorted Atkinson.

"Yes, they have, but only one in the Realm of Death. He killed the other two on the Plane of Existence; he could undo everything! We only just stopped it in time the last time he was there," said a worried-looking old deity.

"This is worrying...I told him to deal with the situation, but not like that. Let's just pull him back and see what his intensions are," suggested Atkinson.

"It's not that easy – he has already been in The Realm of Death," answered Dewhirst.

"So if we cannot pull him back, he will have to be stopped," said Atkinson.

"Not by us. Two of us cannot be on that plane at the same time."

Dewhirst was not telling Atkinson anything he did not already know. "Maybe the police might get the final piece of the jigsaw this time," pondered Atkinson.

"If the police get him, he will be put in prison. How will that help the situation?" retorted Dewhirst.

"I'm afraid the only way is for him to die on the Plane of Existence, and he will come straight back here," Dewhirst added.

"I will be ready to collect him, but I have little faith in a human being able to kill him," Atkinson replied.

Meanwhile, Jeff, Paul, and Gavin were piecing things together using the files from the press, police, and the coroner's office.

"Where does John Smith fit into all this?" said D.I. Johnson. "According to the records, Mr. Smith has been living on or about Lindale Mews since the Middle Ages."

"I beg your pardon?" gasped the coroner.

"Take a look for yourself," said the chief.

Both Gavin Jackson and Jeff Clarke looked at the deed that had Mr. John Smith as the tenant of the property, and Atkinson and Dewhirst as the owners.

"I have a plan," said the keen reporter. "I told the guys back at the paper that I had a friend who has regressed people with hypnotism."

"Not more silliness from beyond the veil..." scoffed D.I. Johnson.

"I have seen this done," said Gavin Jackson, "in the university I attended," he added.

"Would you like for me to ask if he is prepared to help us?" Gavin thought it to be a good idea; the chief was sceptical, and enquired how they would talk John Smith into this.

"I will think of a way," assured Jeff.

Tamara filed her beautifully manicured nails as she watched her love of many centuries pace up and down the new office carpet.

"It's not long to wait, my darling. All we have to do is lay low and keep out of the way of the police," said Tamara.

"I think you over-exaggerate their chances of apprehending me. I will crush any who try and stop me!" announced Atkinson angrily.

As Atkinson's rant was ringing round his office, a gentle 'tap, tap, tap' came from the door. "Come in!" raged Atkinson. The door opened slowly, and a very scared senior clerk advised, with a trembling voice, that the police had come for young Mr. Smith.

Pushing Mr. Braithwaite to one side, Atkinson rushed into the clerk's office, where two uniformed police officers were standing by John Smith's desk.

"What's the meaning of this?" boomed Atkinson.

The taller of the two police officers calmly said, "We need Mr. Smith to help further with our murder enquiries, Sir."

"He is very busy at the moment, so he can come this evening after he has finished his shift," said Atkinson hopefully.

"I'm sorry, Sir. He has to come with us right now," explained the police officer.

"Don't say a word until the lawyer gets there!" shouted Atkinson as the bewildered John Smith was led out of the building.

With that, the second officer turned and said to Atkinson, "I thought you were his lawyer, sir."

Atkinson stuttered slightly when a voice came from behind him. "I'm Mr. Smith's lawyer." Tamara winked at Atkinson.

"I will be up at the station presently," she announced.

"Very good, madam," said the officer.

As the police and John Smith left in the car, Atkinson took hold of Tamara's hand and led her back into the office.

"This is unfortunate," said Tamara.

"Merely an inconvenience," replied Atkinson.

"They only need check the registry, and they will quickly learn that I am not a lawyer," she replied.

"My dear Tamara, this is a backwater village constabulary we are talking about; they are set in their ways, hardly the Met."

"They used to be that way, but you have removed the very people who made it like that. Younger people are taking over – younger, eager people with better resources. We have to be careful!" Tamara exclaimed.

On receiving word from his desk sergeant that John Smith was back in custody, C.I. Johnson bid goodbye to the newsman and coroner. Gavin Jackson asked if he could give Jeff Clarke a lift.

"No thanks, Gavin. I'm going to see if my friend is home."

"Ok – keep me informed, and if he agrees to do the regression for us, make sure you video it," said the coroner.

"I will," replied Jeff, making his way towards his friend's house.

Chapter Eight

The cell walls were grey, silent, and very scary to the plain, simple man incarcerated within them. John Smith was desperately trying to piece things together. All he could come up with was waking up that morning, having a shower, and eating his breakfast...then the strange bus trip to work, and a young man who thought he knew him. Smith thought he knew the man, but no matter how hard he tried, he could not recall ever seeing him before.

The quiet in the cell was broken with the turning of a key and the creak of the door opening. Chief Inspector Johnson walked in. "Hello, John...is it ok to call you John?"

"Yes, of course...I'm sorry for whatever I've done," confessed the bewildered John Smith.

"What do you think you have done, John?" enquired Johnson.

"I don't really know," was the reply.

"Would you like to wait for your lawyer?" asked the Chief Inspector.

"I don't think I have anything to hide, sir," replied John.

Across town Tamara finally got Atkinson to calm down; she caressed the side of his cheek and whispered into his ear that she loved him, and that everything would work out. Atkinson put his arms around her waist and kissed her; he always felt good in her arms. He closed the office door with the back of his foot, lifted

Tamara into his arms, and carried her to the office couch. Laying her down, he began to undo his tie, and pulled it through the collar of his shirt. He undid the buttons of his shirt without taking his gaze off Tamara.

His shirt slid away with consummate ease. He stood back slightly to watch her disrobe. She lay there in her underwear, looking like a goddess, her eyes reflecting his incessant gaze. Knowing that Smith would do as he was told, they both fell into a lover's clinch and worried no more about him – or anything else for that matter.

Jeff knocked on the door of his friend Matt's house. He first met Mathew Hamilton at college some two years ago; they got on well from the start, and still quite regularly met at the local pub to see how they were going. Mathew, or 'Matt', as all his friends knew him, had been interested in hypnotism since childhood and now had a show that he played throughout the pubs and clubs in the local area.

After the usual pleasantries and a cup of tea, Jeff got down to business.

"You have regressed people before, haven't you, Matt?" said Jeff knowingly.
"Yes, many times – it's something I like to do. Why?" asked Matt.
"I've got someone who needs to be regressed."
"Why do they need regressing?"
"I – that is, we, think he is involved in a murder."
"Who's 'we'...and did you say murder? It all seems a bit heavy."
"It's ok, Matt, this will be done with the police and the coroner. This guy who has supposedly murdered loads of people is a complete wimp who cannot remember anything. Are you in, Matt?"
"It's heavy, but what the hell, count me in."

On leaving Matt's house, Jeff wondered how he would get John Smith to take part in this experiment he was setting up. Jeff took out his phone to call Chief Inspector Johnson, and noticed a missed call from Cindy. He pressed the red dial button, and Cindy's phone began to ring.

"Hello, where are you?" answered Cindy.

"I've been to Matt's house. Why?" replied Jeff.

"Mr. Steele fired you again this morning. He said you have stolen newspaper documents, and he wants them back. I overheard him talking to his secretary as I took their tea in," said Cindy.

"He won't mind when his newspaper gets its biggest story ever! I've been given exclusive rights, as long as I hold off while the investigation continues," said her very-excited boyfriend.

Gavin looked out of his office window; his gaze was fixed on the only thing making his mind wander from the murders. Sarah was cleaning the autopsy table, bending over it in such a fashion that Gavin could see a glimpse of her knickers. He smiled to himself and put his pen down; he was just about to get up when his mobile phone rang. It was Jeff, telling him that his friend would do the regression. Gavin put the phone down, took another look at Sarah's rear, smiled again, and got back to work.

Back at the police station, Paul Johnson had brought a coffee for the accused and himself. "Are you sure you don't want your lawyer, John?"

"I don't think so. Just ask your questions. If I can, I will answer them."

"Ok...did you help somebody kill those young people in your flat?" was the chief's opening gambit.

"What young people? I don't know what you mean," replied John Smith.

"The slain young people in your flat. Remember...dead bodies on the bed?" said Johnson, raising his voice slightly.

"Dead bodies in my flat? I really don't know what you mean," was Smith's quivering reply.

"How long have you lived there?" said the Chief Inspector in a calmer voice.

"I don't know," said an exasperated Smith, with his head in his hands.

"We will take a break until your lawyer gets here, because you are not doing yourself any favours," explained Paul Johnson.

On leaving the interrogation room, Chief Inspector Johnson made his way to the front desk.

"Get me a list of all the lawyers working within a two-hundred mile radius of here, with Atkinson or Tamara in their name," ordered the Chief Inspector.

"Tamara?" asked Glenn Simpson the desk sergeant.

"Yes, Tamara, I heard Atkinson call the lady by that name, and it appears she is his lawyer. Work fast! I want the results before they get here."

As the chief was at the front desk, Jeff Clarke walked in.

"Can we talk?" asked Jeff.

"It will have to be quick. I've got John Smith in the cells."

"My friend will hypnotise him as soon you're ready," reported Jeff.

"I'm still not sure about that. This guy is strange. If we do this, I'm not going to be involved," replied Paul Johnson.

"We're ready when you are. Just give me a ring," replied Jeff.

"Sir!" shouted the desk sergeant. "I have the search results and they are very interesting."

The Chief Inspector took the piece of paper, and his eyebrow lifted as he read. "Come with me, Jeff," said the Chief Inspector.

The two men made their way up to Chief Inspector Johnson's office.

"Take a look at this – it's a list of all the working lawyers within a two-hundred mile radius; there are only two Atkinsons. One is fifty-nine, and the other is practically an octogenarian, and none of these lawyers have a first name of Tamara."

"I don't understand," answered Jeff.

"Quite simply, Atkinson and a woman named Tamara posed as his lawyers, an offense in itself, but I want to know why. As far as John Smith is concerned, have your man be ready. The name 'Atkinson' is turning up too many times for my liking," said Johnson.

Across town, Tamara stood naked in front of an adoring Atkinson. "I had better put some clothes on and go to the police station," she said softly.

"Just leave him there; I don't need him for at the very least a quarter of a century," grumbled Atkinson.

"This is not the time to get careless, my love – we have to tie up this loose end," pleaded Tamara.

"I grow weary of all of this. Why don't I just take them all out?" grimaced Atkinson.

"And then what? More people will follow, more questions will have to be answered. This is already becoming a mess...killing more will just make it worse," she replied.

"I'm going out!" raged Atkinson.

"Ok, you go out, but remember this: you have taken people who were not on my list. Do not take any more! You might be a God, but know this, I'm the Listmaker, and you reap the souls on my list. You don't kill at will! That's murder, and until you are fully awakened, you will abide by my list, and that means no more killing. Your father installed me as the Listmaker, and only he can alter that. I love you, but I can't see you fall, and fall you will if you don't change!" screamed a Tamara that Atkinson Junior had never seen before. Atkinson looked at Tamara, shook his head, and stormed out of the office.

An hour later, Tamara turned into the parking lot of the police station just as Jeff Clarke was leaving. They caught each other's glance as they passed in the entrance lobby. "Have we met before?" asked Tamara.

"I don't think so," replied Jeff.

"I have a feeling that we will very soon," said Tamara softly.

Jeff was unnerved by this strange but elegant lady, and he just put his head down and left the building. Once inside, Tamara asked if she could see her client.

"There's no one here who needs financial help, Miss err..." said Chief Inspector Johnson as he came down the steps to the front desk.

"My name is Tamara Helen Stapleton, and I don't understand what you mean," said Tamara, removing one of her driving gloves.

"Do you want to do this here, or in my office? It makes no difference to me."

"After you," said Tamara.

"No, my dear, after you," was Chief Inspector Johnson's cool reply.

Once inside the office, he asked Tamara to sit down. Moving to the other side of the desk, he sat down, put his forearms on the desk, clenched his hands in a praying fashion, and looked straight into Tamara's eyes.

"Do you want to see your client – or shall we discuss the register of the bar?" asked Johnson.

"I studied law in America," was Tamara's quick response.

"Fine! Just tell me when and where, then thanks to the wonders of this modern computerised age, we can have your credentials e-mailed straight to this very computer! I will even print out a copy to save you this confusion at a later date! Of course, none of this is important because Mr. Smith said he didn't need to wait for his lawyer...because he had nothing to hide," smirked the Chief Inspector.

"I demand to see him right now!" retorted Tamara.

"No problem, my dear, just as soon as we get a reply from...which college am I requesting this information?" said the Chief.

"I have never been so humiliated!" scorned Tamara. "I am leaving, but I will return," she added.

"I am counting on it, Madam. I will be right here. Do pass on my regards to your Mr. Atkinson, and tell him that he might have to make do without Mr. Smith for a few days, as we need him to help us further with our inquiries. Good day, madam," said the chief coldly.

Jeff shrugged off the strange feeling that the woman at the police station had given him and made his way back to the newspaper building. On entering the building, he had to move to one side because someone was being stretchered out by paramedics. He made his way to Don Steele's office. He noticed the building was unusually quiet but couldn't quite make out why. He knocked on the editor's door and recoiled in anticipation.

"Come in," said someone with a gentle voice. Jeff opened the door slightly, and looked inside. In Donald Steele's office were three people he had never met. "Hello, can I help?" said one of them.

"Hi," said Jeff. "Who are you?"

"My name is Eugene Black. I'm the assistant editor. Who are you?" inquired Mr. Black.

"I'm Jeff Clarke."

"The young reporter," interrupted the assistant editor. "You are the last person Donald was shouting about before he burst a blood vessel. The paramedics have just left," continued the assistant editor.

"Is he dead?" gasped Jeff.

"No, but he won't be back for a few days. Now, I am going to have a lot to do to keep things running, so can I ask, do you have something of Mr. Steele's or are you this week's firing person?"

Wow, thought Jeff, *I'm off the hook for a few days.* "Err no, sir, I don't have anything. He has fired me three times this week."

"Ok, son, you just go down to the power plant and interview some of the protesters. Get to know the background of their group," said the very calm deputy editor.

Jeff flew out of the editor's office and ran to the canteen; Cindy was collecting trays of cutlery from the tables. He snuck up behind her and threw his arms around her waist, instantly making Cindy drop all her trays. "Jeff!" exclaimed Cindy. "What are you doing? The editor has had a heart attack!"

"No, he's burst a blood vessel. He will be back in a few days, so this means he is off my case, and the new editor doesn't know anything about what I'm doing, so I can work on my story without worrying about what's happening back here. Let's go out tonight to celebrate" suggested Jeff.

"Sounds good to me!" replied Cindy.

At the pathology lab, Gavin Jackson had acquired the DNA evidence from the saliva found on the bite wounds of the first victims. He picked up the phone and called the Chief Inspector. "Hello, Detective Inspector Johnson, can I be of assistance?"

"Don't you mean 'Chief Inspector'?" said Gavin quirkily.

"It's taking some getting used to," said the new chief. "How can I help, Gavin?"

"Can you get a warrant so I can get a swab of John Smith's saliva?" enquired the coroner.

"No need, he is in custody and cooperating with us, so just come over and take your sample," said the chief.

Gavin came out of the office and asked his assistant, Tom Harper, for the whereabouts of Sarah.

"She is in fridge number one," replied Tom.

"I know I shouldn't probably ask, but why is she in the fridge?" asked Gavin with a smile.

"She's been grossing me out again with her gore stories. She's been at it all day," grumbled Tom.

"Shall I take her with me?" asked Gavin.

"I would be most grateful, and consider it a personal favour if you did," sighed Tom.

Gavin opened fridge number one. The drawer slid open, and Sarah was lying quite still with her arms across her chest. As the drawer came to a stop, she opened one eye, expecting to see Tom, but it was Gavin standing there. "Err, hello," giggled Sarah.

"I have never asked anybody in one of these fridges this before, but have you ever taken a saliva sample?" said the coroner, desperately trying not to smile.

"He he, err, nope." Sarah giggled again.

"Come with me, then. It's time you did," said Gavin.

As they were leaving, Tom turned on the radio, tuned it to the classical channel, and smiled.

Sarah ran out, shouting, "I'm alive! I'm alive! It's a miracle!"

Gavin calmly strolled out, wondering what it must be like to work in a normal mortuary.

Gavin Jackson's Jaguar pulled up outside the police station. Sarah got out, carrying the black leather case containing the coroner's instruments. The coroner got out, walked around the car, and joined Sarah, then they walked into the station together.

"We are here to take samples from John Smith," said the coroner. The desk sergeant had been foretold of this arrangement, and asked them to follow the police officer to the cells. Police Officer Linda Harper, the coroner, and the coroner's assistant all entered John Smith's cell.

John Smith stood up and enquired as to what was happening. Gavin Jackson calmly said, "We are here to prove or disprove your innocence; we need to take a swab from your mouth. Will you allow us to do this?"

"Is it going to hurt?" said John Smith in a quivering voice.

"Not at all," assured Sarah, feeling sorry for this pathetic, nervous man in front of her. Sarah opened the case and passed Gavin a pair of surgical gloves, and put a pair on her own hands. Gavin pointed at the sterilised Q-tips and asked her to pass one to him.

With the Q-tip held between his right thumb and index finger, he moved in front of John Smith, and asked him to open his mouth. Turning to look at Sarah, he asked her to pass him a test tube. He took the test tube in his left hand and gently dragged the Q-tip along the inside of John Smith's cheek. The coroner asked the assistant to take the rubber bung out of the top of the test tube. Sarah carefully took off the rubber cap. Gavin Jackson then gently dropped the Q-tip into the test tube and passed it to Sarah, who put the top back on.

"Easy and pain-free as that!" smiled the coroner. "We will be off now. Thank you for your cooperation," said Gavin Jackson in a comforting voice.

As Gavin and Sarah came out of the cell and made their way back to the front desk, they were joined by Paul Johnson.

"Have you got what you need?" he asked.

"We have, and as soon as I have the results, you will be the first to know."

The two men parted with a handshake and a knowing nod of their heads; Sarah waved and made her way out with the cases.

Tamara, by now, had arrived back at Atkinson, Atkinson & Dewhirst, to find that Atkinson had not returned. She took out her mobile phone and pressed the menu button; Atkinson was at the top of her contacts list. She highlighted the name and pressed 'call'; she calmly put the phone to her ear and waited. The phone rang twice and Atkinson answered.

"Are you alright?" asked Tamara gently.

"I'm fine," said Atkinson.

"Where are you, my love?" enquired Tamara.

"I won't be long. I'm at the power plant. It's an impressive building...you were talking about the modern world. I think the modern world isn't as safe as the old world. The good people outside have been telling me how dangerous it would be if one of these power plants went into what they call 'meltdown'. It was very interesting. There would be nothing standing for a ten-mile radius. Don't you find that fascinating, Tamara?" said Atkinson with a chill in his voice.

On Tamara's phone was another button that wasn't on any other phone. She slid the cover at the bottom of her handset; a failsafe so it couldn't be pressed by mistake. She hovered her thumb above the button shaped into the letter 'A' and depressed, instantly transporting her to the Other Realm, where Atkinson Senior and Dewhirst were waiting.

"What is going on, Listmaker?" growled Atkinson Senior.

"He is not himself. I'm trying to get him to lay low, but he isn't listening to me," said Tamara, with an air of panic in her voice.

"Need I remind you that I made the decision to let my foolish son take part in our business because you said he would be an asset to our existence?" Atkinson Senior added.

"I know. I will get him under control, my Lord. I promise," said Tamara in a not-too-convincing voice.

"He will not be allowed back on the Plane of Existence once his Administration is over. I was wrong to let this happen!" snarled the very angry old deity.

As Tamara was about to leave, he chillingly told her, "If he isn't brought under control, I will terminate your existence. Now get out of here!" shouted Atkinson Senior as he sent her back.

Tamara had seen the old Atkinson in action, and didn't fancy him turning on her, so she stayed at the office and awaited Atkinson's return.

The old, oak-panelled front door of Atkinson Atkinson & Dewhirst slammed shut, announcing his return. The old men in the office kept their heads down as he strode through to his own. On entering, he saw Tamara sitting at her desk and closed the door behind him. Throwing his long black coat onto the coat stand, he looked at Tamara as he made his way to his desk. He sat in the chair, put his feet onto the desk, and rocked onto the chair's back two legs. He looked at Tamara and raised an eyebrow quizzically.

Tamara enquired, "Why were you at the power plant?"

"I was just having a stroll," replied Atkinson nonchalantly.

"The power plant is quite a way off – hardly a stroll," she retorted

"Maybe I was just checking my options..." said Atkinson.

At this point, Tamara put her pen down, put her hands on her desk, and eased her wheeled chair backwards. She stood up and walked gracefully over to Atkinson's desk. Putting her hands onto the desk and leaning forward, looking straight into his eyes, and said, "That's enough of this – why were you there and what is going on?"

Atkinson had now placed his hands behind his head and was rocking his chair. "What do you mean?" he muttered innocently.

"You know exactly what I mean! You weren't down at the power plant on a stroll; you're still thinking of removing these people in your way. I've already said, if you do that, it will make things worse!"

"Not if I remove everything! According to those people, nothing will be standing. Nothing, that is, except our building," he beamed.

"That in itself would bring the authorities down on us. Atkinson and Dewhirst has stood in this same spot since the Middle Ages...since before accountancy companies existed."

"But everything would be gone – there would be no record of this place."

"You idiot!" screamed Tamara. "The records at this police station are all held on a central computer database! You're at the beginning of a new century – nothing is local anymore!"

Atkinson removed his feet from the table, stood up, and banged his fist on it whilst still looking at Tamara. "Why do you think you can now order me around?" growled Atkinson.

"Why do you think you are doing what you're doing? Who do you think paved the way for you to work with Atkinson and Dewhirst, and who do you think is now being held responsible for this?" shouted Tamara.

"What do you mean? You are a Listmaker," clipped Atkinson.

"The Listmaker that got you from where you were and pleaded with your father to let you work with him until he agreed; now if you don't toe the line, my existence will come to an end," said

Tamara sadly. Her usual confident stature was now that of a girl beaten into a corner, running out of options.

"Nothing will happen to you during my Administration, Tamara."

Tamara snapped back to her usual state. "You are no match for your father. He could end all of this in the blink of an eye!" said Tamara sharply.

"You underestimate me," said Atkinson.

"You grossly underestimate your father! All we have to do is lay low these couple of days – what is so hard in that?"

"Why should I be told what to do? This is my Administration – not my fathers!"

"Not yet! You haven't started! As I have said before, you are vulnerable! Get that in your head! Your unwillingness to see what may happen is going to be your downfall!"

"Have you finished, Tamara?" enquired Atkinson, "Because this conversation is over. Go back to your desk and do what you do, little lady – go make a list."

The silence was thick and heavy in the office space between Atkinson's desk and Tamara's. Tamara just sat there, looking straight over at the flamboyant beast sitting at his desk, with the soles of his boots facing her over the shiny inlaid desktop. An hour had passed since Atkinson's last words when he removed his feet from his desk and stood.

"Ok, so if I play this your way, I just wait here until it's time to do the first list. Once I start that first list, all these problems are behind us, am I right?" enquired Atkinson.

"Yes, as soon as this list is compiled and I give you the go-ahead, then you are ready to begin. Then once again, nothing will be able to touch you."

"Ok, then we will just wait here. I won't go out anymore; I won't cause any further disturbance."

"That's all I wanted," said Tamara, beginning to smile again.

"What if I'm called about John Smith? What then?"

"Then you simply go and you play the worried employer. They know now that we aren't his lawyers, and nothing he can say can harm us because he's only conscious of work and what little home life he has."

An air of calm fell over the main office of Atkinson, Atkinson & Dewhirst.

Chapter Nine

Chief Inspector Johnson sat at his desk, holding a cold cup of coffee in his right hand, jotting on a piece of paper with his left. He put the cup and pencil down, and removed a piece of paper with Jeff Clarke's phone number on it from his inside jacket pocket. He picked up the phone and dialled the number.

Jeff was having a coffee with Cindy in the cafeteria at work when his phone began to ring. On answering, Chief Inspector Johnson said, "Hello, Jeff...why don't you bring that friend of yours to see me? I've changed my mind."

"I thought you wanted the police kept out of it," stated Jeff.

"Well John Smith is talking freely, and he doesn't want a lawyer, so what the hell? Just let me know when you can arrange for it to be done."

The chief bid the young reporter good day and put the phone down. He stood up and left his office, went down the stairs, and made his way to cell Number 2, where John Smith was residing. On entering, he noticed that Smith was trembling. He sat at his side, and asked him what was wrong.

"I'm going to go to jail for murder," stated Smith.

"Something tells me that you won't be doing that," assured the chief.

"But everything seems to be pointing to me!"

"Not everything is, as it seems," said the chief. "There has been an idea brought forward that may help. You say that you can't remember certain things that have happened. There's a way that we can help you recall those things, but you have to be willing to do it. You have to participate of your own free will."

"If it will prove my innocence, I'm willing to try anything," said Smith.

"Have you ever been hypnotised before?".

"No sir," was the answer.

"Well, if you will agree to it, I would like to have you hypnotised by a professional. This is just in case the DNA evidence is inconclusive," reassured the Chief Inspector.

John Smith put his head down and softly agreed. "I'll try anything, just to get back to my life."

"I will arrange things," said Johnson, patting John Smith on the back.

Jeff finished his coffee, gave Cindy a hug and a kiss, and said, "I'm off back to Matt's house," and left the strangely quiet Donald Steele–free building.

Paul Johnson rang Gavin Jackson and informed him that he had given Jeff the go-ahead for the regression. Gavin asked if he could be there when it took place; Johnson had no objection to his request.

When Jeff arrived back at Matt's house, his mother answered the door.

"Hello, Jeff, come in. Mathew is in his room. Just go up."
"Thanks," replied Jeff as he made his way upstairs to Matt's untidy but homely bedroom.

"The guy has agreed to be regressed," announced Jeff. "Will you be able to do it tomorrow?" he continued eagerly.

"I am free all day tomorrow. You're sure he's not a psycho?" answered Matt.

Jeff laughed. "You will see tomorrow. Shall we say ten o'clock at the police station? I will meet you outside."

"Okay, ten it is, then," agreed Matt.

Gavin Jackson was on the phone to the lab to see how long the DNA test would take, and if there was any way it could be sped up. It just happened that the lab was not busy, and they were already working on it, but it would be much later that evening before they had the first results. Gavin was desperate to have them before morning.

As he put the phone down, it instantly rang. He put the receiver to his ear. It was Jeff informing him that the regression was taking place tomorrow at ten o'clock at the police station. Gavin thanked Jeff for letting him know and said he would see him tomorrow.

Gavin looked out of the interior office window at Sarah giving Tom a hard time, and he noticed that every time he looked at her, it made him smile. He had never had this feeling before. All he knew was that he wanted to be with her. Feeling sorry for Tom, he asked him to come inside his office. Once inside, he asked Tom what Sarah was like to work with.

"She's fine – you're not thinking of letting her go, are you? I know she's quirky and she has a strange sense of humour..."

"Let me stop you there," interrupted Gavin. "You know her best. If you think she is cut out for this work, I will put her through college," continued Gavin.

"Academically, I don't know. All I can say is she does her job well, and is always asking questions," answered Tom.

The two men continued their conversation for about fifteen minutes when the front doorbell sounded.

"I had better go see who it is," said Tom.

"Let Sarah answer the door," suggested Gavin.

"This place is frightening enough without Sarah greeting people at the door," laughed Tom, as he got up and left the office. Gavin just laughed and thought, *I'm going to enjoy being the coroner here.*

Tom answered the door; two girls dressed like Sarah were standing there. "Can we talk to Slabgirl?" enquired the taller of the two black-clad Goths.

"Slabgirl?!" exclaimed Tom.

"Yes, Slabgirl. You know, Sarah," said the shorter girl.

"Just one moment, I will get her," said Tom.

"Can we come in and look around?"

"Certainly not! It's bad enough with one of you people in here, never mind three," said Tom, shaking his head.

"Who is it?" asked Gavin.

"It's two girls who look like they should be in one of our fridges, wanting to talk to Slabgirl," informed Tom.

Sarah immediately took off her white coat, threw it on the table, and ran out, shouting, "I'm off for my break!"

"Slabgirl?" asked Gavin.

"I know...frightening, isn't it?" acknowledged Tom.

Sarah came out to the two girls and gave them both a hug. "Where have you been?" asked Sarah. "I haven't seen you for ages!"

"We've not been going out since that Goth turned nasty."

"What do you mean, Goth turned nasty?" asked Sarah.

"You know, that guy that ripped all those people apart – he was a Goth. He'd been at the Wendy House that night," said Sophie Narey, the taller of the two visitors.

"How do you know?" asked Sarah.

Jenny Archer, the shorter of the two girls, said, "My sister saw what happened."

"What did she see?" asked Sarah.

"My sister and her friend were walking back home from the Wendy House when they were set upon by a group of people. Then, out of nowhere, came this tall guy wearing a long black coat and calf-length boots. She says that she saw him kill one of the people with his bare hands just before she passed out."

"Did she tell the police?" asked Sarah.

"She was too frightened – she's hardly spoken a word since," said Sophie.

"I think my boss would like to hear this…" Sarah interjected.

"No Sarah! We don't want to be involved!" They both exclaimed at once.

"Please wait here – you won't be involved – I'll just go and see him."

Sarah ran back indoors and knocked on Gavin's door. From behind the door, she heard Gavin say, "Come in." Sarah burst through the door, sputtering excitedly.

"My friend's sister witnessed the murder – she knows who did it – it was a tall man – he had a long coat – she saw him kill…"

"Whoa! Calm down!" interrupted Gavin. "Sit down and tell me again, calmly."

"My friend's outside. She tells me that her sister witnessed what happened when those Goths that were attacked that night. Her sister was one of them!"

"Well," said Gavin, "Why don't you bring her inside? Let's have a talk with her."

Sarah immediately got up, left the office, and ran to the front door. But to her disappointment, her friends had left. She looked everywhere, but they could not be found. Coming back inside dejectedly, she entered Gavin's office.

"They've gone," she said, with her head hanging down.

"It's ok," said Gavin. "Come in, and let's talk about this. You're saying that your friend's sister actually witnessed the first of those people being killed…and saw the man who did it? What we need to find out is, would she recognize this man if she saw him again?"

"How will I find that out?" asked Sarah.

"It's not down to you, Sarah, the police will find that out. We all need this man off the street, and the best way to do that is for the police to talk to your friend's sister."

Sarah put her head down. Gavin got up from his chair, and coming around the desk, stood at her side. He put his hand under her chin and gently raised her face so he could look into her eyes, trying to comfort her.

"It will be ok. This is the lead that the police have been waiting for, and you have helped greatly. You have done the right thing, bringing this to my attention. And don't worry if your friends don't like you anymore – I care for you more than any of them ever could."

A tear fell down Sarah's right cheek, slipping onto Gavin's hand. Gavin gently leant over and kissed her on the eyelid, as if to make it better. Sarah put her arms around him and the couple embraced.

"You go off now, and have a break," comforted Gavin, "I'll phone Chief Inspector Johnson."

Chief Inspector Johnson was at his desk, thinking about what hypnotism would do to help the case, if anything – when his phone began to ring. He answered to hear the coroner's voice.

"Hi, Gavin," said the chief.

"Hi," replied Gavin, "Are you busy at the moment?"

"No, I'm not busy. I'm just pondering tomorrow's circus event."

Gavin chuckled. "I take it you mean the regression?"

"Yes," was the reply.

"I may have something else..."

"Has the DNA evidence come back?" asked the chief.

"No, but I am assured that I will have it later this evening. This is something different, and I want to talk to you personally. Can you come over?"

"No problem," said the chief. "I'll be round in half an hour."

"Excellent! I'll look forward to seeing you then," said Gavin.

The Chief Inspector came downstairs to the entrance lobby, putting on his coat. He told the desk sergeant, "If anybody needs me, I'm at the mortuary."

He made his way to his car, and drove off. The traffic in town was unusually light, and a trip that normally took a half-hour was completed in twenty minutes. He parked his car at the side of the coroner's Jag and made his way to the door. Tom let Chief Inspector Johnson in, showing him to Gavin's office.

The coroner asked if he wanted a cup of tea.

"Who will be making it?" Johnson enquired.

"Well – it will be Tom, because Sarah's not here."

"Yes, in that case, I'll have a cup of tea," said the chief.

Gavin smiled. "Actually, Sarah's the reason that you're here."

He began to relate the events of the afternoon.

"So, you're telling me that this girl actually did witness one of these killings? Because she told us that she saw nothing."

"I'm telling you what the girl's sister told Sarah. It would be interesting to know if the girl in question would recognize the murderer from a photograph. That's why I rang you."

"Well, yes – I'm certainly going to have the young lady back in for further questioning."

"If I might just say..." said Gavin, "the Gothic community seems a placid type of people who don't much make or like trouble. It just seems to find them. I'm certainly not trying to tell you how to do your job, but you might want to be gentle in the way you ask your questions. Evidently, she is somewhat traumatised by what she has witnessed. This is probably the reason she preferred to say nothing at the time."

Paul Johnson acknowledged the coroner's request, and said, "I will bring her back, but I will be very gentle. She can look at the photographs we have of John Smith."

The two men continued their conversation for the next hour. When the Chief Inspector's phone rang, it was Glenn Simpson, the desk sergeant relaying a message that Superintendent Viktoria Malik from headquarters had been in touch, wanting to speak to him. On receiving this phone call, Johnson and the coroner parted company, and the Chief Inspector made his way back to the police station.

After dealing with police HQ, he asked the desk sergeant to bring the young couple back in for further questioning. "There is someone here to see you, Sir," said the desk sergeant.

"I will be right down."

Standing at the front desk was the woman that HQ had been talking to Chief Inspector Johnson about.

Detective Inspector Donna Lambert was Johnson's new assistant. Standing five feet eleven inches tall, she had a figure of Amazon proportions with shoulder-length red hair and a freckled complexion. "Chief Inspector Johnson," said the distinctive redhead as she shook her new boss' hand.

"A pleasure to meet you," replied Johnson, straightening his tie. "Follow me," he continued, as he reminded the desk sergeant about getting the two witnesses back.

"I've got a unit on its way, Sir," was the sergeant's reply.

"Where are we going, Sir?" asked D.I. Lambert.

"I'm taking you to where my Chief took me when we first met, McDonald's."

"The burger bar?" inquired the D.I.

"Yes, the burger bar. Big Mac with extra cheese!" enthused Johnson.

"Please, no doughnuts," said the D.I.

"No doughnuts," agreed the Chief Inspector.

The new Chief looked at the new Inspector eating her Big Mac and remembered his first day with Chief Inspector Thompson. Thompson was of larger stature to Johnson and had an air of confidence about himself. He was a man of impeccable dress sense, and one to look up to and admire, and he recalled how much he grew to admire him. Chief Inspector Thompson had taught him so much. He learned to check and double-check, always asking questions, no matter how insignificant. Thompson had told him that questioning was not just about finding facts, it was to wear the subject down. Yes, indeed – D.I. Johnson's Chief was a giant among men in his eyes, and now, he had to wear his old bosses shoe's and had to be the same. He suddenly felt older.

"Your phone's ringing, Sir," said the young D.I. as Johnson snapped out of his inner thoughts.

"We have them back, Sir," reported the desk sergeant.

"Well done, we will be right there," replied Chief Inspector Paul Johnson.

Sarah arrived back from her break. Tom asked her how she was. "I'm ok, Tommy," said Sarah with a cheeky grin.

"There's blood all over the table…" said Tom with a smile.

"I'm on it!" said Sarah, as she ran towards the table.

"Sarah!" shouted Tom.

"Yes?" replied Sarah, looking back.

"White coat," said Tom.

"Oh, yes!" giggled Sarah.

Tom just smiled and shook his head as he always did. He went to the office and announced Slabgirl's return.

"When you have finished the table, would you come in my office?" asked the coroner.

"Nearly done!" she shouted. Sarah flushed away the remaining blood from the table, washed it down with a cloth, ran towards the coroner's office, knocking on the door.

"Come in," invited Gavin. Sarah opened the door and walked in. She stood in front of the coroner with her hands clasped together behind her back.

"Sit down, my dear," said Gavin.

Sarah quickly sat down and looked straight at Gavin.

"How do you like working here?" asked Gavin.

"I love it – it's great," replied Sarah as the ends of her lovely pink lips turned upwards into a beautiful smile.

"I'm pleased," said Gavin. "I've been talking to Tom, and we both agree that we should send you to college."

"Oh no, sir, my dad won't pay for me to go to college…he said it would be a waste of money owing to me being stupid," she said dejectedly.

"I heard your father when I dropped you off at home. I would rather listen to what Tom says about you, than listen to your father's opinion," replied the coroner.

"How would I afford it?" asked Sarah.

"You will attend on day release twice a week on a scholarship," explained Gavin with a smile.

"A scholarship? You have to be clever to get a scholarship…"

"You are clever, my darling little girl. You are witty, and fun, and your scholarship will be private. I will invest in your future, and by doing so, I will be hoping to invest in our future, my beautiful little girl," said Gavin, looking directly at her.

Sarah's pale blue eyes widened. "I…I don't know what to say," she stuttered.

"Just say yes to the college proposal, and tell me that you'll at least think about the other proposal."

"Yes! Yes! Yes!" exclaimed Sarah. "Eh – our future?"

Gavin leaned across the desk and grabbed her hands, carefully placing them in his. Looking deep into her eyes, he said, "Our future – you and I – and I'm not talking about cutting bodies up. I've only known you a very short time, but I'm feeling things I've never felt. You make me tingle…you make me not know where I should be…I'm thinking about you all the time. Sarah, I think I love you…"

Sarah's hands tightened around Gavin's as tears welled up in her blue eyes. Her top lip began to quiver. She felt tightness in her chest. She tingled from head to toe. Then, all of a sudden, she let out a scream as she climbed up onto the table and jumped onto Gavin's torso, wrapping her arms and legs around his midriff. When the weight of the lover's embrace was too much for the chair that Gavin was sitting in, it fell backwards.

As they hit the ground, Gavin said softly, "Can I take that as a yes?"

To which, Sarah placed her hands on each side of his face, pressed her lips against his, kissed him passionately, and let her lips move gently to his ear. She kissed his ear once, and then whispered, "I love you, too."

Tom Harper had just lined up several samples from the hospital, all ready to be filed away. He picked them up gently as the door to the coroner's office exploded open, propelling an over-exuberant Sarah, who was screaming at the top of her voice, bursting through the front door. Tom's painstakingly-prepared material was now in a state of confusion all over the floor, with him holding onto the table. Tom turned around and looked toward the coroner's office.

Gavin Jackson was standing there.

"We're in love, Tom!" smiled the coroner.

"And I thought it was complicated before," said Tom. "It's really going to get interesting now! I'd better put the kettle on!" he said, smiling and disappearing into the kitchen.

Gavin simply floated back into his office with a huge smile on his face.

Tom was filling the kettle when he heard the front door burst open again. He winced at the clattering sound of Sarah's large boots hurtling towards the kitchen. The next second, he felt a grizzly-like hug around his chest.

"I can't breathe...Sarah, let me go!" grimaced Tom with the air being squeezed from his lungs.

"He loves me! He loves me! He loves me!" exclaimed Sarah.

"I know! I know! I know!" said Tom. "Now put me down and let me make the tea! May I remind you that mortuaries are not supposed to be this exciting?!"

Sarah just laughed and skipped back to the table that she had just cleaned, jumped on it, and sat down with her legs swinging, feeling very happy with her little self.

Chapter Ten

L ater that evening, Jeff arrived at Cindy's house. It was a cold, clear night as Jeff waited for Cindy's imminent arrival at her front door. The wait was soon over, as Cindy emerged from the warm light of her mother's late Victorian hallway leading to her awaiting boyfriend. They greeted each other with a kiss and a loving hug, then made their way out through the garden gate and off to the town centre night life.

Cindy's mother's house was not far from the southern end of town, where most of the small pubs were situated. It was this end of town that Cindy and Jeff frequented the most, preferring it to the more affluent northern end of town, where the clubs were the 'place to be'. After a ten-minute arm-in-arm stroll, they arrived at the Adelphi, an old public house near the river that split the town centre in half. After ordering two lager and limes, they took their seats in one of the small rooms – the one with the jukebox in the corner. The sound emanating from the jukebox was that of the Sisters of Mercy, a local band that had risen to great things two decades earlier. This public house was known for its ambiance, its fine ale, and its legendary jukebox that attracted different types of people. Tonight, it had attracted two people in love, who didn't mind people knowing. Within two minutes of taking their seats, their lips were busying themselves on each other.

"I love you," said Jeff, running his fingers through Cindy's hair.

"And I love you right back, Jeff Clarke," replied Cindy.

The two young lovers carried on kissing and drinking – but mainly kissing, through the night. They left the Adelphi as the time bell rang out last orders at the bar, and took a taxi back to Jeff's mother's house, knowing that Mrs. Clarke would have long since retired to bed. The couple had done this on several occasions before, and had perfected their technique of entering the Clarke residence undiscovered.

Once inside, safe behind the locked door of Jeff's bedroom, the couple began to get intimate. Cindy had not had many boyfriends, and out of them all, Jeff was the only one she had felt totally at ease with, as she was shy when it came to be being naked. Cindy was a larger girl with a fuller figure and had become self-conscious about her body, but Jeff made her feel like a cover girl, he adored her curves.

Jeff lay on the bed as Cindy put her coat on the hanger behind the door; she turned to her lover as she undid the zip at the back of her dress. The dress fell away from her ample bosom, revealing a large but incredibly beautiful bra, and then fell to the floor as she carefully stepped out of it. She seductively walked towards Jeff in her bra and knickers. Undoing the bra, her large breasts were emphasised even more by her arms being behind her back, undoing the clasp. The clasp came undone, and the full beauty of Cindy's firm breasts lay in front of his eager eyes.

Cindy pushed Jeff back onto the bed and let her erect nipples brush across his mouth. He instantly began to suck while his hands slid down the sides of her body and his thumbs found their way inside her knickers on each hip, and began to pull them down. As Jeff removed Cindy's pretty pink underwear, he realised how beautiful she was and how much he loved her. He undressed quickly. Cindy was now lying on the bed, unashamed and naked, her legs slightly open and inviting. Jeff turned out the light and joined his Cindy on their bed of dreams; they were lovers, deeply in love.

Earlier that evening, the coroner was in his office, awaiting the DNA results, when his phone rang – it was Sarah, and she was crying.

"Whatever is the matter, Sarah? Please don't cry," said Gavin.

"My dad has told me that I can't go to college, and he says I've to stay away from you. What am I going to do? I don't want to stay away from you!"

Your father is a complete idiot, thought Gavin. "It's going to be alright, Sarah. I will deal with your father," he assured.

"Are you sure?" whimpered Sarah.

"Of course I'm sure. Now you just come into work as normal tomorrow and leave everything to me."

Sarah felt better; she said goodnight to her new love, put the phone down, blew a raspberry at her father, and ran upstairs to her room.

The coroner put the phone down, and it instantly began to ring again. It was the pathology lab with the results. "Unfortunately, the results were inconclusive. There are some similarities, but not enough to be a complete match," said the pathology technician.

"How do you mean? I thought good DNA evidence like the type we have would show that it is the assailant or it isn't. I don't understand how there can be similarities. Isn't everybody's DNA different?" asked the coroner.

"I would normally say yes to that question, but I have never seen a strand of DNA like this one in all my ten years at this lab," said the puzzled technician. "I can only think there must have been some contamination...or he is some kind of alien," said the now nervous tech.

"I'm afraid it's too late in the evening for jokes," snapped Gavin Jackson as he said goodnight and slammed the phone receiver down. *Alien indeed. I can just imagine what the Chief Inspector would say if I passed that report onto him,* thought the coroner. He turned out his desk light, picked up his Jaguar keys, and left the office, wishing Sarah was going with him.

As midnight approached, Atkinson Junior knew that by this time the next day he would be untouchable. All of what had happened since Tuesday would be gone and wiped out.

Tamara looked at Atkinson and realised, for the first time since she gazed upon his stature and fell in love, that love had been somewhat tainted by recent developments. For the first time, she felt uneasy in his presence. She did not know why; it was just different. Maybe she worried about what would happen if the police caught up with him, but more worrying was what would happen if they didn't. She had always enjoyed being Atkinson's girl, not caring about having what mortals called fun, but this was going a stage further. He wanted to be the only Reaper, and keep his father and Dewhirst as scribes. He would be unstoppable, answering to no one but himself. *I can't let this happen*...thought Tamara as she picked up her phone.

'You can't let what happen'? said a voice in her head as Atkinson looked straight at her.

"Another day to pass without a manicure," instantly answered Tamara. "And please, stay out of my head. I need a clear mind to construct my lists," continued Tamara with a confident pose, her head cocked to one side and both of her hands on her hips. Atkinson just smiled and continued planning his future – with or without Tamara.

The office light was still on in Chief Inspector Johnson's office as he looked out of his window. "I know you're out there," muttered Johnson over his teacup as the church clock chimed midnight. There was little movement outside. The old guy who feeds the birds in town was making his way home; he looked up at Johnson's window. Paul Johnson saw that he was saying something to him, so he opened it. "What was that you said?"

"You have to get him today," said the birdman. "Today, or it's all over," he continued, as the church bell rung out the final chime of twelve and he walked away up the hill.

The hairs on the back of Paul Johnson's neck stood up, just like a hound's when something is wrong. He stood back from the window as if he had seen a ghost – or should that be, heard a ghost? It was the birdman outside who the Chief Inspector saw, but the voice was that of his Chief, Jack Thompson. He suddenly felt cold and uneasy. A strange awareness that he was no longer alone in the room fell over him like a cold, damp shroud. He gingerly turned around. Sitting in his old, non-swivelling chair was a grey spectre of what used to be Chief Inspector Jack Thompson. Johnson was rooted to the spot; his lips tightened and his mouth went very dry. His tongue stuck to the roof of his mouth, and he felt an overwhelming fear of what sat in front of him.

"Why do you fear me?" asked the apparition.

Johnson was speechless.

"Just listen, my boy; John Smith will reveal what you need. Listen to what he says, no matter how ridiculous it sounds. The young guys are on to something. Don't use police logic on this case, it will hamper you. Your time is short – and much depends on the few of you."

The apparition of his fallen Chief leaned forward and emphasized, "Everything depends on these next twenty-four hours. Use your judgement, not the book."

The office door could be seen opening through the spectre of Jack Thompson as he disappeared and the young Detective Inspector walked in.

"Are you ready, Sir?" asked D.I. Lambert.

"Am I ready for what? It's midnight," said Johnson.

"It's 09:00, Sir," said his efficient underling.

"My god, I must have fallen asleep. Yes, I'm ready. Have me a cup of tea and two slices of toast sent up, and let me know when Jeff Clarke and the coroner arrive."

As Donna Lambert left the office, Paul Johnson was left wondering...did last night happen or was it a dream?

JOHN PAUL BERNETT

Chapter Eleven

att was waiting outside the police station when Jeff arrived. He picked up his skateboard and walked towards Jeff, and they both entered the police station. Gavin Jackson had already arrived and was waiting. All three were taken to Johnson's office, and Jeff introduced Matt to the Chief Inspector and the coroner, and then Paul Johnson introduced his new D.I.

"How are we going to do this?" asked Johnson.

"Tell them what you will do, Matt," said Jeff.

"I will first gain his confidence. Will you guys be behind the two-way mirror?" enquired Matt.

"Two-way mirror? Where do you think you are?" laughed Paul Johnson. "This isn't television. We will run a video feed into the room next door. Two-way mirror...indeed," scoffed the amused Chief Inspector.

A restrained titter came from the coroner and even Jeff giggled.

"I thought all police stations had two-way mirrors and torture chambers," said Matt, slightly put out. "Well, anyway, once I have his confidence and he is totally relaxed, I will then put him under my influence."

"How will you do that?" asked Johnson.

"I can't tell you. It's a hypnotist's secret," said Matt.

"Don't be an idiot. I'm a police officer, not a competitor. I ask a question, you answer – that's how it works," said Paul Johnson, losing his patience.

Gavin put his hand on Paul Johnson's arm and said to Matt, "He means your professional secrets are safe. We will not disclose your technique."

"I see," said Matt. "I use my old granddad's pocket watch," he continued.

"I'm sorry to let you know – your secret's out, pocket watch...go to sleep," scorned the Chief Inspector.

"I don't have to do this!" exclaimed Matt.

"Sorry," laughed Johnson. "It's been a strange last few hours. Go set yourselves up. I will bring Smith when you are ready for him."

"What does he mean, the secret's out?" asked Matt.

"Everybody knows about pocket watches, Matt," said Jeff, as he put his arm around his friend's shoulder and led him down to the waiting room. "You did really well in there, mate," assured Jeff to his friend.

"What am I doing, Gavin?" asked Paul Johnson, shaking his head.

Gavin just laughed and said, "I'm sure everything will be fine. Shall we go see if our Mr. Smith is still eager to talk?"

The two men left the room, closely followed by a confused-looking Detective Inspector Lambert.

Looking around the room, Matt told Jeff that it was perfect. There were no windows or pictures on the walls, so that meant no distractions. Jeff smiled and said, "So, do you think you can do it?"

"I don't see why not," replied Matt.

"I think it's time to bring him in," said Jeff, as he left to inform the others.

John Smith was led into the room and introduced to Mathew. Matt had a friendly face and was easy to feel at home with. John Smith had already been informed of everything that was going to transpire, so the two men spent the next hour talking, and getting to know each other.

Chief Inspector Paul Johnson looked at his watch and wished they would hurry up; the words of his dream had started popping into his head...and this was taking too long. He looked at the video monitor and saw that Matt was now working on his subject with his grandfather's time piece.

Back in the other room, John Smith was already falling asleep. Matt was instructing him to close his eyes and relax. He was counting down from ten, offering words of encouragement between several of the counts. "When I arrive at number one, you will be fast asleep and ready to travel back – back an hour, then back a day, and then anywhere we want to go. 5,4,3,2,1." A snap of Matt's thumb and middle finger, and John Smith was away.

Mathew made sure the tape was running in the video camera and began.

"Today is the 31st of December, 1999 at 10:15 am. May I ask where you are, John?"

"I'm in a room talking to you," was the answer.

"It's nice being in this room talking, isn't it, John?"

"Yes," was the reply.

"Are you comfortable?" asked Matt.

"Yes," was the reply.

"I would like to go back one hour," said Matt.

John Smith's eyes twitched and he shuffled in his chair. "Bacon and eggs...I'm eating bacon and eggs," John replied.

In the other room, a police officer said, "That's what he was eating an hour ago."

"Where are you, John?" asked Matt.

"In my cell, sitting at my table eating my breakfast," replied John.

"Is it good?" asked Matt.

"Yes," was the reply.

"It's now the 30th of December, 1999 at 10:15. May I ask where you are, John?"

"I'm scared...in a police car...what have I done?" said John with a raised voice.

"Relax, John, you are safe. They are just bringing you here to see me," comforted Matt.

Although beads of sweat were appearing on John Smith's brow, he began to calm down.

"Are you ok, John?" asked Matt.

"Yes," was the reply.

"Are you ready to journey back further?"

"Yes," was the reply.

"Let's go back to a good time. Tell me some of the things you remember, and when and where you were at the time. Do you understand the question, John?" asked Matt.

"Yes," was the reply.

"He's good," said Gavin to Jeff.

"It appears to be working," agreed Paul Johnson.

John's eyes opened and he looked straight at Matt.

"Are you ok?" asked Matt.

"Yes," said John, smiling.

"Where shall we go, John?"

John sat back and looked thoughtful. "Anywhere?" he enquired.

"Yes, you can go anywhere and anytime in your life," encouraged Matt.

"It's my first day at work," announced John.

"Good, what year is it, John?"

"1999."

"Well done, John, what is the date?" asked Matt.

"December 30th – 8:30 in the morning, to be precise," was John Smith's answer.

"I think you are getting confused, John. We have already visited that date," said Matt with a puzzled expression. "What about a little earlier?" he continued.

"How much earlier would you like me to go?" asked John. "That's totally up to you, John," answered Matt.

Across town at Atkinson, Atkinson & Dewhirst, the Reaper Elect was putting on his long black coat as he made his way to the door. "Where are you going?" asked Tamara gently.

"I have business out of town. It will take me much of the afternoon, so you be a good little Listmaker, and make me a very large list for tonight."

Back at the police station, John Smith was regressing further. The Chief Inspector, coroner, newsman, and D.I. were all riveted to the portable video screen displaying the event — like a set of football fans watching the last few minutes of the F.A. Cup final.

"Where are you now, John?" asked Matt.

"1977, another first day at work," said John.

"How old are you, John?" asked Matt.

"I'm 22 years of age," answered John.

"This can't be right," said Johnson in the other room. "He is only that age now. How could he be the same age then?" he continued, shaking his head.

"Let's just let Matt get on with it. He has only just started," suggested Gavin.

Johnson just shook his head.

At this point, the desk sergeant came in the room. "We have received an alarm from the power plant. It seems someone has broken into the plant. It's all a bit sketchy; we have already dispatched a unit."

"It's probably those damned protesters. Go along and see what's happening, Lambert. Take a police officer with you to show you where it is," instructed the Chief to his D.I.

"Ok, John, let's forget about work. Let's talk about your family," said Matt.

John looked puzzled. "Family," he simply said.

"Yes, your parents, brothers, sisters, etc.," encouraged Matt.

"I don't have any," answered John.

"What was your mother's name?" asked Matt.

"I don't know – I can't remember," said John.

"That's ok, John. We will leave your family and we will travel back to a time beyond your mortal memory. Just try and remember something before you were born," said Matt softly.

"I remember...seeing...Mr. Atkinson."

"Is that your employer?" quizzed Matt.

"My father...Mr. Dewhirst's partner."

"I don't understand, John. You told me you couldn't remember your father," said Matt.

"Why do you call me that name?" said John Smith, looking at Matt.

"Isn't John your name anymore?"

"No," replied the man sitting in the chair. Matt looked at John Smith and realised that he might have multiple personalities. Matt's mind was racing; he had never had a multiple before. He was going to enjoy this.

"So to whom am I talking now?" asked Matt.

"Wouldn't you like to know?"

"Yes, I would," said Matt.

"I am who I am when I'm not stupid John Smith," he said with a grin.

"What is your name?" asked Matt.

"Atkinson," smiled the man in the chair.

"One, two, three, four, five, come back, John. It's time to wake up," counted Matt.

John Smith's eyes opened and Matt smiled at him.

"Have we finished?" asked John.

"We're just getting started," said Matt. "Let me go talk to the others. I won't be long." On saying that, Matt left the room and joined the people next door.

"Did you get all that on tape?" asked Matt.

"We got all of it. Why did you stop?" asked Chief Inspector Johnson.

"He needed a rest and I want to check on something," answered Matt. "Jeff, when we discussed this case at my house, you said there were also some murders years ago. When was it?" asked Matt.

"1977," said the chief, raising an eyebrow.

"Hmm...that's the time my man in there was just starting work. Is it coincidental that the murders have started again this second time he has started working there?" asked Matt.

"You sound like you believe what he's saying..." said the Chief Inspector. The coroner and newsman stayed quiet.

"This is hypnotherapy; you are dealing with the subconscious mind. You are not inviting the person to tell you stories. They have no idea what is going on, never mind making something up. When I go back, if you want a demonstration, I can ask him who the prime minister was, or anything relating to that exact time period. But you said we don't have a lot of time, so I think a lesson proving how hypnotism works is a waste of time. Don't you, Chief Inspector?" quipped Matt.

Jeff and Gavin agreed with the hypnotist; the Chief was still unconvinced.

D.I. Lambert arrived at the nuclear power plant; the other officers were already there and awaiting instructions. The protesters were nervous at the police presence and one of them stood forward and asked why they were here.

"As if you didn't know," answered one of the uniformed officers. D.I. Lambert and Police Officer Tony Batley made their way through the protesters and on to the front gate. Once through the electronically-secure gate, they were led to the main control centre. They were introduced to the main plant technician, Jerome Patterson, and he escorted them to the CCTV room. Once inside, they all sat by one of the screens and began to watch what the security camera had captured. The pictures were hazy, but it looked like the shadow of someone setting small charges and attaching them to the main reactor; he also had set one on the only door in and out of the reactor room, and then the image faded.

"Did the sensors turn the camera on?" asked D.I. Lambert. "No, one of the security guards saw it on the monitor and ran the tape," answered Jerome Patterson.

"If someone got in, wouldn't it have triggered an alarm?" enquired the D.I.

"Usually, I would say yes; he would have triggered several alarms on his way to that room," said the technician.

"If you can let me have a copy of that tape, I will have it tested, and we will see what we come up with," said Detective Inspector Lambert.

Jerome Patterson gave her the tape, and she made her way out and back to the car.

"What do you make of that?" queried Police Officer Batley.

"It's all strange, but what the hell. I just left a young chap being regressed to his previous life, so maybe not that strange – just normal for here, perhaps," said the D.I., smiling.

Tamara sat at her desk, combing her long hair; she wore a worried expression and her eyes were transfixed on Atkinson's empty black chair, when the silence was shattered by the opening of the door to the Realm of Death, and out strode Atkinson. "Good afternoon, my dear," said Atkinson.

"I had no idea you were in that realm," exclaimed Tamara

"A little experiment, Tamara. I'm just…hedging my bets," he said, as he put a detonator down on the desk.

Tamara stood up and shook her head. "What have you done?"

Back at the police station Matt resumed his experiment.

"Hello, John…and where are you now?" asked Matt as John Smith went under again.

"I'm here with you," smiled John.

"I would like you to go back to the very first time you met Mr. Atkinson," asked Matt.

"I am collecting sticks in the forest for my parents," answered John.

"What are you wearing?" asked Matt.

"My winter sacking with straw underneath."

"What is your job, John?"

"I be a stick collector," said John. "There is something coming..." he continued in a frightened voice. "Please don't strike me, Sir!" said John, covering his head.

"It's ok, John. I won't let anyone harm you. Who do you think wants to harm you?" asked Matt.

"The dragon...he looks angry," replied John Smith.

"What year is it, John?"

"1352," was his reply.

"It's not a dragon, John. Look closer," said Matt.

"It's Mr. Atkinson. What do you want from me?" trembled John.

"For you to stop collecting sticks and twigs, and come with me forever."

"Why me?" asked John.

"To live forever as my Apprentice."

"Are you a sorcerer?"

"I'm like a sorcerer...take my hand and I will deliver you from all this squalor, and like me, you will live forever."

"Come forward, John, one hundred years. Where are you?"

"I'm in the new offices of Atkinson, Atkinson & Dewhirst. I have a meeting with Mr. Braithwaite at ten o'clock; it's about a new account that I'm to look after."

"Is it, by any chance, your first day there, John?" asked Matt.

"It most certainly is! How did you know?" asked John

"Just a guess, John. What is your position there?" asked Matt. "Mr. Atkinson's surrogate," replied John.

"Surrogate?" repeated Matt.

"I didn't say surrogate. I said apprentice," laughed John Smith.

"Ok, John, my mistake. Where do you live?" queried Matt, quickly scratching some words in his notebook.

"I live at Lindale. It's a fine house," answered John.

"Right, John – I'm building up an idea of how things are for you. Let's travel forward to one of the times when you are not yourself."

"How about right now? Do you think this little journey of yours is going to be of any help? By this time tomorrow, this will all be a barren wasteland with a town population of nil!"

These words bellowed through the room, and after they finished echoing, the shadow-like figure of Atkinson emanated from the trembling body of John Smith. It raised itself away from Smith and walked through a statue-like hypnotherapist, whose only movement was his vocal chords, screaming.

"My god – was that Atkinson"? said a stunned Chief Inspector. "Ok, I have seen enough. Get him out of there!" instructed the Chief to the officers. He then checked to see if any of this has registered on the video.

"We will pull Mr. Atkinson in for further questions, and ask him why his Mr. John Smith is 650 years of age – and more importantly – when he will reach retirement age. I think we have our man."

Matt looked at John Smith and shouted, "One, two, three, four, five!" A snap of thumb and middle finger, and again, John Smith was back. "Are you ok, John?"

"I feel different, but fine," said John.

"I'm just going next door." Matt ran in just as Jeff was rewinding the tape.

"Did we get it all?" screamed Matt.

Jeff took his finger off the rewind button and pressed the play button, and just like magic, everything that took place in the room was perfectly transferred to the magnetic tape of the video recorder.

For a minute, nobody wanted to say anything, but the quiet was softly broken by Gavin. "What the hell are we dealing with here?"

"Hell might have something to do with it..." muttered Jeff.

At this point, D.I. Lambert returned with her own video. "You won't believe this waste of time," she said, throwing it onto the table.

"Get both of these tapes down to the lab. have them enhanced and back to me within the hour, and I will decide what is a waste of time. Remember, time is short. The lab stops everything and has my results back in one hour. Now go!" No sooner had the chief's words ended when the new D.I. was out of the door with the videos. "You guys, my office – right now," said a now non-sceptical Chief. "Take care of Mr. Smith," the Chief instructed the desk sergeant.

As the Chief, the coroner, the newsman, and the hypnotherapist sat down in Chief Inspector Paul Johnson's office, an uneasy calm settled with them. Nobody wanted to open what would be the strangest conversation any of them had ever had.

The policeman stood and took charge, saying, "Mathew, please tell me what we all just witnessed. We did witness it, didn't we?"

"We all witnessed it," answered the coroner, passing the conversation over to Matt.

"I have been hypnotising people for a lot of years, and have successfully regressed many people, but I have never had an entity exit someone like that. I hope it all comes out on the tape."

"What is going to happen now?" asked Jeff.

"All I know is this has to be sorted out before midnight tonight," answered the Chief.

"How do you know that?" asked Gavin.

"It's awkward. If I tell you, it will make me sound like some sort of idiot," said Johnson.

"Come on, Chief. We all just witnessed something from the Twilight Zone. I don't think what you have to say will shock us," answered Jeff.

"Ok, I was told this by my dead Chief Inspector last night at the stroke of midnight."

An uncomfortable silence fell in the office as everybody looked at each other, not quite knowing what to say. The silence was ended by Johnson.

"Ok boys, I'm letting it get silly. Let's wait until the videos get back. We will meet up back here in an hour. Go have something to eat. I think we have a busy day in front of us."

Gavin and Jeff got up to leave, but Matt stayed in his seat. "Aren't you coming, Matt?" enquired Jeff.

"No, I'm going to stay to see how John Smith is; he went through a lot back there."

"We will see you in an hour, then," said Jeff as he left with the coroner.

As the two men vacated the dimly-lit police building and emerged into the bright December midday sun, they both shaded their eyes from the it's glare. Sitting on the wall just opposite were two girls, both very different in appearance, but both smiling straight at the two men. One of them had a knee-length Laura Ashley floral print dress with a pink cardigan over it; in her hand was a bunch of flowers. The other had a black t-shirt with 'Goth Bitch' written across the front, a micro Royal Stuart tartan skirt and ripped black stockings with the tops showing, and a short black jacket with 'Grave Robber' on the back. Both girls ran to their respective boyfriends and hugged them.

"What are you doing here, Cindy?" asked Jeff.

"I'm on my way to see Mr. Steele at the hospital, and I thought I would call and see if you were here. I met up with Sarah, the lady we met the other night at the pub, so we waited together."

"Same for me, Gav, but without the flowers and the Mr. Steele thing," echoed Sarah.

The coroner just shook his head, smiled, and said, "Lunch, anyone? My treat." The four young people left the police station in Gavin Jackson's Jaguar and went to lunch.

Back in the police station, Matt had taken a tray of tea and biscuits into John Smith's cell.

Matt said, "Hi, John, are you ok?" as he placed the tray down on the plain wooden table.

"I feel great. You know those murders in my flat had nothing to do with me..." said John in a rushing kind of voice. "I was at work...and guess what I do at work, Matt."

"I don't know what you do for a living," answered Matt.

"Absolutely nothing. I just sit there, day after day, and do nothing at all. I have a bit of excitement every twenty-five years or so, but mostly nothing."

"Why are you remembering this now?" asked Matt.

"I'm not sure. This is the first time I have remembered. Maybe you have awoken something within me," said John excitedly. "Atkinson isn't human, you know..." he continued.

"May I get the Chief, so he can hear this, John?" asked Matt.

"The more the merrier!" said the now loose-lipped grey man. Matt ran up the stairs and into the Paul Johnson's office.

"Chief, Chief!" shouted Matt.

The Chief's half-cup of coffee was now all over his shirt.

"What the devil is the matter?" exclaimed Johnson, wiping Nescafe from his shirt.

"It's John Smith – he is singing like a canary, sir."

"Singing like a canary, two-way mirrors...is Humphrey Bogart about to appear? You really do watch too much TV, son," said a disgruntled chief.

"No, sir, please come and listen to him!" encouraged Matt as he ran back out of the office and down to the cell.

"Singing like a canary..." muttered Paul Johnson as he left his office and followed the excited hypnotist.

Gavin, Sarah, Jeff, and Cindy parked outside the Lounge Bar & Grill. This place had the reputation of having the best chef in town, and it was the restaurant where Gavin liked to eat. The four people walked inside, and were greeted by the head waiter, Mike, who instantly acknowledged Gavin with a knowing smile and showed him to his favourite table. After perusing the menu, Jeff ordered the fish and chips with mushy peas. Cindy ordered the char grilled rib eye steak with slow-cooked tomatoes, salsa Verdi, and rocket salad. Gavin ordered the pan-seared salmon with tomato and olive tapenade on basil mash, and Sarah ordered burger and chips with extra chips and tomato sauce.

Nothing was mentioned about what the two men had witnessed that morning, but Sarah had a definite buzz about her. She was bursting to say something, and Gavin finally said, "Ok, my little one, what is it?"

"Do you remember saying you would come to the Wendy House with me sometime?" she asked.

"Yes," said Gavin with some trepidation in his voice.

"There is a special on tonight...It's going to be ace. Will you come? will you come?" pleaded Sarah, fair bouncing in her chair with excitement.

"You will enjoy it, Gavin," said Jeff with a little smile.

"Of course I will, Sarah. I know – why don't we make it a foursome? Why don't you two come along?"

"Alright," said Jeff. "It's a date. What's happening tonight, Sarah?" asked Jeff.

"There is a band on and I've heard they are great!" said Sarah excitedly.

"Sounds like fun," said Gavin; Jeff and Cindy agreed.

At the police station, Chief Inspector Paul Johnson joined Matt in John Smith's cell. He looked down at Smith. He looked calm and very unconcerned about what had just transpired.

"Are you alright, John?" asked Johnson.

"Never better, Paul," said John Smith.

The Chief Inspector looked at Matt and smiled.

"What can you tell me about your boss?" asked Johnson.

"What's to tell? He is an ancient God, a lesser one of three."

"What!?" exclaimed the Chief.

"I'm his surrogate body. Tonight, he will enter my body and begin his term of office...his Administration, if you will," explained Mr. Smith. "He will enter my body and I won't remember anything until he is replaced by Mr. Dewhirst in twenty-five years, when I will start work again," said Smith with a smile.

The Chief nodded his head and smiled. "Singing like a canary? More like crowing like a cuckoo! You have fried his mind, and on police grounds! My god, if anyone wants me – I will be playing with crayons in my padded cell."

D.I. Lambert's car screeched to a halt in the car park outside the police building. She exited and ran through the doors, past the desk sergeant, and up the stairs without stopping. Running straight into Chief Inspector Johnson's office, she placed the two video tapes, and the enhanced version, on his desk, saying, "Take a look at that."

The Chief Inspector instantly put the enhanced version from the power plant first into the video player.

"Jesus Christ..." gasped Johnson. "That's Atkinson – and he is planting explosives! Take a look at this one Lambert,"

"It's him again...coming out of John Smith...but how?" said the young Detective Inspector.

"John Smith told me, not ten minutes ago, he was used as a surrogate. What the hell are we dealing with?" said Johnson.

At this point, the three other musketeers walked in. "Gavin, take a look at this!" said the over-excited Chief Inspector.

"It looks to me like it's all down to police work now. This could be your man! It's all down to you arresting this guy, and Jeff writing about it, and hopefully, nothing for me to take care of," said the coroner, hoping his life could return to normal so he could focus on Sarah.

Across town Tamara knew that she could not let Atkinson continue on this folly. Something had to be done, and fast.

She retired to her home, and opened her vast wardrobe. She unzipped the back of her gown and let it fall, then gracefully picked it up and hung it on its hanger, and placed it on the rail. She pulled down her knickers, folded them, and placed them in the laundry hamper. Standing naked, she opened the special part of her wardrobe, the one that contained her leather armour.

She took the leather pants with attached short kilt – the type gladiators used – and pulled them up and over her tight behind. She stood looking at herself in the mirror – a tall, slender woman, with firm small breasts and square shoulders.

Next, she put on her shin and thigh protectors, fastened by leather buckles at the back. They were hand-tooled and showed signs of combat. She strapped a pair of ankle-length boots on and stood there naked from the waist up. Taking her breastplate out of her wardrobe, she looked at the scarred leather, and thought back to the many battles she had had at Atkinson's side.

As she slipped her dainty arms through the leather breastplate that perfectly matched her own body shape, she felt utterly and completely alone. For the first time in her existence, she felt the chill of fear. She did not strap her scabbard to her waist and thigh, for she knew a sword would be of no use; she knew nothing in her personal arsenal would be powerful enough to stop Atkinson. She just knew she had to try.

Holding back a rare tear, she lay down on the couch to gather her thoughts and wait for her beautiful foe; whatever followed, she was ready to accept. As her eyes closed, she thought of happier times of love and friendship, of a partnership she thought would last a thousand millennia... of Atkinson.

Chapter Twelve

hief Inspector Paul Johnson and Detective Inspector Donna Lambert pulled up outside the offices of Atkinson, Atkinson & Dewhirst with two marked police cars arriving in unison. When all the cars had been exited, the six members of the police entered the building, headed by Chief Inspector Johnson holding a warrant for the arrest of Atkinson Junior.

The police were greeted by the ever-faithful Braithwaite, who informed them that Mr. Atkinson was out of town for the afternoon.

"Please be more specific," demanded the Chief.

"Mr. Atkinson does not tell us his whereabouts," answered Mr. Braithwaite.

"What about his mobile phone number?" enquired the Chief.

"Alas, that won't do any good, as he has left without his phone sir. I'm sorry I cannot be of more assistance to you," stalled Braithwaite.

"As soon as he returns, phone me immediately," ordered Johnson, throwing his card on the table.

After searching the premises Johnson marched out of the building, closely followed by his D.I. and the uniformed police.

"Do you believe him, sir?" asked D.I. Lambert.

"What sort of fool do you take me for? I most certainly don't believe the doddering old fool. He is clearly covering up for his boss, or whatever he is," was the Chief's grumbled reply. "Let's go to the power plant. I want a look for myself," he continued, trying to gather his thoughts. The small convoy of police vehicles made its way three miles north of town to the power plant.

As the police arrived at the plant, to their dismay, the protesters had increased their numbers tenfold and they were blocking the gate. The Chief Inspector got out of the car and ordered them to move, but they all began to sit down and link arms.

"I do not need this, Lambert. Get some reinforcements up here and I want them all moving, every last one," he barked.

"On what charge, sir?"

"Obstruction, damage, wasting police time...any of the above – you choose. Just get rid of them and let me know when they have gone!"

He got back in his car, turned it around, and two protesters had to leap for their lives or be crushed under his wheels, as he sped away back to the police station.

On arriving at the station, he nearly collided with four transit vans used for crowd control, speeding off in the direction from which he had just come. Johnson parked his car, put his jacket on, and walked into the police station. He went straight to the desk sergeant and asked if there were any calls. "No," was the reply.

He asked how John Smith was.

"He is in his cell with that circus guy," answered the desk sergeant.

"Circus guy? You mean the hypnotherapist. We are nearly in the 21st century, you know," answered Paul Johnson.

He then went to the cell, where John Smith and Matt were deep in conversation.

"Hi guys. John, if you would come up to my office and help me identify a person I have on video at the power plant, I should be able to let you go. You come along too, Matt," he continued.

All three men went up the now-familiar steps to Johnson's office and sat down by his video player. He pressed the 'play' button and what had happened at the plant earlier was displayed on the video.

"That's Mr. Atkinson! He is obviously in the Realm of Death, but it is him, Sir," John Smith confidently said.

"Realm of Death?" repeated Johnson.

"Yes, that's why you can see through him. He wanted you to see him, because on that plane, he can be totally invisible – so he wanted you to see him for some reason," said Smith.

"What is the Realm of Death?" asked Johnson.

"There are many realms...the one we are on is the Plane of Existence. There is also the Realm of Death, where the Atkinson's and Mr. Dewhirst do their work. The third is just known as the Other Realm, where the elder Atkinson and Dewhirst reside when they are not in the other two realms. Then, there is the Dark Realm. I have no knowledge of that place."

"Are you following this, Matt?"

"Yes sir, John has been telling me all about it while you were gone."

"The paperwork on this one will be interesting," remarked the Chief with yet another smile softening his face. "Do you have a passport, John?" he continued.

"No, sir," was Smith's simple reply.

"Then you are free to go – but I may need to pull you in again next week," said Johnson.

"Unfortunately, by midnight tonight, I will be gone, Sir," answered John.

"There we go again with midnight – what is it about midnight?" asked Johnson.

"That's when Mr. Atkinson will use my life force for the next twenty-five years, and I will have no memory of what is happening," said Smith.

"How are you both existing alongside each other then, or am I not following this?"

"Mr. Atkinson came back early for some reason, and it upset things, causing Mr. Dewhirst to die and go back to the Other Realm...but things weren't ready and people were here who shouldn't have been, and it's left me with these few days of ordinary living," said John Smith.

"But what are Atkinson and Dewhirst?" asked Johnson.

"Quite simply, they are the Reaper and the Scribe," said John Smith.

"When you say Reaper and Scribe you really mean it literally, don't you?" enquired Johnson.

An unequivocal, "Yes," was Smith's answer.

"Well, as I said, you are free to go, John. You might want to go with him, Matt, and tag along. Sounds like an interesting ride."

As John and Matt went to the front desk to get John's belongings, Paul Johnson was left sitting in his office, wondering where to go next. He phoned D.I. Lambert for an update at the power plant; it wasn't the update he wanted. D.I. Lambert reported that the more they arrested, the more protesters were turning up; they were coming from all over, and the police were beginning to lose control of the situation.

"If it gets any worse, call me, and I will get the army in," reassured her Chief Inspector.

Paul Johnson sat back in his chair and tried to piece everything together. It was impossible; if John Smith was right, no matter what happened, Atkinson would become this Reaper at midnight, despite not owning a horse, a scythe, or an hourglass. If this is what happens, then why was there a problem? Why did he have to be stopped?

The Chief Inspector lifted himself out of his chair, pushed it away with the back of his legs, put on his jacket, and made his way out of his office. He went to the house of his late Chief Inspector, ducked under the police incident tape, and into the kitchen where his boss had laid, trying to get a message to him. Johnson pulled up a chair and sat with his hands together and his head down. He sat there for an hour and finally said, "Are you there, Jack?"

"I've been here all the time," was the instant reply.

Paul Johnson jolted back onto his chair, breathing in short bursts of air, his eyes wide open and nostrils flaring. "Where are you?" stuttered Johnson.

"I'm here. Do you need to see me, or do you mistrust your own ears? Relax – please breathe normally or nothing can be achieved here," the ghostly but comforting voice said.

"How do I deal with this, Jack? I don't really understand what's going on," confessed Thompson's replacement.

Matt and John were now away from the police station and in a café in town. It was a small, friendly café where time wasn't rushed and the two new friends sat talking and drinking frothy coffee; John had the proof of that on his upper lip.

"Do you fancy going out tonight, John?" asked Matt. "We could go to the pub, or something. We could see if Jeff fancies a night out," Matt continued.

"I've never been out, I would like to very much," he said with a smile.

With that, Matt took his phone out and fingered through the names in his contact list; when Jeff's number was highlighted, he pressed the 'call' button.

"Hi, Matt, how's John?" asked Jeff as he answered.

"He couldn't be better. He is the reason I'm calling. Do you guys fancy coming to the pub with us tonight?"

"I can't tonight. I've already made arrangements – but there's no reason you guys can't come with us. We are going to the Wendy House to see a band. Are you up for it?" asked Jeff.

Matt lowered his phone from his mouth, looked at John, and asked him if he would like to see a concert; John Smith readily agreed. "Jeff", said Matt, after lifting the phone back to his mouth, "shall we meet at the Pack Horse about 8 o'clock?" he continued.

"Eight o'clock it is – See you then," said Jeff

Matt pressed the 'off' button on his phone and the conversation was over.

"Ok, Jack, you have my undivided attention. Please walk me through this," said Paul Johnson to the unseen phantom.

"This Atkinson that you will duel with tonight is the same one I chased across town and up the alleyway at the side of Atkinson, Atkinson & Dewhirst all those years ago. That is what I was trying to tell you about on the night of my demise. I now agree with my old friend Sid, having witnessed things from this side of the fence. It seems this troublesome Atkinson is different from his two partners and is wreaking havoc – the kind which nobody wants – most of all, his partners. If he succeeds tonight, it will be disastrous for all mankind. Have you worked out the John Smith angle yet?" asked his deceased Chief Inspector.

"Yes, I had a hypnotist regress him, and all sorts of strange things came to a head – most of which I didn't believe at the time. But now, as my bounds of reality have been stretched to their limits, I believe it all. The only problem is that I don't know Atkinson's whereabouts, so I can't bring him in."

"There will be no bringing him in, Paul. He has to be killed, and killed by midnight tonight. You must find a way of doing it for the sake of all Humankind. If you fail, it all ends tonight. Use whatever allies you can, and be strong, my boy, be strong."

The ghostly voice was silenced by the chiming of the church clock as it tolled five bells, and Johnson made his way back to the police station.

Chief Inspector Johnson called down to the front desk to see if there were any messages; none had arrived. He picked up his phone and called D.I. Lambert. On answering, she informed him that the situation was now under control and that they could now gain entry in to the power plant.

"I will be right there," said the Chief, jumping out of his chair and making his way downstairs. Pulling out onto Park Road, he turned right and headed back to the power plant.

John Smith didn't want to go back to Lindale Mews, because he had no intention of running into Atkinson – so he accepted Matt's invitation to go have tea at his mother's house. On arriving at Matt's house, Matt made his way into the kitchen and informed his mother that they had a guest for tea. John Smith was standing in the hall when Matt and his mother came out of the kitchen. Matt's mother was wiping her hands on her apron.

"Hello, John, come inside and make yourself at home. Tea won't be long," she said in a welcoming way.

"I'm having the best day I can remember!" enthused John.

"And it's going to get better tonight!" smiled Matt.

"Well, until midnight...but I will try to put that to the back of my mind," said John, sporting a happy face.

"While we are waiting for tea, let's go and pick you something to wear for tonight. We are about the same size," said Matt.

John Smith followed his new friend up the stairs, and wished this could be his life permanently, but he knew all too well that it would end at midnight, and he hung his head and sighed.

Matt saw John looking sad and he lifted John's chin up and looked straight at him and asked, "What's the matter?"

John smiled and looked back at Matt and said, "I feel strange."

Matt smiled and said, "That's something you will get used to, John. Have you ever been with a woman before...Or for that matter, a man?"

John Smith blushed as he realised that what he was feeling for Matt was affection; he coughed and felt awkward.

Matt said, "It's ok, John. It's not taboo anymore, and if your feelings are like mine, we should have a beautiful friendship."

Again, John Smith smiled and realised he had smiled more in one day than he could ever remember smiling before.

The moment was shattered by Matt's mother announcing that tea was ready.

Tamara's slumber was ended by the ringing of her phone. "Only six more hours to go until midnight, and I want to make up for the misunderstanding earlier, my love," said Atkinson.

"I'm just glad to hear your voice. When are you coming back?" answered Tamara.

"I will be back in time to take you out this evening," said Atkinson.

"Ok, honey, I will look forward to it," said Tamara. As she put the phone down, she thought, *you will take me out or I will take you out.*

The Chief Inspector arrived at the power plant to chants of "Fascist pig!" and "Save our planet!" The latter he was used to, but 'fascist' and 'pig' were new to him. He paid them the same mind as he usually did, by simply smiling at the people being held back by the thin blue line, and driving straight past them, up to the gate and inside, where D.I. Lambert was waiting for him.

"What took so long?" asked Chief Inspector Johnson.

"They all just came from nowhere, and they had no idea why they were here. All of them just kept on saying, 'We need to be here,'" said the exhausted D.I.

"That's ok. You have got it under control, well done," praised the chief. "Let's get inside now and have a real look at what is happening," he continued.

Once inside, Chief Inspector Johnson and Detective Inspector Lambert made their way to the main building again, but this time, Johnson wanted to see the main reactor room – not a facsimile on a screen. Reluctantly, the technician agreed and led the two police officers to the east wing of the building through another security-locked gate, and on through a pair of double-glass doors, into the main reactor room. The main reactor itself was encased behind glass, with only one door leading into it. Chief Inspector Johnson and D.I. Lambert walked up to the door and Johnson asked to be let in.

"Impossible!" claimed the startled technician. "The room could be radioactive, and we cannot allow anybody to go in!"

"But we need to check for explosives in there!" said Johnson.

"How possibly could there be explosives in there? Nobody can get in!" answered Marie Harrison, the technician.

"We need to check anyway. I'll take the responsibility myself," said Chief Inspector Johnson.

"Unfortunately in the main reactor room of a nuclear power plant the technician makes that decision, not the police, and I will not allow you to go in there!" demanded Harrison.

Chief Inspector Johnson looked at D.I. Lambert. Realizing that to enter would be folly anyway, he agreed with the technician. Having closely looked at the main reactor, and then the inner chamber where it resided, no physical evidence could be seen. The charges that he saw on the video film in reality weren't there. He decided to go back and have another look at the video, because it was clear that he wasn't going to gain entry, so there was no point in wasting time.

After leaving the building, Chief Inspector Johnson and Detective Inspector Lambert got back into Johnson's car and made their way to the police station.

"This might be a bad time to bring this up, Sir," began D.I. Lambert.

"Bring what up?" asked Chief Inspector Johnson.

"I haven't eaten since I got to the power plant earlier today, and I am rather hungry. Could I perhaps take a ten-minute break to grab something?"

Chief Inspector Johnson, realising what time it was and how long she had been there, said, "No, we can do better than that. Let's go find a café."

They drove through town and stopped at a little café on Park Road. On entering the café, everything on the Specials board appealed to D.I. Lambert. She asked a slightly rough-looking man behind the counter which of the specials took the least time to prepare, and she ordered that one. The Chief just ordered a cup of tea. They both sat at the only available table, near the window. The Chief's tea arrived, slightly stewed, but once he put his three sugars into it and took a mouthful, it could have been the best champagne.

"It was strange…" he said, "all of those people turning up today, today of all days."

D.I. Lambert agreed. "It was the strangest thing, I really believed them when they were telling me that they didn't know why they had to be there. They just needed to be there."

"This is the strangest police work I've ever done! Maybe we'll have to look at it differently from normal police work," he said

"How do you mean?" asked Donna Lambert.

"There were no clues, there is no evidence. Everything is in front of us, yet we have nothing hard to go on. All we've got are phantoms on a videotape, hypnotised journeys through many centuries, an accountancy building that has stood the test of time, surrogate bodies for ancient Gods and messages from beyond the grave," mused Chief Johnson.

"Messages from beyond the grave, Sir?" repeated D.I. Lambert.

The chief shook his head and took another gulp of tea.

"Never mind, I'm just babbling."

At that point, D.I. Lambert's food had arrived, and she heartily tucked into it.

Gavin Jackson stepped out of the shower and strode across his marble floor to the mirror. Opening the cabinet, and pulled out his shaving gel and razor. Lathering the gel in his hands, he creamed the lower part of his face. Gently scraping the razor across his chin in a deliberate fashion, he removed his five-o-clock shadow.

Replacing the shaver and foam into the bathroom cabinet, he took out a bottle of Polo cologne, unscrewed the cap, and put it on the countertop. Placing some into his left hand, he replaced the bottle on the counter, rubbed his palms together, and massaged the lower part of his face. He withdrew his breath sharply as the alcohol in the cologne bit into his skin. Replacing the cap back onto the cologne, he placed it back into the cabinet.

He then put on his robe, made his way back into his living room, turned on his CD player, and listened to Mozart's 'Magic Flute'. He then sat back in his chair and wondered how Sarah was doing.

Cindy was already dressed and made up, and was knocking on Jeff's front door. Jeff answered and she came inside.

"You're early, I was supposed to come and pick you up," he remarked.

"I got bored, so I got ready early, and here I am!"

"I'm glad you are," said Jeff. "I'm not sure what to wear tonight, and maybe you could help me."

They both went upstairs to Jeff's bedroom.

Across town, shouting could be heard from the ground floor of a run-down, back-to-back terraced house.

"Turn that godforsaken noise down!" bellowed a gruff voice from the living room.

Upstairs, Motorhead's 'Ace of Spades' was fair bowing Sarah's windows as her head moved vigorously backwards and forwards in the middle of her room. She stood there in just her black knickers, singing into her hairbrush, matching Lemmy word for word – taking no notice of the shouts from downstairs. Looking at her clock, she realised it was time for her performance to be over, and the crowd would have to wait until next time. She exited stage left onto the landing and went into the bathroom, where she removed what little attire she had on and stepped into the shower.

Gavin was now dressed in black trousers, a black shirt without a tie, and a pair of high-shine, black leather shoes. As he checked his appearance in the mirror, he picked up his car keys, placed his Rolex onto his wrist, and pressed the elevator button. The elevator arrived to the sound of a bell. He stepped in and made his way down to the car park, strode confidently to his gleaming Jaguar, and drove up the ramp, and then off to the other side of town.

Jeff and Cindy exited the front door and went down the garden path, turning towards the centre of town, arm in arm.

Two rather smart-looking young men emerged from Matthew's mother's house. Matt was looking his usual cool self, and with him was a young man, clean-shaven with gel-spiked hair. John wore a pair of blue jeans, sneakers, a blue shirt and a Levi jacket. They made their way to the bus stop for their short journey to the university end of town.

Sarah dashed out of the steamy bathroom, wearing only a towel around her head, and ran into her bedroom, where she sat at her dressing table. She removed the towel from her head, took out a hairdryer, and started drying her hair. She held her head upside-down and ran her fingers through its wet strands, making it stand on end. She then added a small amount of holding gel, sat back up, and finished her hair with the dryer.

Standing up in her full glory she wandered over to the wardrobe, where she removed a pair of fishnet stockings, a very short skirt, an embroidered top and the briefest thong that she owned. She first put on the thong with no apparent method – just one foot then the other – tugging it straight up with a bit too much gusto, so that she had to fish the string from her bum with her forefinger and thumb. Then she put on her stockings, first the right one and then the left. She didn't need a suspender belt because the stockings were hold-ups. Quickly, she fastened her little skirt with a zip and side straps with buckles, then donned the black and purple embroidered top. She jumped into her German military boots with the tops left open wide and the laces unfastened, and finished her look with her favourite 'Grave robber' jacket.

Grabbing the items that she would need for the evening – purse, lipstick, eye makeup, et cetera – and placing them in her Shaun the Sheep backpack, Sarah made her way downstairs to the front room. Bursting open the door, she stood there with her arms raised and shouted, "TA DA!" Her entrance was greeted in the same way it was always greeted by her family, with contempt.

Sarah's father said, "You look like a slut – all the old men will be slobbering after you."

"I'm used to that. It's no different to being here with you!" she said, looking right at her disgusting father. "But that's not going to be for much longer..." said Sarah, sticking out her tongue at him.

"Keep on, girl, and I will give you a spanking."

"Your days of spanking me are coming to an end, because I'm moving out soon and getting married," announced Sarah, as she ran out of the room towards the outside door, quickly chased by her father.

He shouted, "Who in the hell would marry a cheap tart like you?" just as Sarah opened the door, and a distinguished voice from the front step said, "That would be me."

Sarah's father stopped in his tracks and Sarah looked up at Gavin in amazement. "I didn't know you were there," swooned Sarah. She felt like a medieval lady whose brave knight had come to save her.

"From here on, if I hear you have been disrespectful in any way towards my fiancée, you will have me to deal with, not a little girl. She won't be back tonight, but she will return tomorrow for her belongings, because tomorrow, she moves in with me and will no longer have to deal with your tyranny," said Gavin Jackson in a firm voice.

"Wow – I don't understand most of what you just said, but it must have been good, because my dad just stood there with his mouth open. Am I really moving in with you tomorrow?" beamed Sarah.

Gavin nodded his head without taking his gaze off this reptile of a man. "Come on, Sarah, let's go meet the others." Sarah grabbed Gavin's arm and they both walked to his awaiting Jaguar.

Chief Inspector Johnson and Detective Inspector Lambert arrived back at the station and made their way up to Johnson's office. Turning on the light, they were both startled by someone sitting in the Chief's chair. Johnson was just about to call for help when he suddenly recognized who it was.

"How did you get into my office?" asked the Chief.

"Let's not waste time on such talk, Chief Inspector. Tell me what you know of Atkinson," asked the elegant lady sitting in his chair, wearing a long black coat that seemed to be hiding something bulky underneath.

"You appear to have something concealed under your coat, madam," said the Chief Inspector.

"Nothing that need worry you, Mr. Johnson, and please, call me Tamara. If I may ask again, what of Atkinson?" she quietly asked.

"I know he isn't an accountant," said Chief Inspector Johnson in a matter-of-fact tone. "I know that his two partners are Gods and I know John Smith is 650 years old. Atkinson has put some sort of explosive charges all over the power plant that we cannot get to because they are in another realm. Need I go on?" said the chief.

"Then what I say will not distress you too much, Chief Inspector. I aim to kill him tonight. The only reason I tell you this is because what I'm trying to do is almost impossible, so I don't need the police getting in my way. I don't mean any offence by that, but while I'm trying to what – in effect, will be saving the world, I don't want my concentration broken by people shooting me all the time...if you understand what I mean," said Tamara, as if she had just announced that she might be getting a parking ticket.

The Chief looked stunned.

"My dead Chief Inspector told me that I would need to be helped in this investigation," said Johnson in a low, slow voice.

"I know he did. I released him so he could talk to you. I'm glad you listened."

"What do you mean, you released him?"

"He was entered on one of my lists without my consent, so I was able to release him to talk to you. Remember, please, no interference," said Tamara as the lights went out.

The lights instantly came back on but Tamara was gone, and all that was left were two members of the police force, looking at each other, neither knowing what to say.

At the Pack Horse, Jeff and Cindy were joined by Matt and John. Jeff got the drinks and they all sat in the downstairs room, which was already filling up with all sorts of Goths and alternative dressers. Cindy took a sip of her lager, as did Jeff. Matt and John just sat there like two small boys who knew a great secret.

"Ok, Matt, what's going on?" said Jeff.

Matt said, "You know I've been single for over a year now." "Yes," said Jeff.

"I'm not anymore!" said Matt with a cheeky grin.

"What, you and John?" said Jeff.

Matt just nodded his head.

"That's great!" exclaimed Jeff, shaking his hand. Cindy gave John a kiss on his cheek, which made John blush and started everyone laughing.

"So tonight will be a great night! We have something to celebrate," announced Matt, looking at John.

Sitting in his Jaguar, travelling down Low Road towards town, Gavin asked Sarah what she wanted to do before they met up with Jeff and Cindy. "We're early. I had planned on staying awhile at your house to get to know your father," he said with a little smile.

"You stayed long enough to find out exactly what he's like," said Sarah with a giggle.

"You have no idea how much you are filling my life. I am so happy," he confessed.

"Me, too, I love you Gavin. I just want to be with you. You don't have to marry me. I will be glad to have the time you can spare me," said Sarah, putting her head on Gavin's shoulder.

"That sounds like your father's talk. I want to marry you. I think I've known that ever since the first day I saw you," said Gavin.

Sarah just smiled. "Let's go somewhere for just us for an hour. How about your place?" said Sarah.

Back at the police station, Chief Inspector Johnson was addressing all the officers who were on night duty.

"All of you have been issued with photographs of the man and his assistant, who we have to apprehend tonight. On seeing either of these people, you will contact me straight away. On no account must you try to arrest them, even if they appear to be doing something unlawful – you just keep in eyeshot and contact me. Is that understood?"

"Yes!" was the resounding answer from the uniformed officers. With that, he left them to their night duty and climbed back up the stairs to his office with his Detective Inspector.

"What do we do now, Sir?" asked D.I. Lambert.

"Now we wait for the first sighting," said the Chief.

Gavin's car pulled into the underground car park of his apartment block and Sarah and he exited the car. As they walked to the elevator, hand in hand, Gavin pressed the button on his key fob and the car horn and lights indicated that the car was locked and alarmed. The elevator arrived to the sound of a generic voice saying, 'Doors opening'. They both entered the elevator. Gavin put in his security key and pushed the penthouse button.

As the upward motion could be felt, Sarah smiled at Gavin and took off her jacket. She then undid the straps and button at the side of her mini-skirt and it fell to the ground. Grasping at the bottom of her loose-fitting top, she pulled it up and over her head. Then grasping the sides of her knickers, she pulled them down and kicked them into Gavin's penthouse with the rest of her clothing as the elevator doors swished open. Sarah stood there naked; she took Gavin's hand and led him into his bedroom.

As Sarah lay down on his bed, Gavin paused a moment to look at this beauty lying in front of him. For the first time, he could see the artistry of the tattoos that covered about twenty percent of her body, with fairies on her left arm. She had a tattoo of Pan on her right arm, and other tattoos about her legs and abdomen.

He was now familiarised with her more discrete piercings; she had a ring through each of her erect nipples, one in her belly button with a dragonfly on it, and a vaginal hood piercing, none of which she was too shy to show him.

Gavin unbuttoned his shirt and removed it; he quickly unfastened his belt and pulled it through its loops. Slowly unzipping his trousers, he looked up at Sarah as she lay in front of him. As he stared at her beautiful body, he felt a swelling in his unzipped trousers, a swelling that caught Sarah's eye and transfixed her gaze on that area. She wanted him so badly that she could not wait for Gavin to take his trousers off. She grabbed them and wrenched them from his legs. Gavin gasped as she grabbed his boxer shorts in the same barbaric fashion and pulled them to the ground. Gavin's erect penis was now directly in front of her face, so she took hold of it with her right hand and slowly caressed it with her tongue.

She looked up at Gavin, whose eyes were closed, and he was trembling with excitement. Slowly, she let Gavin's phallus enter her mouth, and she rubbed gently with her hands at the base of it. Gavin's hands clenched as he looked down at his fiancée looking up at him, her mouth busy on his manhood. Several minutes passed and Gavin felt his penis throbbing in time to Sarah's mouth movements, and he knew that he would not be able to hold back the oncoming surge, so not knowing Sarah's preference, he withdrew from her mouth.

Sarah lay back down on the bed and Gavin joined her. He kissed her lips and let his tongue press up against her pouting mouth. Quickly, her mouth opened and Gavin's tongue was granted entrance and was immediately welcomed by Sarah's own tongue. Sarah's mouth tasted sweet and refreshing as Gavin put his arms around her naked body. After that first French kiss, Sarah let her tongue slip over Gavin's face, first to his nose and both of his eyelids then back down the left side of his face, then slipping back into his mouth.

Gavin's tongue did the welcoming this time, and his hands had started mapping out the contours of Sarah's body. His fingertips moved slowly from her chin to her neck, then down to her breasts that were heaving in anticipation. Gavin's hand cupped her firm right breast, and his mouth followed his hand downwards to that wonderful area. As the tip of his tongue touched her nipple and ring, Sarah's back arched and she moaned softly. He tantalized her nipple by flipping the ring up and down with his tongue. Quickly, Gavin's tongue took a side step to her left breast. This breast had a Celtic ring tattoo around her areola, which perfectly followed its round shape; his tongue busied itself on that nipple to the same moans as the other. His tongue's natural migration south found itself licking at her belly button, teasing the dragonfly jewellery in the same way as he had her nipple ring.

Sarah, by now, was trembling with anticipation as she felt his tongue go over the soft waxed skin just above her vagina. Gavin stopped at the very top of her vagina for a moment to remind himself that she was a virgin, and that he should be very gentle. He felt Sarah's hands on his head, encouraging his entrance to her unblemished area, for her virginity was something that she wanted to finally part with that very night.

Gavin's busy tongue was now opening her small tight pussy; the movement of his tongue was like a cat lapping at cream. Sarah screamed with delight as the first thing that didn't belong to her entered her vagina. Gavin's industrious tongue had now reached her hood piercing; he had readjusted himself so that his head was now between her legs. Sarah's moans were turning into screams of absolute delight. She was laughing and crying at the same time. Sarah noticed that something had joined Gavin's tongue; she was experiencing a man's finger inside her for the first time. It was slightly uncomfortable, but it felt so good. Sarah could feel that she was going into orgasm when Gavin withdrew his forefinger and tongue and reared up from between her legs. "Are you ready, my beautiful Sarah?" asked her lover.

"Yes, yes!" she screamed.

Gavin gently moved his hips into position, widening her legs and lifting them up with his hands just behind her knees. He made his first thrust forward, just enough so that the tip of his penis touched her slightly open, moist pussy. Gavin then eased forward, his foreskin being pulled back by Sarah's small opening; this made both lovers wince at the same time. Sarah no longer had a smile on her face. This was painful, but she knew it was a pain that all women must go through, so she held on to the bed sheets and put her head back deep in the pillow.

Gavin saw that she was in pain, so he whispered in her ear, "Are you alright, my darling? If this is too much, I will stop," comforted Gavin.

"No!" shouted Sarah. "Keep going." She pushed herself hard down onto Gavin's erect penis. She screamed, and then something seemed to give, and Gavin's penis slid fully inside her vagina. As Gavin eased his hard penis out and then back in, he noticed the tell-tale scarlet sign that Sarah had lost her virginity.

Feeling very special that he had been offered this wonderful girl's virginity he knew, there and then that he would never hurt her again, and at the first possible moment, he would make her his wife. Gavin looked at Sarah and wiped away a tear from her cheek; he put his arms around her and squeezed her. "I love you, Sarah. I love you," said Gavin with a tear in his eye.

Sarah giggled and said, "We will be doing that lots, won't we?"

"Anytime you want me to," replied a very satisfied coroner.

Tamara's mobile phone rang, but it wasn't Atkinson; it was the other number on her phone. She answered, and was transported to the Other Realm.

"Things don't seem to be going as planned," observed Dewhirst. "You are aware that you only have until midnight to sort out this mess?" he continued.

"I see you are wearing your armour, but you have no sword. How will you kill him without your sword?" asked Atkinson Senior.

"My sword is useless against him; it is supposed to protect him!" shouted Tamara, holding back her tears.

"The reason you do not wear your sword is for the opposite of what you say. You know that if you get a thrust into him with your sword, his existence will end, and you don't want that. You think you can get him back here and reason with him?" argued Dewhirst.

"I can reason with him. He is just like a spoiled child. Let me dispatch him back here," pleaded Tamara.

"No!" was the unanimous answer from both Reaper and Scribe.

Chief Inspector Johnson was pacing all around by his chair.

D.I. Lambert was staring out of the window.

"I can't believe that with all the police officers patrolling tonight, there has been no sign of this man," said Johnson.

"He's obviously laying low, Sir," answered D.I. Lambert.

"I don't think he'll lay low. Sooner or later, he'll show himself, and as soon as he does, we will have him."

The conversation was broken by the ringing of his phone, and he quickly picked up the receiver. It was the front desk saying that nobody had reported anything yet. The chief just growled and slammed the phone down.

Over by the university in the Pack Horse, Jeff, Cindy, Matt and John left the pub and made their way towards the Wendy House. On arriving, they had to queue; it looked as if New Year's Eve was going to be popular.

In a high-rise apartment in the centre of town, Gavin escorted Sarah into their elevator. It travelled downwards; the main difference between the journey upwards was a flush in Sarah's cheeks.

To the generic voice of 'Doors opening', they exited and got back into the Jaguar, which they had left an hour earlier, and made their way to the university, and a rendezvous with Jeff and Cindy.

At the police station, Paul Johnson put his coat on and asked D.I. Lambert to follow him. They came out of the office and went down the steps. He informed the sergeant that they were going out on patrol.

"I can't stand this anymore!" said frustrated Johnson to D.I. Lambert. "We'll go out and grab a coffee, so, when we get the call, we can get straight on it."

They both got in Johnson's unmarked police car and drove off up Park Road, stopping in the all-night café.

"Sorry to hear about Jack," said a familiar voice.

Paul Johnson looked up from counting his coins to see the owner of the café, who wasn't usually there nowadays.

"Yes, it came as a shock to us all," said Chief Inspector Johnson, picking up the coffees and going to the table.

"Who was that?" asked D.I. Lambert.

"He's an old friend of Jack Thompson. I met him the second day that I was with my old Chief, and I used to speak to him on a daily basis, but then he got staff and I've hardly seen him since. It makes me realize every time somebody says his name that I no longer have Jack Thompson when I need him."

"I'm sorry you feel that way, Sir," said D.I. Lambert.

"For both of our sakes, I hope you never feel it," said the chief with a hollow laugh.

Tamara entered the offices of Atkinson, Atkinson & Dewhirst. Even though it was 8:30 in the evening, everyone was there, doing their jobs. Tamara strode through the posse of old men into Atkinson's office, which was still empty. She sat at her desk, took a nail file out of the drawer, and attended to her perfectly-manicured nails. Not too long after she arrived, the door to the Realm of Death creaked open, and Atkinson confidently strode in, in his finest gothic attire.

"I see you are already dressed," observed Tamara.

"Yes," replied Atkinson. "And what wonders do you have under your coat for me, my darling?"

"Oh…this is an old number I'm wearing. I thought it might befit the evening. It certainly goes with the Gothic feel."

"Then show me," said Atkinson.

"You've seen this a hundred times before," was Tamara's reply. "Now you have me intrigued – I really would like to see under your coat," said Atkinson in a slightly demanding way.

Tamara stood up and pulled on the belt of the coat. As it opened, she let her shoulders fall back, and it fell to the ground, revealing Tamara in her full battle attire.

"Isn't there something missing?" quipped Atkinson.

"I hardly think they will let me in a concert with a broadsword strapped to my side," was Tamara's quick reply.

"You have me slightly perplexed…the only time I've seen you wearing that outfit was because violence was about to ensue."

"As I said – it goes with the Gothic feel. You have also made many enemies in the short time you have been back. I may be needed to protect you."

"I think you overestimate your powers on this side of the fence," remarked Atkinson.

"So should I just stand by, and watch others attack you while you can still be hurt? Should I not be at your side, to protect you?"

"What's the worst that could happen? If somebody shoots me, I'll instantly be back with the old guys, therefore, instantly back here… unless you have other plans…"

"What other plans could I have? I am what I am – I am your Listmaker. If you're not here, I'm not here. What do I gain by your demise?"

"I take your point. But, in my opinion, the outfit looks ridiculous without the sword. If you are indeed wearing it to protect me, then we must stop off and get your sword to complete your outfit."

"If that's what you really want, my love, then we will call for my scabbard on our way to the Wendy House?"

"It will be busy I suppose with it being New Year's Eve"

"I suppose we had better be on our way in that case. I shall phone a taxi."

"Fine, I'll just quickly freshen up and I'll be back here in five minutes."

Tamara called a different taxi company than the one she had used last time, and waited for Atkinson.

By now Jeff, Cindy, Matt, and John had made their way inside the Wendy House. They went downstairs and showed their tickets to the attendants, who let them down another flight of stairs and into the lower room of the club. As they walked in, they made their way to the balcony overlooking the dance floor, with the best view in the house for when the band came on. Matt had gone to the bar to get the drinks when Gavin and Sarah arrived. Gavin seemed shocked to see John Smith standing in front of him, looking extremely different.

"Hello again," said Gavin, shaking John's hand. "Nice to see you're a free man."

"Yes, it's lovely to be here! I've never been to this place before."

"Then we shall be newbies together," said Gavin, "for this is my first time, too."

At that point, Matt came back with the drinks. Sarah joined the four young people while Gavin went for their refreshments.

The dance floor was starting to fill up with the people who liked to be close to the stage. There was no room for dancing. The band was due on at ten o'clock, and the auditorium was already almost full.

Back at the café on Park Road, the Chief and his D.I. left and got back into their car. The police radio was quiet. It was almost as if the town had gone to sleep. Chief Inspector Johnson looked at his watch and recorded the time as being 21:45. Then they pulled away slowly and headed towards town.

A black and white taxi pulled up to the offices of Atkinson, Atkinson & Dewhirst and sounded its horn. Atkinson Junior asked Tamara to go to the taxi while he dealt with something at the office. Atkinson pressed the button on his phone and asked, "Has Tamara contacted you today?"

Atkinson Senior said, "Yes."

"That's all I needed to know." Atkinson put the phone down. He opened his drawer and pulled out a bone-handled, stiletto-type knife and placed it in his pocket. Turning off the lights, he exited the building and joined the love of his life in the taxi cab.

"We need to make one stop, and then we want to be taken to the university."

"It's very busy there," said the cabbie.

"Yes, it's going to be a good night," said Atkinson, "the likes of which this town has never seen."

Tamara bit her lip and looked out the window, her breath showing on the cold pane. The cab soon arrived at Tamara's residence. She left the taxi and went inside. The bedroom light went on as she made her way to her wardrobe. She picked up her scabbard, wrapped it in a black shawl, turned off the bedroom light, and made her way back to the taxi.

"Ok, let's get down to the Wendy House," said Atkinson.

Tamara thought to herself that it was outside the Wendy House where all this trouble started, and how she had joined in and helped him, not knowing she was helping the possible end of existence. Tamara hung her head and sighed.

"Penny for your thoughts," said Atkinson.

"I thought you could read my mind," said Tamara.

"You asked me to keep out of your thoughts," answered Atkinson.

"My thoughts...when have I had thoughts that weren't concerned with lists, or you?" she said, with an air of bitterness about her answer.

"Let's make tonight a night to remember; after all, we go to work tomorrow, and all this fun comes to an end," said Atkinson.

"Fun, is that what we've been having?" muttered Tamara.

"Do I detect a tear in your eye, my love?" asked Atkinson.

"No, I have something in my eye," she replied, wiping away a solitary tear – a tear for her soon-to-be lost love – because before the night was over, one or both of them will have been wiped from existence.

"Enough of this gloomy conversation, we are here. How much is that, my good man?" Atkinson asked the driver.

After paying, they got out of the taxi and made their way through the university campus to the Wendy House. Tamara was strapping her scabbard to her waist and thigh when she caught the attention of one of the doormen. He came over to the couple and asked what Tamara was doing with a sword.

"It's just part of my costume. Take a look..." she said, opening her coat. The doorman's eyes opened wide when he saw how little of her body was covered with clothing.

"You see, I'm a warrior woman – and besides, the sword is stuck in the scabbard," she said, offering her sword to him.

"That's ok, madam, you can see it's plastic a mile off. You have a good night," said the doorman.

"We intend to," replied Atkinson, taking Tamara by the arm and leading her past the ticket collectors. Downstairs at the cloakroom, she deposited her long coat and he left his leather trench coat. Turning away from the cloakroom, they walked towards the main room and onto the balcony. Many people observed their dramatic entrance, especially six people standing not ten feet away.

Gavin took out his mobile phone and called Chief Inspector Johnson. He made his way into the hallway, so he could hear. The Chief answered, and Gavin asked him if he knew where Atkinson was.

"I have no idea...I have officers all over town," he answered honestly.

"He's right here," said Gavin.

"Where?" asked Johnson excitedly.

"He's at the university, at the Wendy House – and we have John Smith here with us," said Gavin in a worried voice.

"Is anyone with him?" asked the chief.

"Yes, that woman is with him."

"Tamara!" shouted Johnson.

"Yes," said Gavin.

"One last question – is she armed?" asked the chief.

"She has a broadsword, but I assume it's a toy one," answered Gavin.

"We are on our way. Keep away from them!" said the chief in an authoritarian voice. "This is Chief Inspector Johnson to all units – make your way to the university, and rendezvous with me there as fast as possible, but no sirens, Johnson out." The chief's car sped down Hunslet Road towards town, and reached the rendezvous point first.

Inside the club, Atkinson and Tamara made their way to the bar and ordered two absinthes. They took their drinks and went into the main room, when Tamara caught sight of someone she recognised. She told Atkinson that she was going to mingle, and he said he would do the same. Tamara made straight for the balcony to the six people standing there, all looking at her.

"What are you doing here?" she asked John Smith.

"I'm here to see the band," he answered.

"What do you know about bands?" asked Tamara.

"I invited him," said Matt.

"Who are you, and why are you spending time with our employee?" demanded Tamara.

"I'm Mathew – and surely it's up to John who he sees when he is not at work."

"Hmm...standing up for our Mr. Smith. If you want to protect him, I would get him out of here before Mr. Atkinson sees him. That isn't a threat; it's a bit of good advice. I don't think Mr. Atkinson is as understanding of the gay scene as I am. Please, John, you and your friend had better leave."

"I don't want trouble," said John, "but something is telling me I should stay."

"Alright, just keep out of his way," said Tamara, offering John a smile as she walked away.

Outside, the police were now in full force, awaiting Chief Inspector Johnson's word to move in. Johnson sat in his car, knowing that Tamara had asked him not to hinder her in the work she had to do.

"What do we do now, Chief?" asked Donna Lambert.

"I don't know; you heard Tamara. I will have to give her a little time to do what she has to do," he replied.

"But what if she is just buying time for her boyfriend?" asked D.I. Lambert.

Johnson showed a worried frown.

"Don't think that thought hasn't been rattling around in my head since she disappeared," confessed the Chief. "Either way, if I get it wrong, I dare not think of the outcome. We have until midnight and it's only ten o'clock. She has one hour – and then we end this," stated the chief.

As the chief finished talking, his phone rang. It was the police station patching through a call from the power plant. "Hi, Chief Inspector, this is Ed Simpson. I am the Night Chief Technician at the power plant. Ummm...I think we have a problem here. Now, I know that this will sound crazy, but several devices just appeared out of nowhere in our main reactor room – One of which has just disabled the door that is the rooms only entrance. Can you advise us on what to do?"

"I think you better hit the stop button, and turn off the reactor," instructed the chief.

"Oh – you don't understand, sir. It will take 48 hours to power down the reactor."

"48 hours? What will happen if those devices go off with the reactor...err, reacting?" enquired Chief Inspector Johnson.

"We will have, in seconds, what Oppenheimer took years to perfect," said the very worried technician.

"Oppenheimer? Who the hell is Oppenheimer...and what does he have to do with this?" asked Johnson.

"He split the atom, sir, paving the way for the first atomic bomb, which I might add was like a roman candle compared to the explosion that will occur if these charges go off in our reactor room," said Ed Simpson in a trembling voice. "The problem is that there is no point in alerting anyone, because the nearest airport is an hour away, and it is in the range of the destructive blast and fallout that will occur," he continued.

"I thought he was just trying to put out the lights as a decoy! I will send the bomb squad at once; you get your radiation people onto it as well" ordered the chief.

"As I said earlier Chief Inspector, we cannot gain entry; the door is not operational and it really is the only way in," interrupted the tech.

"You are all intelligent there! Find a way of opening the door for when the bomb squad arrives, and call me when it's done!" instructed Chief Inspector Johnson, now feeling the pressure even more. He looked at D.I. Lambert. "That nuclear plant has just become a ticking atom bomb."

"It would seem that the protesters have been right all along," said D.I. Lambert.

"Protesters! We need to get them out of there," said the chief.

"How will we do that? They will not move for us, and if we say the plant is about to blow, they will panic!" said D.I. Lambert.

"If that guy is right, it doesn't really matter where the protestors are," said the chief. Taking his phone in his hand, he called the station. "Patch me through to the bomb squad," he insisted.

"Sorry, sir, did you say...bomb squad?" said the voice at the other end of the phone.

"Yes! The bomb squad, now!"

"Right away, sir," answered the desk sergeant.

There was a click, a long unbroken tone, and then a dial tone. A very efficient-sounding man answered. "31st regiment, Brigadier Ashton speaking, may I be of assistance?"

Chief Inspector Johnson hesitated for a brief moment and then introduced himself; he explained his current problem, to which the brigadier asked what kind of charges they were.

"I really don't know – I have no experience with bombs," confessed the chief.

"That's ok; please clear those civilians from the front gates so we can gain entry."

"Consider it done. I'm dispatching units right now," said the Chief as he got out of the car. The Chief told three of the uniformed officers to take their car and partner to the power plant and make sure the gates were clear for the army.

"The army, sir?" asked one of the officers.

"Yes, the army! Just go do as I ask!" barked the Chief.

The officers got back in their patrol cars and headed off towards the power plant. One of the doormen had noticed the police build-up outside the club, and came over to find out what was going on.

"We have had a tipoff that there will be trouble here tonight," said Johnson.

"Trouble here?" laughed the doorman. "These are Goths; they don't go out looking for trouble. These are the easiest nights of the week for us," scoffed the doorman.

"That might be the case, sir, but I think you will find that trouble looks for them this evening," advised Johnson.

The doorman looked puzzled and went back to his spot by the door.

The three police cars arrived at the power plant. Most of the protesters were asleep in their tents, but a few more militant ones were sitting around the fire, comparing stories of sit-ins and camping outside American bases. They got up to see what was happening as two of the cars parked side by side, each touching a gate post. The police quickly exited and stood in front of the two cars, blocking the protesters from the gate. Soon, the headlights of the army vehicles could be seen speeding towards the gate. By now, more of the protesters had gotten up to see ten army trucks speeding through the police cars and the open gate. The police got in their cars and followed the trucks just before the gates closed, leaving the protesters up against the bars, looking in.

It was now 22:30, and the band had finally taken the stage. The lights had gone down, and the opening guitar riff echoed throughout the room. Everyone surged forward, spilling onto the already-crowded dance floor, leaving the balcony area quite clear. In fact, there were only two groups of people standing there now; a group of black-clad, long-haired girls, screaming at the lead singer of the band, and a group of six people who had just come to the attention of the rather distinguished man sitting with Tamara. He stood up and began to make his way over to them, knocking people out of his way, leaving a wake of upturned tables and an ocean of drinks on the floor.

Tamara suddenly saw what was happening, and ran to where the six young people stood, standing between them and the oncoming Atkinson.

"What is going on here?" demanded Atkinson.

"What do you mean?" asked Gavin.

"We're here to see the band. What's the matter with you?" said Jeff.

"I'm not talking to you – my question is aimed at him," said Atkinson, pointing straight at John Smith.

"He's with me; I brought him to see the band," said Matt.

Tamara looked at Atkinson and said, "Stop drawing attention to yourself. What does it matter why these people are here?"

"Why are you here?" Atkinson shouted at John Smith.

"I told you, he is with me. Now leave us alone!" insisted Matt.

Atkinson glared at Matt and grabbed him by the throat. Matt began to choke, as Jeff and Gavin both wrestled with Atkinson's arms. One swish of Atkinson's arm sent both of them flying to the ground. At this point, several security guards moved in to stop Atkinson, but they were dispatched in the same way. As the scuffle turned into a fight between Atkinson and the hopelessly outgunned group of young men and more security guards, the band left the stage, as the crowd was now paying more attention to the ensuing fight rather than their music.

Now it was Tamara's turn. She took hold of Atkinson's hand and wrenched it away from Mathew's neck; he fell to the floor in agony, leaving herself, Atkinson, and John Smith standing there. "What the hell are you doing, bitch?" snarled Atkinson, looking straight into Tamara's now loveless eyes.

"Stopping this folly – something I should have done earlier," she said as she drew her sword.

"But I am unarmed," said Atkinson, with his hands now in his pockets.

"Let's leave here and settle this outdoors!" demanded Tamara.

"Anything you say, my dear," said Atkinson, as he grasped the knife in his pocket. In a flash, he pulled it out and slashed it across her face. Tamara recoiled and knocked the knife from Atkinson's hand. It flew through the air and came to rest in Sarah's arm. Sarah screamed as the blade dug into her flesh, falling to the ground. The cut on Tamara's face was agonisingly painful, for that was no normal knife – it was made of the same material as her very own sword. She put the pain to one side as she pointed her sword towards the now weapon-less Atkinson. He took hold of John Smith and put him between himself and Tamara.

"What are you doing, you coward?" said Tamara disgustedly.

As she withdrew her sword, he threw John Smith at her, and made his escape

Outside, a doorman came running towards Chief Inspector Johnson. "There is trouble inside and we can't get it under control."

"Ok – listen up, everyone! Just get everybody out. Leave the two people who are fighting alone," instructed the Chief as they ran into the club en masse.

John Smith crawled over to Sarah. "Are you alright?" he asked. Sarah had tears of pain running down her cheeks as John picked her up and took her to a safe part of the club. Sarah had already removed the knife. "Where is Gavin?" she shouted.

"He is alright. He is over there with Jeff. He has been knocked out, but he is fine. I'm going to check on Matt now." But as he reached his newfound love, he discovered that Tamara had not been quick enough in releasing him and he lay dead on the floor. John sat rocking on the floor, cradling Matt in his arms, and for the first time in his existence, he experienced the pain of loss and the emotion of hate.

Tamara got up and gave chase. As she caught up to Atkinson, she lashed out at him with her sword, catching his chest and drawing blood from his pectoral area, making him fall backwards. She leapt to where he fell – but he had already gotten out of her way. He emerged behind her, punching her in the small of her back and smashing a bottle over her head. She cried in pain as she flew over a table and into the wall; blood was now pouring from her head.

The police were helping people escape from the club when Chief Inspector Johnson saw Atkinson right in front of him. For the first time in his career, he drew his handgun and pointed it straight at him; unfortunately, he hesitated and the chance was lost.

As Atkinson went for the killer blow on Tamara, she turned and hit him full in the face with the hilt of her sword. This sent him spinning backwards, and he fell once again. Tamara drew back her sword and was about to place it deep into his chest, when he kicked her legs from under her, sending her to the floor. Atkinson stood up and kicked Tamara full in the face and in her stomach; she groaned in pain. He was just about to do it again as D.I. Lambert smashed a chair over his back, and John Smith kicked him between the legs. Without flinching, he hit John Smith with the back of his right hand and sent him spinning to the floor.

Atkinson's onslaught was halted just long enough for Tamara to regain her senses. As she stood back up, Atkinson had just fisted the D.I. square in her face, breaking her jaw, cheek bone, and several teeth. Once again, Tamara lashed out with her sword, catching his neck; if she had been an inch nearer, it would be all over, but Atkinson just backed off again as Tamara tried in vain to thrust her sword into his abdomen. She kept moving forward, but Atkinson eluded her every move. Once again, the Chief got a clear view of Atkinson and discharged his firearm, catching Atkinson in the right arm. Atkinson screamed in pain as he realised what Tamara had been trying to tell him about human frailty.

Tamara lurched forward and stuck her sword into the same arm. At this point, Tamara should have finished him, but this time, it was she who hesitated as she remembered the love and good times they had. Atkinson used this moment of weakness, stood up, and kicked her between the legs. She fell to her knees as Atkinson kicked her once again in her face, sending her backwards onto the floor. He picked up a jagged leg from one of the broken tables and was about to sink it into Tamara's chest when he caught sight of Johnson pointing his gun at him once more. He quickly dropped the table leg and grabbed one of the innocent bystanders, a young girl who was crying. He picked her up and put her in front of himself as a human shield. The Chief instantly lowered his weapon. Realising their weakness, he took the girl with him for added security and ran out of the club.

At the power plant, the bomb disposal unit was ready to gain entrance to the main reactor when an alarm began. "Oh no!" shouted Ed Simpson.

"What's the matter?" said Brigadier Ashton.

"That alarm went off because one of the rod doors is automatically opening in there."

"That means precisely what?" demanded the brigadier.

"It means that whole area in there is now radioactive, and nobody can go inside."

"But we have to go inside to do our work!" announced the brigadier.

"Nothing can survive in there," said the distraught technician.

"How did that happen?" asked the brigadier.

"I don't know – it's impossible. It takes two security keys turning at the same time to open those rod chambers; I have one of them and it has not been turned," explained Ed Simpson.

"Right," said the brigadier, taking charge. "Get me whatever suits you have for going in the vicinity of radioactive materials. You, you, and you – make a start on that door! We need to be in as soon as those suits arrive," he ordered. The three privates got started on the door.

Chief Inspector Johnson ran over to Tamara and helped her to her feet. She had blood pouring from her head and mouth.

"At least we know now that you are not buying time for him," he said, as he wiped the blood from her mouth.

"What do you mean?" asked Tamara.

"It doesn't matter, my dear. Are you alright to carry on? We need to get that girl off him and you appear to be the only one strong enough to get near him."

"It's nothing to do with strength, Chief Inspector. It's to do with the fact that you people are all human; and as for the girl – she is as good as dead – he will just use her to stop bullets. Speaking of which...you're not the best shot in the world, are you?" said Tamara, managing a little smile. "Where did he go?" she added.

"He has run out of the club – with the young girl," answered Johnson.

Atkinson ran out of the club with the girl limp under his arm, shouting, "If anyone comes near, I will kill her!" He ran over to an awaiting taxi and wrenched the driver out. He put his human shield inside and drove off, with two police cars in pursuit.

The lead car informed Paul Johnson of the direction they were headed. With Tamara at his side, the Chief ran over to where Jeff and Cindy were. Cindy was holding Jeff in her arms. He had blood oozing from a cut on his lip and his wrist looked like it was broken – but apart from that, he was alright. He saw Gavin and called over to him, "Are you alright, Gavin?"

"I'm looking for Sarah," said Gavin.

"She will be outside with everybody else. Are you ok?" he reiterated.

"I'm fine; you get off after him. We are all alright here. When I get Sarah, we will take Jeff to the hospital," said Gavin.

As Chief Inspector Johnson made his way towards the door, he saw his Detective Inspector lying on the ground with massive wounds to her head and face. He called over to one of the uniformed officers and asked her to stay with the D.I. until the ambulance arrived. He then got up and left the club with Tamara.

Police officer Linda Harper sat with Donna Lambert, trying to keep her conscious until the paramedics arrived.

At the power plant, the suits had arrived, but there were only three of them that had the spec to be able to be used in such radiation.

"Right, men, gather round!" shouted Brigadier Ashton. "We have four bombs and three suits, and 45 minutes to defuse them. Sergeant Collins, Corporal Stevens, and myself will do the defusing. As soon as we are in, I want a phone link with the police. All of you must now retreat to the safety of the control room, so we can enter this chamber. Mr. Simpson – is the room we are in sealed when you leave?" asked the brigadier.

"Yes, sir, as soon as we leave, I will turn on the air lock," answered the technician. One of the three men working on the door informed his superior that the door was now unlocked.

"Good work, men," said the brigadier. "Can we have everyone out now, please?" he continued.

Chief Inspector Johnson and Tamara sped down the road, following the directions of the leading chase car.

"He seems to be heading towards the Town Hall, Sir," was the message from the front car.

"We will be right there," answered the chief, followed by six police cars, all with their sirens blazing out loud.

Atkinson's car arrived at the steps to the Town Hall. He jumped out with his insurance against any more shooting under his arm. He looked up at the clock and grinned as he waited for the police to arrive. He took out a trigger device from his pocket and switched it on.

At the power plant, one of the devices had been defused when, all of a sudden, it started up again. "Sir!" shouted Corporal Stevens. "Come over here! It's started up again! I had stopped it!" claimed the corporal.

"Damn!" shouted the brigadier. "It's also got a remote device, which means that even if we get all of these done, someone can still detonate them remotely. Get me the police on the line," he ordered the technicians in the control room. "We still have a job to do here, men. All four of these must be defused, and then we will have to put our faith into someone getting that remote detonator," said the brigadier.

As the Chief Inspector and Tamara pulled up at the Town Hall, Johnson's phone rang. "Chief Inspector... listen very carefully. We have defused most of the bombs here."

"Brilliant! Well done!" praised the chief.

"No, I said listen carefully. We have defused them, but they have all come back online. Somewhere, someone has a remote detonator. We can't do any more here. You will have to find the person with the detonator."

Chief Inspector Johnson told Tamara what the bomb disposal people had just informed him.

"Atkinson has it. I saw it earlier when he returned. He intends to wipe out all the records of what has happened here by blowing up that plant."

"That's suicide!" said Johnson.

"Not to him – if he is killed by something that isn't divine, he will be transported straight back here, so he has nothing to lose," informed Tamara.

"And what happens if he is killed by that sword of yours?" asked Johnson.

"Then his existence is over. Dewhirst becomes the permanent Reaper, Atkinson the Scribe, and me the very lonely Listmaker," sighed Tamara.

"Well, my dear, I wish you well. Go kill him," said the Chief.

"If it was that simple..." murmured Tamara, as she headed up the stone stairs to the balcony, where Atkinson was standing, holding his little shield in front of himself.

At the power plant, a vigil had begun outside the gate, almost as if they knew what was going on. All the protesters were now standing at the gate, looking in like some kind of doomsday crowd. The technicians were sitting around in the control room, waiting for the core to go into meltdown. The army remained in the reactor room looking at the devices with red lights going off and on, counting down the seconds to their annihilation.

All that was left now was a tired, heavily-wounded female warrior, making her way up the steps to meet her fate, each step causing pain to every part of her body. The eyes of everybody there, who were caught up in all of this, watched this tired, brave lady climb step after step. Atkinson stood there, confident and aware of how wounded his love of many centuries was. She looked at the man she knew as her soul mate; she tried to look in his eyes to see if there was some kind of spark still there, but there wasn't – just a cold blank stare.

"Why not let the girl go? You don't need her anymore," pleaded Tamara.

"She will stop those fools down there shooting at me...and what does it matter? They will all be dead soon," said Atkinson Junior, showing Tamara the remote detonator in his hand.

The town hall clock began to chime as midnight approached. The huge bell in the clock tower resonated once, twice, three times.

"Stop this!" cried Tamara. "It's insane! What can you gain?"

The bell continued to toll the fourth time, fifth time.

Tamara lunged forward with her sword, only for Atkinson to move to one side and grab her neck.

The sixth and seventh bell rang out into the night.

She desperately tried to get one last thrust of her sword and managed to puncture Atkinson's stomach.

The ringing bell kept its count with the eighth and ninth resonance.

Atkinson finally dropped the poor girl he had used as a human shield, and with rage in his eyes, he screamed. "You have failed! This wound won't kill me!" He readied his detonator.

The tenth and eleventh bell of doom rang out.

"No it won't, but this will, you evil bastard!" screamed Sarah, as she plunged the knife that had stabbed her arm deep into Atkinson's temple. Atkinson's grip on Tamara eased, but then his hand started to tense and his thumb began to press the red button on the detonator. Tamara, with her very last ounce of strength, took off Atkinson's hand with her sword, instantly separating the hand and detonator from his lifeless body. The hand and the detonator flew over the edge of the clock tower and hurtled downwards. Atkinson fell to his knees, and then onto his face as the bell tolled its final ring for Atkinson.

At the foot of the building, the bruised Chief Inspector Johnson looked up to see what was happening; he had been joined by a crowd of onlookers, including John Smith. "What's happening, sir?" he asked.

"All I know is that it's midnight and we are all still here. Shit! What's that?" shouted the Chief.

At that point, Sarah looked over the balcony and shouted, "Catch the detonator!" The Chief, followed by John Smith and the rest of the police, all ran to where the small box-shaped item was falling.

"It's mine!" cried out John Smith as the rest stopped. Beads of sweat could be seen on everyone as they watched him dive majestically to catch the falling detonator, as well as a West Indian wicket keeper dismissing a batsman at cricket. John Smith stood up and proudly gave the detonator to Chief Inspector Johnson, who immediately turned it to the off position. He ran up the stairs, with Smith and police officers following.

At the top of the tower, Tamara rested against a short wall. On the floor at her side was the slain Atkinson, with his own blade embedded deep into his temple.

"Well done, Tamara," said the Chief, still panting.

"Not me – I think this brave little girl needs a lot of thanks from everyone," said Tamara, as she closed her eyes and slumped over her dead lover, and then joined him.

"How did you get here, Sarah?" panted a very out-of-breath Chief Inspector Johnson.

"I don't know; I was in the club and I pulled the knife out and someone threw me over his shoulder. A voice in my head said...*your sister needs you*...and I was dropped on the floor here with the knife in my hand and I just, well, you know..."

"That's ok, you did a fine job," said the chief to the sounds of ambulances arriving.

The paramedics arrived and ran to Atkinson and Tamara, pronouncing them both dead at the scene. They then turned to Sarah and treated her arm. They told her that her arm would heal fine, but that her tattooist would have some repair work to do. Sarah just giggled as Chief Inspector Johnson passed her his phone and said, "Someone would like a word with you."

Sarah put the phone to her ear and shrieked, "Gavin!"

Sarah was taken down on a stretcher, and Burke and Hare arrived in their van to remove Atkinson and Tamara. The Chief walked down the steps with John Smith, and asked him what he was going to do now.

"I don't know, Chief Inspector," he answered, as he saw a woman he knew standing in the shadows. He left the chief and walked over to her.

"Hello," said John Smith.

"The main boss at Atkinson, Dewhirst, & Smith would like to talk with you. I think they have a promotion in mind."

"But...but...Tamara, I've just seen you put in a body bag and taken away with Mr. Atkinson."

"Welcome to the management of our company, John. You will find many things are possible...even the impossible," said Tamara with a little grin.

The champagne was flowing at the power plant as the technicians and the army personnel realised that the police had stopped the detonation, and they were all still alive.

Gavin put down his phone and told his two friends that Sarah was alright.

"She has something exciting to tell us when she arrives."

Jeff was pleased that Sarah was ok, but he felt a deep sadness over the loss of his friend, Matt.

Chief Inspector Paul Johnson decided to walk to the hospital to check on D.I. Lambert. As he walked, he had the feeling that he wasn't alone. "Is that you, Jack?" asked Johnson.

"You did good, son. You have learned many things tonight. Take what you have learned, and use it in your everyday police work, and it will make you a better copper."

"Thanks, Jack, I couldn't have done it without you. See you again, old friend," said Johnson.

"Yes, but not too soon. Bye for now, lad. Sid, wait, I'm coming!"

At the hospital, Sarah arrived. She leapt off the stretcher and ran into Gavin's arms. "I did it! I stopped him! I waited my time and I totally kicked his ass!" she yelled in his ear.

"Alright, my love, you can tell me all about it later. Let's get your arm attended to first. Jeff has to stay in the hospital tonight to make sure he is ok; he has just gone into the ward," said a relieved coroner.

In ward ten at the general infirmary, the curtains were pulled back on Jeff's bed by the two nurses. The person in the next bed asked him if he was ok. On hearing Jeff's voice, the guy shouted, "You're fired!"

JOHN PAUL BERNETT

Chapter Thirteen

Two weeks had passed, and things had begun to settle back into a quiet, low-key routine. That put a smile on the now-official Chief Inspector Johnson's face. This was how it should be – no demons from other realms, ghosts, bombs or sword fights...and especially no murders. Yes, police work was back to how it should be.

D.I. Donna Lambert strolled into Chief Inspector Paul Johnson's office, her facial scars still red but healing. Her dentist had worked wonders on her teeth, and her best dress was all cleaned and pressed.

"You're looking glamorous, Lambert," observed Johnson.
"We have to look our best for Sarah this afternoon," replied the D.I.
"Yes, we do. It's not often someone gets the key to the city, especially someone as young as Sarah. Imagine the impact on the youngsters of our city, having a hero of their own age group. I only hope she doesn't swear in front of the Lord Mayor," said Johnson with a smile.

Cindy was busy tying Jeff's tie.
"There, you look very smart, good enough for the Civic Hall."
"I feel all trussed up...I can hardly move in this suit," complained Jeff.

"Be quiet, Jeff. You couldn't go in a T-shirt and jeans," chuckled Cindy.

At that point, a car horn sounded outside. "The taxi's here!" said Cindy excitedly, and the couple made their way downstairs and out to the taxi.

The limousine was parked outside Gavin Jackson's block of apartments, awaiting the appearance of the town's hero. Unfortunately, the girl of the moment was locked in the bathroom.

"I'm not coming out, and you can't make me!" said Sarah.

"Why won't you come out? The car's here and everybody is waiting at the Civic Hall just for you, my love," said Gavin gently. "If you come out, I will let you assist me all day tomorrow. I might even let you make an incision..." offered Gavin.

The bathroom door suddenly unlocked and the door opened slightly.

"Promise?" pouted Sarah.

"Scout's honour," replied Gavin.

"Ok then, let's go!" shouted Sarah, as she burst out of the bathroom and ran to the door giggling.

"I see you have dressed for the occasion," said Gavin with a smile.

"Yep," was Sarah's reply.

Her 'occasion' attire was a black mini-skirt with pink rabbits on it. She wore a black shirt with a tie. The tie was black with pink rabbits on it, and pink tights with black rabbits. The finishing effect came from a little pair of black plimsolls with no rabbits at all.

Gavin joined her at the door in his dinner suit and black tie. He thought to himself...*what a striking couple we are*, and once again smiled. Gavin helped Sarah to the car, and they slowly made their way through the streets to the Civic Hall.

As they made their way into the city centre, the streets were lined with people cheering, all trying to get a look at the special person who had saved all their lives. The crowd was not aware of the supernatural part; they just knew this girl had stopped a terrorist from blowing up the nuclear plant, and they were grateful.

The occasion was getting grander as they neared the civic buildings, because the army had a guard of honour arrayed up the stairs to the hall.

Watching from a top-floor window of one of the tower blocks was John Smith, who was preparing for a meeting himself. In the two weeks since the stand-off with Atkinson, the rejuvenated Tamara had been instructing him about what he had done up until then. But more importantly, he learned what Atkinson Senior and Dewhirst wanted him to do from now on. To suddenly find out that he was the human part of what was basically the Grim Reaper was hard enough to take in, but then to be asked to carry on his work was extreme, to say the least. Then she explained that she was taking him to this meeting in another realm, and that when he returned, he would no longer be human; that was the icing on the cake.

"You are going to be just fine, John," comforted Tamara.

"Am I? I don't share your confidence, Tamara," he confessed.

"All you have to do is come with me this afternoon and everything will be alright. Just trust me, John. You will feel things you won't believe. You will see with the eyes of a God. Everything will be at your disposal...and I do mean everything, John," said Tamara, in a very suggestive way.

As the limousine stopped at the foot of the stairs to the grand Civic Hall, a brass band began to play a version of 'Holding Out for a Hero'. Gavin exited the car first, made his way around to Sarah's door, and opened it. As Sarah stepped out of the car, the crowd cheered, and the guard of honour stood to attention. Sarah was overcome with emotion and she cuddled Gavin for support.

They both made their way up the red carpet on the steps, but Sarah kept her head buried in Gavin's chest. At the very top of the wide stone steps stood the Lord Mayor, flanked by council dignitaries from every political party, all of whom wanted to shake Sarah's hand.

Away from the party at the Civic Hall, Tamara took hold of John Smiths hand and asked him if he was ready for his date with destiny.

"Can I refuse my date?" asked John hopefully.

Tamara walked up to him and straightened his tie. "No," she said, and gave him a kiss on the cheek.

"Ok, then lead the way," said John Smith, quite timidly.

Tamara depressed the 'A' button on her special mobile phone, took John Smith by the hand, and they both were instantly transported to the realm where Atkinson Senior waited for their arrival.

By now, the handshakes were over on the steps of the Civic Hall and the main party had gone inside. The crowd outside began to leave as the speeches inside began with a tribute to the youth of today by the Lord Mayor. Many tributes followed, but none was like the one that the new Chief Inspector gave. Paul Johnson waxed lyrically about how civilians played an epic part in all of this, and in particular, young civilians such as Jeff Clarke, the new coroner Gavin Jackson, and the girl of the moment – Sarah. But he paid the biggest tribute to Matthew..."Or Matt, as we all knew him. When he arrived at the police station, I thought he was a freak. I knew nothing of hypnotism, and was going to have nothing to do with it, but the young people sitting here before you convinced me to give him a chance. He was so successful regressing our subject, that the investigation was saved precious time – time that we could ill afford to lose. Then nearing the end, he paid the ultimate sacrifice to protect his friend. He lost his young life in that struggle by the madman we were pursuing. I don't know many hardened police officers who would have gone against this beast, but Matt had no hesitation. Thanks to this selfless attitude shown by Matt, his friend John Smith's life was saved. Unfortunately, John Smith, who also played his part in the team effort that brought this madman down, cannot be with us today, so with no further ado, I would like you to raise your glasses to our saviours – Sarah, Matt, John, Jeff, and Gavin." The assembled masses all rose, raised their glasses, and saluted the town's young heroes.

Atkinson Senior was sitting in his throne-like chair as Tamara introduced John Smith to him.

"You must forgive Mr. Dewhirst's absence, but you did play a part in him being back in your domain," said the old deity, with a voice resembling someone suffering from laryngitis. "My son's untimely exit from your old domain has left me with a problem, Mr. Smith. Dewhirst should be resting and spending time here with me, but he has had to go back to carry on our work. Now what can we do about that, Mr. Smith?" continued Atkinson Senior.

Smith looked straight into Atkinson's eyes and answered, "Are you offering me a promotion? If you are, is the benefits package the same?" He turned and looked at Tamara.

"Know you this: all he had will be yours. His powers yours, his benefits yours. Should you fail and be unworthy, his fate will also be yours. Tamara is your Listmaker. She will show you the ins and outs of your new position; your office awaits. Now be gone. I grow weary of all this change," said the shadowy figure.

As they left, Tamara said, "Two things bother me."
"What bothers you?" asked John.
"Atkinson Senior said 'untimely exit'. Usually when a being has ended its life, he says it's dead. That leaves me worried. He knows everything, and he did not confirm his son's death – he just said 'exited the domain.'"
"It's probably a slip of the tongue. What's the other thing?"
"I thought you liked boys. I saw how you looked at me when you asked for Atkinson's benefits," she said with a smile.

"I did look at you, and I don't know why I'm like this...it seems everything is different and still the same. My whole life has been turned upside down," waxed an unsure Mr. Smith.

Tamara smiled, and somehow, the confused John Smith was reassured. The Listmaker and new Reaper watched the firework finale above the Civic Hall with a glass of Dom Perignon from a hotel balcony.

Chapter Fourteen

The front door at the offices of Atkinson, Dewhirst & Smith opened and John Smith walked in.

"Sorry to hear of Mr. Dewhirst's untimely demise," said old Mr. Braithwaite, the usual announcer of a change of figurehead. All the old pen-pushers put their heads down and continued their work.

How strange, thought Smith. *It was Atkinson who had just been removed, not Dewhirst. But Dewhirst had to come back when Atkinson was removed.* He then realised that was twice he had thought the word 'removed' instead of killed. He would have thought no more of this had he not witnessed Tamara's death, and then moments later, was reunited with her. *Hmm...strange indeed,* he thought. *Was a rejuvenated Atkinson awaiting him around the next corner?*

"Enough of this nonsense!" cried out Smith, and all the clerks looked up simultaneously. John Smith looked slightly embarrassed as he made for his office.

Only now he realised there were no young, upwardly-mobile members of staff to send each other e-mails; that must have been a quirk of that strange Tuesday when all this began. It was just the 700-year-old Sunny Acres Mob. *Maybe some of these fossils could retire; after all, eternity was a long time to share with this workforce,* he thought to himself.

"Coffee, tea or me?" offered Tamara.

John Smith just looked at her as he slammed the door closed and fell back on it, looking quite scared.

"Whatever is the matter, John?" enquired Tamara.

"Why did you think it odd that Atkinson Senior didn't use the word 'dead' when describing the demise of his son?" quivered John Smith.

"Relax, John," assured Tamara.

"What if he is back? He will come for us both," panted John Smith.

"Remember, John, there cannot be two Reapers at the same time. You are quite safe," she comforted. "Now, back to my original question: tea or coffee? I don't think you are in the mood for me." She laughed.

"Tea, please," said Smith.

Jeff Clarke walked into the lobby of his newspaper building, knowing his boss was back. Jeff had set a new record of getting fired, not counting Sid of course, but Sid had been there a long time. However, Sid had never been fired in a hospital; Jeff alone held that distinction. He looked into the canteen to say hi to Cindy.

"I'm not looking forward to this," announced a nervous Jeff. "You will be fine," reassured Cindy. "Do you want a cup of tea before you go up?"

"No thanks, I had better get this over with," said Jeff.

In his office, Donald Steele was tapping a tune on his desk with a pen when he heard Jeff knocking on the door.

"Go away!" he roared. Jeff took a deep breath and walked into the editor's office. Steele looked at Jeff. For a moment, he held his gaze, and then he put his pen down.

"What am I going to do with you?" he said with a surprisingly quiet voice. "You got the story, but you didn't do what I told you to do. So, if you are hell bent on acting like your friend Sid, you leave me no alternative. I want you to go and clear your desk. Somebody else needs it now."

Jeff's head fell, as all that he was expecting was unfolding before his eyes.

Then a wry smile came to Don Steele's face as he announced, "And move your stuff into Sid's old office. That was reporting from the seat of your pants, boy! You can't teach that kind of reporting, it is born into you! My god, you will probably get a Pulitzer Prize for this story!" grinned the editor.

Jeff was elated, and thought to himself that now was probably not a good time to tell his editor that he had signed a paper at the police station, saying he would not write the story, as it would cause too much unrest.

Sarah's eyes opened wide as she assisted Gavin in her first real autopsy. She watched and admired the young coroner going about his duties. Gavin had never known a more wonderfully strange girl in his whole life, a life that had started a new chapter, having arrived at this town only a few short weeks ago.

The police station was quite busy. A woman was at the front desk, complaining of boys in her street playing football and her greenhouse window having been smashed. Three cats had gone missing. One man wanted the police to intervene in an argument that he and his neighbour had started over the dividing line of their gardens, and a purse had been lost. Yes, everything was truly back to normal.

"Why is it that I know what to do at my new position, Tamara?" enquired John Smith, as he and Tamara drank a cup of tea in his office.

"I have had no training, and yet, I am totally ready to start."

"Relax and don't worry so much. You will be good at this. Your journey to the Other Realm and your meeting with Atkinson Senior is the reason you appear to know everything," assured Tamara, as she sipped her tea without wetting her lips. "Your first list is ready and it is time to go. I know you know what to do, but just let me run through it with you, so there are no mistakes."

"Every living human has an invisible cord that links them from the Plane of Existence to the Realm of Death. Each one has an allotted time on this earth, and when that time is up, you cut their cord, resulting in the death of the individual human. How they die is not important. It's the time that is important, for as you are cutting the cord in the Realm of Death, they die on the Plane of Existence, and their name is inscribed in the Great Book in the Other Realm. Is that how you see it, John?" asked Tamara.

"Pretty much," he replied.

"Then we are as one – the eternal Listmaker and gatherer of souls," said Tamara

The old door behind the desk creaked open. Tamara gave John a kiss on the cheek. John walked into the Realm of Death, and the door swung shut behind him. As he walked into this strange land, he noticed the sound was muffled and it was unusually bright. He had imagined there to be billions of cords all going into one central place, but there weren't. In fact, the only visible cords were the ones to be cut. He took hold of the first one, and with one flash of his giant sword, a life was terminated.

He carried on like this for 12 days and 12 nights, until every cord was severed. Only then did he stop and think of what he had just completed – and he felt good. He turned and looked over his shoulder towards the door that led back into the Plane of Existence. He saw what looked like a tall – muscular man, but he was very faint and had no cord attached to his person. As he walked towards this faint but imposing figure, the man faded away. Smith walked towards the door and went through it.

He gave the strange figure no more thought as he passed back into his old realm, where Tamara was still finishing off her tea, as if he had only been gone for 12 seconds and not 12 days.

Tamara welcomed the new Reaper back and said, "Wow, you did that faster than Atkinson! Did you have a good time?"

The newly-invigorated John Smith smiled and said, "Oh yes."

The phone rang and Tamara answered. "Hello, Chief Inspector, how can I help?" Tamara placed her hand over the phone and asked Smith if it was alright for him to come over. John Smith readily agreed, and she relayed the message. "He will be here in an hour," announced Tamara.

"What does Paul want?" enquired Smith.

"I'm not quite sure, John, but he did say it's off the record," smiled Tamara.

"When he has gone, shall we go eat?" asked John.

"Remember, John, what you want, you get. You are the master now, not the slave," said Tamara.

"I know, but in this realm, I'm used to living a quiet life. For the meantime, at least, I would like that to continue. We have found out what happens when you are too controlling, and I certainly don't want to end up fighting you," he laughed.

The date had been set and the invitations had gone out. Now it was time to meet the parents. Sarah sat in the passenger seat, while Gavin drove his gleaming Jaguar up the long driveway to his parents' country home. Donald and Harriette Jackson sat in their Edwardian drawing room, awaiting the imminent arrival of their darling son...and the rather common girl they were about to be introduced to.

The afternoon quiet in John Smith's office was broken with Braithwaite tapping on the door.

"Chief Inspector Johnson to see you, sir," announced the elderly gentleman.

"Paul, do come in," invited John.

"John, Tamara, hello – nice to see you again."

"Would you care for a beverage?" asked Tamara.

"No thanks, I just wanted a chat with you both...off the record as friends, if that's ok," said Johnson with a worried smile. Tamara offered him a chair.

At the mansion, Sarah enquired "Is this your dad?" As a tall, distinguished gentleman opened the car door.

"No," replied Gavin. "This is Jarvis, my parent's butler. How the devil are you, Jarvis? You look great!" he continued.

"I'm exceedingly good, Master Gavin. May I take the lady's cases?" said Jarvis efficiently.

"She doesn't have any, my good fellow," Gavin replied.

"Cases of what? And what is a butler?" whispered Sarah into Gavin's ear.

Gavin gave his now customary smile and said, "Just say, 'Hello, Jarvis'."

"Hello, Mr. Jarvis. I'm Sarah, and I'm very pleased to meet you," said Sarah, as she did the curtsey she had been practicing. Jarvis' Edwardian posture relaxed for a brief moment, and a faint smile was cracking his stiff upper lip.

Back at Atkinson, Dewhirst & Smith, John opened the conversation. "What can we do for you, Paul?"

"I have witnessed phantom bombs, people emerging from surrogate bodies, and ancient warriors fighting on the Town Hall clock tower. The worrying thing is that the two ancient warriors died, but I am here chatting to one of them. Do you get my point?" asked Paul.

"Are you worried the other one might return?" replied John Smith.

"In a word, yes."

"I will let Tamara handle this, Paul."

Tamara explained about how two soul gatherers cannot exist at the same time.

This gave the Detective Chief Inspector the answer he wanted, and he left with a certain amount of ease.

After he had left, John thought about the shadowy figure he saw on his way back from the Realm of Death.

"Can my cord be cut, Tamara?" John asked.

"We do not have cords," replied the Listmaker.

"How many people don't have cords?" was the next question.

"You and I, Atkinson and Dewhirst are above the life and death thing. We are completely different beings. Why?" asked Tamara.

"That's it, then. It was one of those two checking that I was doing the job right," said a relieved John Smith.

Tamara looked straight at John Smith and said, "What are you talking about? Neither Atkinson nor Dewhirst can enter that domain while you're there."

"Who was the guy standing by the door when I made my way back, then?" asked the new Reaper.

"It was your imagination, John. That domain can play strange tricks on your mind the first time you enter it."

Jarvis opened the grand front door into an imposing reception hall, closely followed by the two young lovers.

"I am so going down that banister rail," said Sarah.

"I used to get scolded for the same thing as a boy," remembered Gavin.

In the next instant, Sarah ran up the stairs, placed her leg over the top of the banister, and slid all the way down. She fell rather unladylike on the floor, with her legs in the air.

"This is Sarah, Mother," said Gavin, as Sarah looked up at the very stern-looking Mrs. Jackson.

"Hi, pleased to meet you, Mum!" smiled Sarah.

"You need to work on your dismount, my dear..." came a booming voice from behind the silently astonished leader of the Allerton Chapel branch of the Women's Institute. Donald Eugene Jackson just smiled, shook his son's hand, and whispered to his son, "You are going to have to work on your mother."

Both men began to laugh. Jarvis left the room as the two ladies looked at each other.

"Come on inside the drawing room, my dear," said Gavin's father, as he put his arm around his soon-to-be daughter-in-law and led her into the room.

"I'm good at drawing!" said the breath of fresh air that wafted into the stuffy old English drawing room.

"I'm sure you are, my dear," said the grey-haired, distinguished gentleman.

Gavin put his arm around his stunned mother and followed them in. Jarvis arrived in the room, carrying a silver tray containing bone china cups and saucers, a grand tea pot, and a cake stand adorned with all manner of sweet delights.

"I took the liberty of purchasing this beverage for the master's betrothed," announced Jarvis.

Sarah just looked at Gavin, bemused. Gavin whispered that Jarvis had just told her the can of coke was for her.

Sarah smiled and gave Jarvis a hug and said, "Thank you very much." Jarvis' cheeks lost their paleness as he gave a slightly embarrassed cough and quickly left the room. Gavin and his father roared with laughter. A crack of a smile appeared on the lady of the house's face; she began to warm, as everyone eventually does, to this delightfully strange but sweet girl. After the shaky start, the afternoon tea went well, and Gavin realised how lucky he was to have found Sarah.

Tamara looked out of the window at the unmarked police car driving away. She had a worried reflection staring back at her from the pane of glass. *What, or who was lurking in the Realm of Death, and what damage could it do?*

"A penny for them."

Tamara turned around very quickly to see a smiling John Smith. "Why did you use that turn of phrase? It's important, John! Why?" shouted Tamara.

"I didn't say anything," a slightly bemused Smith answered.

For the first time, John Smith saw that Tamara looked scared.

"Ok," said John. "I'm worried now. What just happened?"

Tamara slowly sat down at her desk, put her head in her hands, and said, "I've just heard Atkinson's voice in my head."

Tamara and John Smith just looked at each other in the very old office of the even older firm.

In the deepest recesses of the darkest eternity, a shackled lesser God was undoing the chains that bound him to that dark place one by one, getting stronger with each chain that he removed from his body. Eternal revenge was in his cold, dead heart for a lover who had betrayed him, a surrogate who had taken his place, a father who showed he didn't have the killing edge anymore, a policeman, a young journalist, a meddling coroner and the girl whose knife had spoiled what was to be his finest hour. He would enjoy the killing of that individual most of all.

Back at the mansion, it was quickly moving towards bedtime. Gavin knew there was no way that he and Sarah would be allowed to share the same room.

"I am going to show Sarah to her room," announced Gavin.

"I will pour you a brandy, Gavin. We have much to organize," said his father with a smile. Gavin and Sarah began to climb the stairs when Gavin asked her about her brothers and sisters.

"I don't really have any. That is my foster family, and they only ever kept me for the money they received. I did have a sister, but we were separated at birth," said Sarah, looking slightly sad.

"Well, you are going to have a family now, my dear." Gavin took her to the room where the maid was waiting to attend to Sarah.

"Hello," said Sarah. "Who are you?"

"I'm Alice, my lady. I will tend your needs."

The two girls went into the bedroom after Gavin had given her a goodnight kiss.

"Shall I draw you a bath, miss?" asked Alice, as they entered the room.

"Thank you," replied Sarah. "Are you going to be my friend while I'm here?"

"Erm," stuttered Alice, "I don't think the mistress will allow for me to be your friend. You see...I'm not of the same class as you people, and I'm not allowed to mingle with you," replied Alice with her head down.

"That's just silly! We are now friends and if anyone doesn't like it, they can deal with my lovely Gavin!" enforced Sarah.

Tamara's phone rang. On answering, she was instantly transported to the Other Realm.

"What troubles you, Listmaker?" asked Atkinson, sitting on his vast, throne-like chair.

"You know what troubles me, Great One. My mind is at your every whim," said Tamara humbly.

"Your thoughts go to my absent son," snarled Atkinson.

"Again, you haven't dismissed him as being dead," said Tamara.

"We both know the answer to that question," hissed Atkinson. "Where he is, he can do no harm," he continued.

"I hope that's true, because John Smith has seen him in the Realm of Death...and he spoke to me," interrupted Tamara.

"Silence, Listmaker! What you say cannot be! All the events of the recent past have played a part in what you two think you are seeing and hearing. Now be gone. Once again, I tire of you."

Tamara didn't find herself back in her domain she reappeared in Dewhirst's private chamber.

"My Lord, how can I be of assistance?" asked Tamara as she lowered her head.

"Before you go, know you this: should my partner's idiot son somehow return to your domain, seek out your sibling. Only the two of you together are strong enough to protect Smith during this time of adjustment." The old God closed his eyes and the audience was over.

Tamara found herself back in the office, looking at John. She was clearly shaken, as Smith took her in his arms and asked, "What just happened?"

"Nothing, John. Dewhirst wanted to tell me that I had to visit my sibling," she replied, not too convincingly.

"Brother or sister?" asked Smith.

"Until a moment ago, I wasn't aware I had either..." she replied.

At the newspaper building, an eruption had occurred in the editor's office. It was time that the story of all stories should have been on Don Steele's desk, but it wasn't. Worst of all, he had just found out about the paper Jeff had signed.

"Get the lawyers in here now!" screamed the purple-faced editor.

"Calm down, sir," urged his secretary. "Be careful – remember what happened last time?"

"Yes, I can remember, and he caused that too! I want to see if that paper is legal. Clarke! Clarke! Where is that kid?" demanded the editor.

Jeff Clarke was already out of the building. He was on his way to the police station to let them know what was about to hit them.

"Come in, Jeff," welcomed D.I. Lambert. "The Chief is out. Will I do?" asked Donna Lambert.

"My editor has just found out about that paper I signed saying I wouldn't print the story. He was calling the lawyers into his office when I escaped," explained Jeff.

"I don't know the ins and outs of what happened, but the Chief Inspector won't be long, I'm sure he will sort it out," she reassured with a smile.

Tamara sat at her desk, trying to think back to a time when she had a brother or sister. As hard as she tried, nothing was emerging from her past. All she could think of were the many battles she had fought to protect the man for whom she drew up lists, and the final fight she had against him. The only reason she defeated him was because of the help of that strange little girl, who was brave enough to stab him with the knife he had used on her. With that thought, she got up from her desk, put on her coat, and announced to John Smith that she was leaving but would be back before nightfall.

The doorbell rang at the mortuary and Tom answered.

"Good evening," said Tom to the elegant lady standing there. "I'm afraid Mr. Jackson is away for the weekend. Can I be of assistance?"

"I'm a friend of his parents and I was in the area, so I thought I would come and see him," announced the well-dressed woman.

"Oh dear," replied Tom. "That's where they have gone."

"They?" asked the woman.

"Yes, he and his fiancée," said Tom, all of a sudden realising he might be giving away too much information to this stranger.

"Do tell Gavin I called," replied the woman.

"May I ask who called, madam?" asked Tom.

"Tamara," replied the elegant lady, as she walked serenely away.

Tamara took the phone from her handbag and called the office. Mr. Braithwaite answered, and Tamara instructed him to find the address of the coroner's parents and that time was of the essence. Braithwaite set about his task, and in seconds, gave her the whereabouts of Gavin Jackson's parents.

"If I'm not back in time, tell Mr. Smith his list is in the top right hand drawer of my desk."

Braithwaite agreed, and Tamara put her phone back into her handbag.

At the police station, Chief Inspector Paul Johnson arrived back at his office to find D.I. Lambert and Jeff Clarke already there. "Hello, Jeff," said the Chief Inspector. "What brings you here?" he continued.

"My editor has found out about the paper that I signed," answered Jeff.

"Ahh, I think I should pay a visit to your Mr. Steele. My old boss and he had many a run-in over what should and shouldn't be printed," laughed Johnson. "Has his temper improved with age?" asked Johnson hopefully.

"It's got worse," replied Jeff.

Just as they were all laughing, Paul Johnson's phone rang. "Hello, what can I do for you?"

Jeff and D.I. Lambert were still quietly laughing together when Johnson said, "I have one of them with me now, leave that to me Tamara,"

Jeff and Donna Lambert looked at each other with puzzled expressions on their faces. "Ok, I will see you when you get back," said the chief, as he put his phone back into his pocket and looked at Jeff with a worried brow. "I'm going to have to detain you, Jeff."

"What have I done?" replied the startled reporter.

"Nothing lad, it's for your own good. Tamara has just asked me to round up everybody connected with the Atkinson case and to meet up with her when she arrives back with Gavin and Sarah. I'm sure it's nothing to worry about. I was only talking to her today, and she told me that nothing could go wrong."

Sarah had spent the day trying to piece together the strange dreams from the previous night when Gavin asked her, "What's the matter, Sarah? You have been quiet all day."

"I don't know. Maybe it's the strange house. I didn't sleep well, and I feel strange today."

"In what way strange? Do you feel you are coming down with something?" enquired Gavin.

"No, it was as if someone was trying to tell me something..." said Sarah, with a confused expression.

"Nothing that a spot of afternoon tea won't put right," said Gavin with a smile.

"There is a Miss Tamara Stapleton here to see Master Gavin," announced Jarvis, as the Jacksons were settling down to afternoon tea with their soon-to-be daughter-in-law. Gavin and Sarah looked at each other, and Gavin asked his parents to excuse them. They both went to the front door.

"We have much to discuss on our way back to the office," announced Tamara. "We need to be back before John Smith starts work this evening," she continued.

"The office? Why, what has happened? Have there been more murders?" said Gavin with a worried expression.

"Not yet," said Tamara, "but there will be." She looked at the little girl holding onto him.

Sarah said, "I will get our things. You let your mum and dad know what's happening." With a worried look in his eyes, Gavin withdrew to the drawing room and explained to his parents that the weekend had come to an end.

At the police station, Paul Johnson was beginning to feel nervous when he heard shouting from downstairs. Not long after, his phone rang.

"Show him up to my office," said Johnson. The Chief Inspector looked at Jeff Clarke and said, "This is going to be interesting."

There was a knock on the door and in walked Donald Steele.

"Where's Chief Inspector Thompson?! And what is he doing here?" said the editor, holding out a disapproving finger at the young reporter.

"He is helping us with our enquiries" said Johnson.

"Well let me help you with those enquiries! From tomorrow, you will find him at the job centre... and who the hell are you!?" interrupted Donald Steele.

"As an editor, you are behind in the news. My predecessor, Chief Inspector Jack Thompson, is dead. I am Chief Inspector Paul Johnson. Firstly, I would ask you to lower your voice and alter its tone. If you want to know why your employee is here, like I said earlier, he is helping us with our very important inquiries, the likes of which have never been written about in any newspaper. Now you can help us, or hinder us," said the new chief with an air of superiority about himself.

The editor stood for a while with his mouth open. Eventually, he regained his composure, looked at Jeff Clarke, and said, "My office, 9 a.m. This better be good." The door slammed as Steele left the room.

Gavin kissed his mother goodbye and said they would be back soon. Sarah gave Gavin's father a kiss on his cheek and said,

"See you both soon." She jumped into Gavin's Jaguar, where Tamara was already sitting.

"How did you get here?" asked a smiling Sarah.

"I was dropped off..." said Tamara, as astral travel was probably beyond Sarah's understanding at the moment. Gavin got into the driver's seat, turned the key, and the Jaguar roared into life, spraying small stones from under the back wheels as they exited the driveway of the manor house.

"What's going on, Tamara?" asked Gavin as he peered through the windshield at the road ahead.

"Let's just say we are going to a very important meeting about our old friend Atkinson," she replied.

"Atkinson?" said Gavin, taking his eyes off the road for a moment.

"I will explain everything when we arrive at the office," she assured him. "Well, Sarah, did you enjoy your time in the country?" asked Tamara, changing the uncomfortable subject.

"It was great! I met Gavin's mum and dad! They are really nice! I also met Mr. Jarvis, he is a very posh gentleman who makes sure everything works in the house; I think his second name is Butler. I made a new friend who runs me a bath and got my bed ready. It was all really smashing...but I didn't sleep very well," said Sarah, taking in a large gulp of air.

Tamara smiled and held out her hand to Sarah. "That all sounds wonderful. I am sorry you couldn't sleep, why do you think that was?" she gently asked.

"Dreams, strange dreams about fire and swords and fighting and..." At this point, Sarah stopped talking and looked straight into Tamara's eyes and said, "You. You were with me, and we were fighting a monster. I can't remember any more." Sarah put her head down.

This quiet moment was halted by Gavin announcing, "We will be back in about an hour." Sarah lifted her head again and smiled.

Tamara phoned Chief Inspector Johnson. "We are on our way back. Can we meet at John Smith's office in an hour?" asked Tamara.

"No problem, we will meet you there," said the Chief.

Chief Inspector Paul Johnson, Detective Inspector Donna Lambert, and Jeff Clarke arrived at Atkinson, Dewhirst & Smith first, and were shown to John Smith's office by Mr. Braithwaite. "Come in," said John Smith with a smile. "Tamara has told me to expect you guys. It's good to see you again, Jeff," he said, as he shook Jeff's hand.

"What's the problem, John?" said the ever-efficient chief.

"I'm not quite sure, but we will find out presently, I'm sure. Can I offer you all some tea?" asked John.

Not long after, Braithwaite announced the arrival of Tamara and placed a tray of tea on the desk.

In the Other Realm, Dewhirst asked Atkinson Senior what the meeting with Tamara was about. "A small matter that is worrying your Listmaker," answered Atkinson.

"Your son trying to get back into their realm is no small matter," retorted Dewhirst.

"As I told the Listmaker, he cannot get back there," growled Atkinson.

"You know this to be untrue," hissed Dewhirst.

"The chains that bind him cannot be broken," argued Atkinson.

"Did you fasten the chains yourself?" asked Dewhirst.

"I am assured they are secure."

"Secure, you say...I don't share your feeling of security...I am the one who has to go back every time he tries to change the way of things and I grow weary of it all," growled Dewhirst.

"It will be dealt with this time," assured Atkinson.

"If it is not dealt with this time, I will deal with it myself," said a not-too-convinced, tired deity.

JOHN PAUL BERNETT

Chapter Fifteen

After all the pleasantries were over, Tamara called the strange meeting to order like a chairman of the board. But this wasn't business as usual, and she didn't really know what to say.

"What's all this about, Tamara? You have been quite vague about the whole thing," said Paul Johnson.

"Yes, I concur," announced John Smith.

"Where do I fit into all this?" asked Jeff.

"One at a time, please, just let me speak," urged Tamara.

None of the people in that office had seen Tamara this unsure of herself.

Donald Steele returned to his office and called his lawyers in. To his dismay, he was told that the waiver given to the police was enforceable, so legally, he could not go ahead with that particular story. *Hmm, that particular story...*thought Steele. "What about another angle?" announced Steele.

"Another angle?" said Jim Harper, the newspaper's lawyer.

"Jeff Clarke has signed the waiver for his story. Let's get another reporter, and then we can go ahead," said Steele triumphantly.

Jim Harper said, "I will look into it, sir." He left the room with a bundle of papers under his arm.

"Send in Hunter!" Donald Steele blasted into the two-way intercom to his secretary.

There was a knock on the door, and Ray Hunter walked in. The editor gave the new reporter the background to the story so far, and told Ray Hunter that he expected him to remember that he was a reporter and not a collaborator with the police. Ray Hunter placed the dossier with the information under his arm, and assured his editor that he would not let him down.

By now, Tamara had begun talking.

"You all know now what happens at this office. For a thousand millennia, we have done this work faultlessly...until now."

"I don't think I like how this is going," said Johnson.

"Chief Inspector, if I may?" interjected Tamara.

"Sorry, carry on," replied Johnson.

"The man that Sarah so bravely killed is not dead."

At this point, everybody started talking, and the scene was more like a market than a meeting.

"If I may, gentlemen!" screamed Tamara.

The room hushed and Tamara began to speak again.

"When Sarah plunged that weapon into Atkinson's temple, it should have killed him; that was a special blade forged by the Gods many centuries ago. Unfortunately for us, his father intervened, and instead of him dying, he was put in a special place to hold him forever. The place that binds him doesn't appear to be strong enough to hold him."

"How much time do we have before he escapes?" asked Gavin, looking very worried, holding his intended's hand.

"I don't know. I'm going to pay him a visit this very night. I know where his father has sent him, and I will try and reason with him," said Tamara softly.

"That sounds like suicide!" said a shaken John Smith.

"No! If he was free to harm me in that realm, he would be here already," reassured Tamara.

"I will come with you," said John Smith.

"You have a list to take care of, John," said the somewhat scared but efficient Tamara.

The one person who had stayed silent while all this had been going on now spoke. "He will come after me, won't he?" asked Sarah.

"Yes," replied Tamara.

"I will be ready for him this time!" announced Sarah.

"What?" said Gavin. "We will go away – miles from here – where he can't find us," stated the coroner.

"Why do you say that, Sarah?" asked Tamara with a puzzled look.

Sarah just looked at Tamara and said, "You know exactly what I mean. I know what to do this time."

Gavin Jackson, Jeff Clarke, Donna Lambert, and Paul Johnson looked at each other, and then at the two girls staring at each other. John Smith stood back, looked at what was going on, and wondered what his role would be in all of this. Tamara held Sarah's hand, and announced that she needed to talk to Sarah alone. She asked Gavin if he could return for her in two hours' time.

After many reassurances by Tamara of Sarah's safety, he begrudgingly agreed. He took the love of his life in his arms, kissed her passionately, and withdrew.

The meeting broke up, and the worried participants made their separate ways home. John Smith, Tamara, and Sarah were left at the office, looking at each other on the brink of a war, the likes of which mankind had never seen before.

Paul Johnson and Gavin Jackson exited the building, looking stunned, worried, and not quite believing what had just transpired.

"What if he comes back?" said Johnson.

"Don't remind me. I know who he will come for first — my Sarah," was Jackson's fast reply.

"He will get all of us, Gavin," said the Chief inspector. "And when he has sorted his revenge on us, what then for the world? He didn't have a second thought for laying to waste our city, and that was before we killed him. My god, can you imagine? I still don't understand what this thing is, Gavin, and people will be looking to me for answers," announced a worried Chief Inspector.

Down the alley, running by the side of the building, just out of sight but within earshot of the two worried officials, Ray Hunter turned his Dictaphone to the 'off' position and scurried back to his editor.

There was a faint sound of a clock chiming as Tamara pulled out of her desk drawer that night's list for John Smith.

"Take care, John," said Tamara, as he exited the office and entered the Realm of Death.

Sarah looked into the void as the Reaper quietly entered his domain. The door began to close behind him with a slight grating noise and Sarah looked back towards Tamara.

"At last, we are alone," said the Listmaker.

Sarah gave a little smile.

Tamara had walked over to where she stood, and said, "We have only a short time, my brave little girl, and many things we need to discuss."

"I feel strange. Why is that?" asked Sarah.

"You have many tattoos on your body. Do you have one on your left ankle?" enquired Tamara.

"You won't believe this, but I was born with one on my left ankle. Well, I mean, I have a birthmark there," answered Sarah.

"May I look, Sarah?" asked Tamara.

"Of course you can," said Sarah, with her customary smile.

Sarah took off her Doc Martin boot, and turned down her pink and white hooped sock to reveal her birthmark. When Tamara saw her ankle she placed her dainty foot on a little stool, drew up her skirt to reveal her stocking top, unfastened the suspender and gently turned down her stocking all the way to her stiletto shoe, revealing the exact same birthmark. Sarah was astonished that someone had her birthmark; Tamara knew that the birthmark was the sign of a warrior. Until now, only one person had it, so the only other one must be the sister whose coming Dewhirst had foretold. The two girls replaced their hosiery and footwear and sat down.

"Sarah," began Tamara, "I now know your involvement in Atkinson's demise was no accident."

"What do you mean?" asked Sarah.

"I know all this is going to seem strange, but I was told before I came to get you and Gavin to seek out a sibling to help me defeat Atkinson. Somehow – I don't know why – maybe it's divine intervention from Dewhirst, because I know it would not have come from Atkinson – but somehow, I knew that my sister was you. I need you to come to terms with this before Gavin gets back, because I need you."

"I know. Somehow, I've always known, and something tells me I will be ready when the time comes to stand by your side, like back at the tower," answered Sarah.

The two girls hugged as Gavin returned for Sarah, and John Smith returned to their Plane of Existence.

Gavin led Sarah out to the car and asked her if she was ok.

"I'm good," answered Sarah. "I have something to tell you, Gavin," she said in a soft voice.

"Can it wait until we get home, my love? We can talk over a glass of wine," said Gavin. Sarah smiled and nodded as the gleaming Jaguar pulled away from the strange old building with the changed name – Atkinson, Dewhirst & Smith.

Tamara gave John Smith her special phone and said, "If I'm not back in twenty minutes, call Dewhirst – not Atkinson, and tell him what has transpired."

"You can't go in there on your own," announced John.

"How gallant you are, John, but what's needed is a savage killer. That is an edge I have that you don't, sweetie," answered Tamara, with a kiss on John's cheek.

With an air of authority and a beautiful smile, she stepped into a Dark Realm ever so quietly, leaving John Smith alone in the old building, wondering who would step back out of it. Only time would tell.

Gavin's Jaguar whooshed into the underground parking space and came to a smooth halt, precisely in the centre of his allotted space. The driver's door swung open and the elegant Gavin Jackson alighted. He walked around to the passenger's door, opened it, and a somewhat-calm Sarah took his hand and joined him. A press of a button in Gavin's right hand locked the car and set its alarm, and the betrothed couple made their way to the elevator.

Paul Johnson arrived back at the police station. His arrival was low-key, and through the back door, he slipped up the stairs to his office. Taking out his old boss' bottle of whiskey, he poured a glass, took a sip, and wished that he was the Detective Inspector and not the Chief.

"Well, unfortunately you are, sir," said D.I. Lambert.

The chief dropped his glass and turned sharply round.

"I didn't realise I said that out loud or that you were there, Lambert," said Johnson, bending down to pick up his glass.

"Allow me, Sir," said the D.I., as she bent down with him. Their hands touched as they both took hold of the glass. D.I. Lambert looked into the Chief's worried, tired eyes and caught hold of his hand. "Penny for them, Sir," she said softly.

Paul Johnson smiled for a second, and then quickly coughed and straightened his tie and said, "Oh, you know, the usual – cats stuck in trees, arguments about property divides...Armageddon." At this point, the chief sat back in his chair and put his head in his hands. Donna Lambert walked over to the door and locked it. She turned back to the desk and took the phone off its hook. Paul Johnson looked at her as she slowly moved around to where he was sitting and seductively sat on the desk at his side. The downstairs lights at the police station burned all night, but the lights to the upstairs offices, including Chief Inspector Johnson's, were all turned off.

Tamara turned to see the heavy door close behind her and checked that all the armour that Dewhirst had deposited into the Realm of Death was in place on her beautiful body. After sliding the new sword into her left scabbard, and the dagger in the scabbard on the side of her right calf, she was ready to face her foe. That was how she now saw the beast for whom she once had nothing but admiration and love. This time, there was no remorse, nothing he could use against her. He would yield or die, and she now favoured the latter. With the thought in her mind of *I'm ready*, Dewhirst transported her to the deeper, older realm that held Atkinson Junior prisoner.

As Gavin and Sarah cuddled up on the leather couch, sipping their wine, Sarah began explaining to him what had been discussed back at the office. She explained how divine intervention had put her in that club, at that exact time and place, to do what she did. Gavin had now come to some sort of understanding that, however unthinkable it was, there was much more to life and death than his field of science was aware of.

"Knowing that he will come after you first makes me want to just book tickets to anywhere in the world, and get out of here," said Gavin softly in her ear.

"I know, and a part of me thinks that way, too — but we would spend our lives running, and sooner or later, he would find us. If we are going to have a life together, I want it to be just us, and not us and our fears," she replied.

"You are, of course, right, my dear. Just tell me what you want me to do," said Gavin, looking quite sad.

"Just love me. I think love is the strongest weapon you can use against hate, although I will accept all the weapons they give me," she said with a cheeky grin, trying to make her Gavin feel better. The two young lovers cuddled together and watched the sunset from their skyscraper vantage point, wondering how many more they would share.

It was at about this time that Ray Hunter got back to the newspaper building, but to his dismay, the offices were closed, and only the night shift printers were working. Raymond Hunter was a man who had spent a good deal of time working for major newspapers, with offices that were open twenty-four hours a day, and he saw this as unprofessional. He placed his backpack containing his notepads, pens, Dictaphone, and computer in his office and locked the door. He always left his tools at the office, so he could not be called to do extra work — the very reason he didn't work for the broadsheets anymore.

As Ray Hunter left the building, from out of the shadows in his darkened office stepped the ghostly figure of a true 24-hour journalist, who never got the chance that Hunter had scorned. The deceased Sid Jenkins had no idea why he was not at peace, he just knew there was a reason for him being here, and that reason was to remove what was in this backpack to give his living friends time to try and work things out.

The quiet of the room was shattered when the door lock was clicked back and the handle turned. The spectre disappeared back into the shadows as a man with a full-face mask came in the room with a flashlight.

Seeing that the room was empty, the man removed the disguise, revealing himself as none other than Jeff Clarke.

"Breaking and entering...now that's illegal, young Jeff."

Jeff Clarke froze to the spot on hearing his name, and rather foolishly put the mask back on.

"Although it's an improvement, I've already seen you," said the phantom.

Jeff's eyes widened in recognition as the ghostly figure of Sid Jenkins emerged from the shadows.

"Do you want to sit down, lad? You look like you've seen a ghost."

"But...but you're..."

"Dead," finished Sid.

"Err...yes, I went to your funeral," said Jeff, who had now removed the mask again.

"It seems we are both here for the same purpose, which is a good thing. It means I don't have to conjure up a fire to burn the place down. You can just steal it," smiled the old newsman.

"But that's just it – I don't know why I'm here! I was asleep at home when I was dreaming about Tamara. She said I had to meet someone in this room, and here I am," said a confused, scared Jeff Clarke.

"Good, you have just told me the reason I am here. If you look in that backpack, you will find a recording machine. Do not let Donald Steele, or anyone for that matter, hear what is on it," said Sidney Jenkins. At that, the boy took out the Dictaphone and put it in his pocket. The ghostly figure of Sidney Jenkins turned and walked towards the shadows. Just then the police, acting on a tip-off, burst in and grabbed Jeff Clarke, and arrested him for breaking and entering.

It took a short time for Tamara's eyes to adjust to the dimness of the desolate place she found herself in. There were all kinds of sounds echoing around this vast catacomb, but no sign of life or anything that resembled it – just a feeling of dread.

"Why can you not see me, Listmaker?" said a familiar voice.
Tamara swung around but saw nothing.

"You cannot use the eyes you use in that useless domain where you, and all the other little rats, scurry around."

"I don't need eyes. I can smell your presence."

She closed her eyes and used her mind.

"You are foolish to come here, only my father can let you in or out of here…" said Atkinson, as he now stood in front of her, "and still you don't fear me…you grow old, Listmaker. Your senses are not what they used to be. Your armour is new," hissed Atkinson.

"Shut up with all this bullshit. We both know you are still bound, or you would have taken the coward's way and killed me from behind," she retorted.

"Why have you not struck me down then? Do you still hope for the good times we had to come back?" said Atkinson.

"Hush, you fool. I know that this is just an image of you. It was a cool trick – it worked on Smith, but it doesn't work on me. I've come here to talk, but I'm quite prepared to kill – so which will it be, Atkinson?"

The image in front of her disappeared, and in the dimness, she could see him chained to the wall. The wound in his head was untreated, and he was sitting there with all the chains intact. He was bound, and unable to cause any trouble.

"Why have I been sent to kill you if your bondage is holding?" said a confused Tamara.

In a very weak voice, Atkinson said, "Somebody wanted you out of the way for a while."

Tamara quickly thought, *back*, and was transported to the Dark Realm, and then to the Plane of Existence. As she returned through the door, John Smith was waiting, and she ran into his arms. "I think it is going to be ok – he is still bound. It's just the domains playing tricks with our imagination."

Back in that dark place, Atkinson Junior let the chains that had bound him drop to the floor, to the sound of his laughter. He laughed for what was to come, and how easily he had fooled his old soul mate and the two geriatric Gods, who would soon be dethroned.

JOHN PAUL BERNETT

Chapter Sixteen

onald Steele lit a cigar, drew a mouthful of smoke, and exhaled with the cigar clasped between his teeth. He smiled. *I will have my story...*he thought to himself, while slipping off his tweed jacket. He made his way to his desk. As he reached it, the door slammed shut. This startled the editor, but then he heard a familiar voice coming from behind him.

"I don't think telling the world it is about to come to an end is a good idea, Donald."

The editor swung around, and to his astonishment, saw an old newspaperman standing with his back to the door.

"S...S...Sid!" stuttered the editor in astonishment as the cigar fell from his mouth.

"Surprised to see me, Don?" asked the phantom, standing as plain as day right in front of him.

"I'm not seeing you! You're dead!" said Donald Steele, rubbing his eyes.

"Oh yes, you can very much see me, and do you want to know why you can see me?" said the spectre in a louder voice.

"No!" shouted the editor.

"Because I'm dead before my time, which is bad for me, but could be helpful to you, so stop your snivelling and listen to what I have to tell you!" announced Sid Jenkins.

"Ok, I'm listening, but this doesn't mean I will do anything, though..." replied Steele in a child-like fashion.

"Donald Steele – the newsman, the editor – who only got the job because of his wife's connections in Fleet Street. The man with his finger on the pulse of life itself. The one who doesn't even know there was a break-in here last night."

"What?" shouted the editor.

"Be quiet while I'm talking to you! Yes, a break-in and you are going to go to the police station and drop the charges."

"Drop the charges? I will have them put whoever it is away for a long time!" roared a red-faced editor.

"If you do that, I will guarantee to you, here and now, that by the end of the week the Apocalypse will be upon us and you will be responsible!" boomed the now-fearful spectre.

If Donald Steele's mouth could have opened any further, it would have.

"You don't know how near we came only a few weeks ago. Look at it this way – you can have the real headline story or you, and everyone else on this planet, can join me. If you want the latter, do nothing. If you want the story of all time, with you being its editor, go and get Jeff out of prison."

"Jeff Clarke!!" interrupted Steele.

"Yes, Jeff Clarke, and be glad he is signed to your payroll, for he is instrumental in all of this. Oh, and while I have your attention, fire that fool you replaced me with!" demanded Sid, as he disappeared.

At this point, Donald Steele thought further than a story and a headline. More to the point, if he had just had a chat with a ghost and he believed it to be true, then the conversation must be true, too. A strange feeling came over the editor...one he had not felt for a long time...he felt humbled. He remembered starting at the paper around the same time as his then-friend Sidney Jenkins. He remembered how Sid was like Jeff, always asking questions, and how he was always a story behind him...and how he admired him.

The editor picked up the cigar and went to the canteen where Cindy asked him what he would like. He just smiled at her and said, "A cup of tea would be nice, my dear."

Cindy wondered what was wrong with him as he took the beverage and went to the table where Ray Hunter was sitting.

"What do you have for me?" asked the editor.

"I did have a great lead, but someone broke in here last night and stole my stuff," was the quick reply from the journalist.

"You would have had your important stuff on you, though," pointed out the strangely quiet editor.

"No, I didn't. The thief made away with everything I had," was the response.

"This makes things easier for me, then. You see, normally at this point, I would shout 'You're fired'! followed by 'Get your things, and get out'! but I don't need to do that," smiled the editor.

The newsman looked relieved as Donald Steele rose and started walking away. Turning back, the editor said, "As you don't have any things, Just get out. You're fired."

The editor triumphantly left the canteen, and asked Cindy to let his secretary know he was going to the police station.

The Chief Inspector came down the stairs at the station.

"You are in early, Sir," said the desk sergeant.

The Chief just nodded in an embarrassed way and asked if there was anything new. The sergeant informed him that Jeff Clarke was in cell number 4 and that he was in there for breaking and entering.

"Jeff Clarke? Breaking and entering? Give me the keys," said Johnson. Glenn Simpson gave him a bunch of keys, with the one for cell number 4 protruding outwards. Paul Johnson quickly snatched them and made his way through the heavy door to the cells.

The anti-clockwise turn of the brass key revealed the inmate – a very scared-looking Jeff Clarke. Chief Inspector Paul Johnson walked into the cell and sat at Jeff's side.

"What's all this about, Jeff? You were the last person I expected to see in here," said the chief, trying to put his young friend at ease.

"You won't believe me if I tell you," said a despondent Jeff.

"Now, if you had said those words a month ago, I would have agreed with you, but now I think slightly differently," answered Paul Johnson with a smile to try and lighten the moment.

Jeff turned, looked Paul Johnson in the eyes, and said, "To believe me, you have to believe in ghosts."

The Chief Inspector said, "Carry on...I'm listening."

"What? You actually do believe in ghosts? That's amazing!" said Jeff.

At that point, a police officer knocked on the door. "Come in," invited the chief. The door opened and P.O. Linda Harper introduced Donald Steele.

"I'm dropping all charges," said the editor.

"Ok, the boy's all yours. We will have to finish our discussion at a later date, Jeff," said Paul Johnson.

"I would love to!" said Jeff. At that, Donald Steele bid Paul Johnson good day, then he and the young newsman left the building.

Tamara's phone rang. She looked at John Smith, and they were both transported to the Other Realm.

"What news, Listmaker?" enquired Atkinson Senior.

Dewhirst asked why both of them were here at the same time.

"We were called," said Tamara.

"Wrong, you were called!" replied Dewhirst, pointing at Tamara. "You have left a gateway for Atkinson to get back, you fools."

Both Tamara and John Smith looked at Atkinson Senior. He just shrugged his shoulders nonchalantly and said, "I must have pressed both buttons at once."

"It doesn't matter, for he is securely bound. I saw it for myself."

"You have been deceived, Listmaker. Get back at once and make sure the Realm of Death has not been breached!" demanded Dewhirst, as he turned to his counterpart and glared at his profound foolishness.

The Reaper and Listmaker were sent back to the office.

"What are you doing? This is madness!" raged Dewhirst.

"I want to see what they are made of. I'm not just handing the job I made for my own son on a plate to some peasant fool," snapped Atkinson.

"Your son is a power-mad, egotistical idiot!" replied Dewhirst.

"Be careful, Dewhirst. Watch what you are saying."

"It doesn't matter what I'm saying! Do you have any idea what is going to happen up there? The place has changed in the four-hundred years since you walked in the air," said an angry Dewhirst. "They have missiles that can raze whole cities to dust. They do not trust each-other, and nation will turn on nation. You are a fool! An old, out-of-touch fool! What have you done?!"

Dewhirst stormed away, leaving Atkinson to ponder upon what had just transpired.

In an old, derelict farm building in the countryside just out of town, a tall, well-built man wearing black clothes was looking through a cracked pane of glass, musing on what fun to have first.

A grin came to his lips as he thought...*This time, I will have my revenge.*

JOHN PAUL BERNETT

Chapter Seventeen

As Tamara and John Smith returned to the Plane of Existence, Tamara ran to the window and stared out at the town centre.

"What was all that about?" said Smith.

"John, he is out there – and he knows where we are. He could get us at any time," said Tamara.

"Relax, Tamara. Atkinson and Dewhirst won't let anything like that happen," comforted the new Reaper.

Tamara spun around and said, "It's lesson time, John. We are the ones who can do anything here – unless they are here, they are powerless to help. This is a mind game played by an old God who appears to have become slightly bored. He is going to play this to its bitter end, and in this game, we are not the players— we, my friend, are the pawns." Tamara looked at John, who now wore the expression of a school boy about to get a caning.

"If I am here, then how can Atkinson be here?" enquired John Smith.

"Now that's a question I have been asking myself, and the only answer is that his father has removed his Reaper status, which puts him on my level of existence," answered Tamara.

"Will he know that?" asked John Smith.

"I hope so, because if he doesn't, his confidence will be greater than his power, and he will emerge before Sarah and I return. That could be tricky. If that's the case, you will have to deal with him, John," said Tamara.

"Me? What can I do against him?" answered a rather frightened John Smith.

"For three days, you can't be hurt; he can. You have to understand that, John. You have to take it on board."

The front desk phone at the police station rang; the desk sergeant answered and patched the call up to Chief Inspector Johnson's office. On hearing the caller's voice, Johnson froze for a second, for it was none other than the man that he saw being zipped into a body bag a few short weeks ago.

"Can I help you?" said Johnson eventually, after what had seemed a very long pause.

"Dispense with the pleasantries, Johnson. You know who I am," growled Atkinson.

"I know who you are, and I now have knowledge of what you do in the grand scheme of things. What I don't know is why all this has happened...why you need to change things," stuttered Johnson.

"Because when I came back, I wanted to bring the old firm into this 21st century of yours, but you and your meddling people put a slight pause to my plans. However, I am an immortal being, and you will soon be dead," stated Atkinson.

"Well, before I'm dead, let me let you in on a little secret...I know you have to be here for three days before you are invincible. This time, it's not mortals chasing you, so keep a close eye on your back – for you may be a God or a demon, but for the next three days, you are able to be killed. Nobody in your old domain will help you this time, and all my team are now going to be armed, thanks to you letting me know you're back," said Johnson, as he slammed the phone down.

After hearing what Johnson had to say, Atkinson put his phone back in his inside pocket and laughed quietly to himself. *The poor man doesn't know who he is dealing with*, he thought to himself. Underlying his laughter was a very slight worry thought. *Did they know something he didn't?* But he being Atkinson, it was quickly dismissed as nonsense.

Donna Lambert had heard the shouting and joined the Chief Inspector in his office.

"What's the matter, sir?" enquired the D.I.

The cool calmness of how he had just dealt with Atkinson now left him, and he cradled his head in his hands.

"Atkinson's back," said Johnson in a low voice.

"What!" exclaimed Lambert, as she sat down in front of him.

"Come on, get your coat," said the Chief. "We are going to our friendly accountancy firm," said Johnson regaining his momentum. But as they reached to the front door, Tamara and John Smith were just arriving at the police station. All four people looked at each other for a second, and then the Chief said, "Not here, come with me." All four of them left the station and made their way to their cars.

The newspaper building was business as usual when the editor and young reporter returned.

"You go and bring us some coffee from the canteen. I will go up to my office," said Donald Steele. As he got there, his secretary tried to get his attention, but he brushed her aside, saying, "No calls, and I do mean no calls, from anyone."

Soon after, Jeff arrived with the coffee.

"Now lad, come and sit down, and let's start from the beginning, because I'm confused."

Only after the editor had agreed that all of this was between the two of them did Jeff begin to tell the editor what had transpired, in what was to be the story of all stories.

As the two cars pulled up outside a quiet little café, the four occupants alighted and went inside. The gruff-looking man behind the counter, who looked like he hadn't shaved for days, asked them what they would like.

"Four teas, please," said Johnson. He gave the man the money and picked up the tray.

"We will sit over there," he said, motioning with his eyes to a quiet corner of the café. Once seated, the Chief Inspector opened the conversation.

"Atkinson has phoned me, letting me know he is coming after us."

"What did you say?" asked Tamara.

"I told him we were ready for him this time, and that I knew he was vulnerable for the first three days he was back," answered the Chief Inspector.

"What did he say?" asked John Smith.

"Nothing...when I had said my piece, I put the phone down on him," said Johnson.

"Brave man," observed Tamara, raising an eyebrow. "You know that will not have scared him. Fear is an emotion he is devoid of. We have to prepare, and once again, we only have three days, as you all know. Atkinson will lay low, so I am going to use this time to get to know my sister. I will be out of reach for the first day, for what we have to do will not be taking place on this Plane of Existence. John is going to be at the office. Atkinson cannot go there now; his surrogate has taken his place. They cannot be in the same place at the same time, and that might prove to be an edge for us," said a back-to-her-efficient-self Tamara.

The Chief Inspector said, "I will get Gavin and Jeff and bring them up to speed. While you work with Sarah, getting Atkinson on your side of the rainbow, we will work on doing it on ours. Hopefully, we will get him somewhere in the middle," said Johnson, and the tea party broke up.

Not long after arriving back at Gavin Jackson's apartment his phone rang. On answering, he handed the phone to Sarah. Tamara told Sarah that she needed to come for her and would be there in twenty-five minutes. Sarah said she would be ready, and turned to Gavin. Putting her arms around him, she told him that she had to go. Gavin kissed her and said, "Just a few short weeks ago, you were 'Slabgirl', a crazy little thing running around, annoying everyone, but look at you now! You just make sure you come back to me," he said.

"I will," she whispered in his ear.

The quiet of the moment was broken by the intercom buzzer. "We will be right down," said the coroner, regaining his composure.

As Tamara waited in the car parking area, she saw Gavin and Sarah's elevator door swish open. They walked to where she was parked.

"Hop in, sis," smiled Tamara. "Gavin, you might want to make your way to the police station. I think Paul wants to see you." With that, she gave Gavin a little smile and drove out of the car park, leaving tread marks on the ground and him watching, wondering if he would ever see his darling Sarah again.

Paul Johnson was back in his office. Donna Lambert had gone to pick Jeff up from the newspaper building, and Gavin Jackson was making his way to the police station. The only one missing was the one in the middle. John Smith was sitting at his desk, deep in thought, when his special phone rang. On answering, he was summoned to the Other Realm. Upon arriving, a heavy sense of unease filled the chamber where he stood as Dewhirst walked in.

Before Smith could speak, Dewhirst told him to be quiet and listen.

"It is impossible for two of your kind to be in the same spot at the same time; you are going to need help, boy. You are no match for my foolish partner's idiot son. I have never known a situation like this. Even we, down here, do not know the outcome of what has been put in place. If Death does ride out on his own, there can only be one end. For if Death rides, then so too will War, Pestilence, and Famine – in short, the Apocalypse – and not just for Humankind...for everything that we know. Unlike my somewhat unsteady friend of all time, I cannot let this happen, and in the end, sacrifices will be made. For now, protection is needed. Take this chest, and adorn yourself with its contents. The reaping must carry on. You must distance yourself from the ensuing battle, and keep doing what you are here to do. Am I understood?" The old deity stood back, and John Smith found himself back at his desk with the old chest upon it. On opening it, he found a hooded cloak, a sword, a dagger, an amulet, a ring, and a single gauntlet.

The office door began to open, so Smith quickly closed the lid on the chest. Tamara walked in with Sarah, noticing the chest, which was familiar to her. She asked John where he had found it.

"Dewhirst gave it to me," he answered.

"Dewhirst? Not Atkinson?" said Tamara.

"I got the opinion that Mr. Atkinson wasn't aware of what his partner had given me," said Smith.

"I know for a fact that he doesn't know, for that is Atkinson's own armour – the strongest armour in existence, so why would he give it to you?" said Tamara.

"He said something about sacrifices having to be made; I must stick to the reaping, and that Atkinson Junior and I could not be in the same spot at the same time. I think I'm supposed to wear this armour all the time," said John Smith.

"You can wear it all the time, because once it is on, only our kind can see it...but beware, John, because although it will protect you, it will also engulf you. It will take over your thoughts. It is magical armour that will take your life force. That's how the armour gets its power, so be careful, John. Only wear it when you need it," advised Tamara.

This new development with Smith and the armour worried Tamara, but she had a job to do and not long to do it. Taking Sarah's hand in hers, she told John Smith that his list was in the usual drawer, pressed a button on her phone, and was gone. John Smith was left staring at the case in front of him. Tamara was in a place somewhere between the two domains...a place where she could train her sister without having to worry about Atkinson and his whereabouts.

By now, everybody had arrived at the police station, and Paul Johnson was the first to speak. Sitting around the long table in the briefing room were Gavin Jackson, D.I. Donna Lambert, C.I. Paul Johnson, Jeff Clarke, and a man who – up until now – was unknown to everybody but the chief.

"This is Captain James Woodard. He is our liaison with the army, and this is what this meeting is about. The question is, do we try and deal with this ourselves, or hand it over to the armed forces?"

Gavin was the first to speak. "There is a lot at stake if we don't get him this time, Paul."

"I know. That is why I might be handing it over to someone more equipped to deal with it," answered the chief.

"Excuse me, Sir, but who is equipped to deal with it?" asked Donna Lambert.

Jeff just listened, not quite knowing what to think.

"We have to see what Tamara, John, and Sarah come up with," said Gavin.

"Where are Tamara, John, and Sarah?" said James Woodard.

This was now quite awkward for Paul Johnson, because he had not told the captain of their involvement in all of this. Explaining that one of them was teaching the other how to battle in another domain, and that the third one was the Grim Reaper, might prove tricky.

"They are gathering information at the moment," said the Chief, as he realised how hard it would be to explain all this.

"Maybe we will keep things how they are for now, but can you guys be on standby if we need you?" asked the Chief Inspector.

The captain, still not quite sure what was going on, agreed and left, leaving the four of them looking at each other.

The first thing that Sarah heard was a skylark's beautiful song. As she opened her eyes, the first thing she saw was Tamara. Tamara was standing in front of her. She was tall; her hair was long, and flowing down over her shoulders like a waterfall bursting over a cliff. She seemed to have a golden glow all around her. Her eyes were ice blue, her lips cherry red. Her gown was made of golden thread.

The curves of her form were easily visible, immerging from behind her, a pair of beautiful feathered wings. She held out her hand and Sarah, open-mouthed, walked towards her with her hand outstretched. The two girls held hands for a moment, and then Sarah said, "You are an angel!"

"A common mistake, my sweet young thing. I am not an angel. I am The Listmaker, and this is how I look, but human eyes cannot see me; they see the other Tamara."

"Where am I?" was the next question.

"Do you not recognise this place?" asked Tamara.

As Sarah looked around, her eyes opened wide. "It's home!" she yelled. "I haven't seen this place since my mum died!" Tears began to well up in her eyes. "That's my house!" she said, running to the small cottage.

"Sarah, come back. These are but shadows of what once was. They only exist in your memory. That's why I have brought you here, for here is where your strength is; here is where I will teach you," advised Tamara. "Do you remember our mother?" asked Tamara.

"No, but I do remember that cottage is where we lived and I know she loved me," sobbed Sarah.

Sarah looked up at the sky and it was as blue as it could be; the grass was so green, and everything was wonderful. "I want to stay here forever!" she shouted at the top of her lungs, and then she remembered Gavin and the fate that was going to befall everyone back where she belonged.

Sarah turned back to Tamara, and the whole place was suddenly dark. The golden Tamara was gone; in her place stood the one true Tamara, clad in black. She stood seven feet tall. She wore a pair of high-leg boots with armour plating on the front and Achilles plates at the rear, chainmail leggings, a leather and metal-studded kilt, chainmail bodice with black breastplate, and armoured sleeves with one gauntlet on her right hand. Her helmet had a carved black raven adorning it, with black feathers coming out at the very top. Her golden wings were now crow-black; in her right hand was a mighty broadsword, and in her left a black shield. Lastly, strapped tightly to her thigh was the dagger that Sarah knew only too well. The last time she saw it was when it was sticking out of Atkinson's temple. The two girls stood face to face, Tamara looking down, Sarah looking up. "Time is short, so let's get started," announced Tamara.

"I'm ready," said Sarah.

JOHN PAUL BERNETT

Chapter Eighteen

𝕬 solitary drop of water slid slowly down the window pane as Atkinson looked out on the new daybreak. It was a grey start to the day, and he was already feeling stir-crazy, trapped inside this damp farm building that he had slept uncomfortably in for the night.

He remembered the old farm that stood here and how he first came upon the useless, witless imposter that was in his place. He recalled that John Smith was a dirty peasant boy gathering sticks. Was that better than the life Atkinson had bestowed upon him? To think someone as unimportant as that dull excuse of a human was keeping him from what was rightfully his!

"I could end all of this now," he said out loud to nobody but a mouse, shuffling around in the straw. He remembered Tamara telling him that he had to 'lay low' and thought, *What arrogance! Telling him what to do.*

"Yes, lay low. That is what they will all think I will be doing this time. I will show these fools what I can do!" said Atkinson triumphantly; the mouse, however, was still unimpressed.

His thoughts wandered again to Tamara – the good times they had shared, once again reflecting on times past. Part of him wanted that to return... but revenge was all that was important now. He knew he was the God, and everybody else was beneath him, and they were going to be put to his sword.

Chief Inspector Johnson woke up, his neck hurting, still sitting in his office chair. As he stood, he felt the bones in his neck crack into place. He put his jacket on and left the room. Feeling the growth on his chin as he descended the stairs to the front desk, he felt like he had been hit by a train. Fastening his tie into place, he asked if there were any messages.

"No, Sir," was the reply from the fresh-faced young police officer standing behind the desk.

"Who are you?" enquired Johnson.

"Police Officer 58962 Collins, Sir," was the quick reply.

"Whoa, too fast! it's very early. Your first name will do. I will never remember all that," retorted the chief.

"Phillip," answered the nervous bobby.

"That's better. Phillip what?" asked the chief.

"Sorry Sir, Phillip Sir."

The Chief Inspector's head fell down in disbelief. "No boy, your surname. Phillip what?" answered the chief, whose morning was getting worse by the minute.

"Sorry Sir, Collins sir, sorry Sir."

"Ok, Phillip Collins, I'm going to get some breakfast. If anything important comes up, remember to write it down and then phone me, please." With that the Chief Inspector was out of the door.

On his way out, Police Sergeant Glenn Simpson was just arriving back with the morning papers.

"You're early, Chief Inspector."

"Yes, I didn't make it home last night, Glenn. Who's the kid on the desk?" asked Paul Johnson.

"Oh, that's P.O. Collins. He's from London. He got caught up in a bomb raid...and it left him none too well upstairs, if you know what I mean. He has been transferred to us from the Met as a kind of convalescence, so to speak."

Convalescence? Here? My god, if only they knew – this would be the last place on Earth they'd send him, thought the smiling Chief Inspector, as he made his way to the car.

Jeff Clarke was already up and on his computer, writing up yesterday's strange meeting. This was going to be Jeff's role; he was to document everything that was happening, but not divulge anything to his editor until all of this was over, by which time he would have the story of a lifetime, and he would be able to choose what paper to work for. His fingers danced majestically across his keyboard as yesterday's facts were transferred from his notes to his hard drive. He wore a smile on his face – the smile he always wore when Cindy would soon be there. They had arranged a picnic in the park; the weather wasn't really nice enough for that, but he knew that whatever they did, it would be great. Jeff's concentration was broken by his mother shouting him to breakfast. Jeff pressed the 'save' button on his computer, and headed towards the righteous smell of bacon and eggs.

Gavin Jackson hadn't slept, his mind was racing. Only after he let Sarah go off with Tamara did the realism of what they were going to do hit him. Being a scientist, all this went against everything he had been taught. He was left wondering if he could carry on, knowing what he now knew. He wondered where science could fit into all of this, and, more to the point, he wondered where it was all going to end. And what about the wedding? Would Sarah be different when she returned? How would he go on if she was different? He stopped himself at that point, and the calm Gavin returned; clearing his head, he took a shower. After drying himself off, he put on a dressing gown and made his way to the kitchen. From his tower, the grey wet roofs of the buildings below seemed to emphasize the greyness of the day, and his mood.

Having finished his breakfast, he dressed, left the penthouse, and made his way to work. This was his day off, but he wanted something to do. The place seemed empty without Sarah dropping a tray of instruments or harassing Tom Harper. He soon decided that this was no good; all he could see was Sarah. She was everywhere. As he threw his jacket over his shoulder, he told the ever-efficient Tom Harper that he was going, and he would see him tomorrow. As he left his place of work, he walked over to the parked Jaguar and threw the jacket onto the passenger seat. After driving around aimlessly for a while, he arrived at Atkinson, Dewhirst & Smith. He pulled into the alley at the side of the building, then put his jacket back on, locked the car, and made his way to the entrance.

"Mr. Smith is expecting you, sir," said Mr. Braithwaite.

"He is?" said Jackson, looking slightly confused.

"This way, sir," said the elderly gent, as he slowly walked through the room towards John Smith's office.

"Come in, Gavin," greeted John Smith. "It's always nice to see you," continued the Reaper.

"How did you know I was coming?" asked Gavin.

"Sarah has gone off with Tamara. I thought it wouldn't be too long before you came asking questions. It's very natural that you would come and see me. I would have done the same thing in your shoes," said John Smith with a smile.

Gavin managed a smile and an acceptance of what his friend had just said.

"Tamara and Sarah share the same parents, and you will have to let go of your scientific way of thinking to understand this. They were both born many centuries ago, but they were parted at birth to keep one away from Atkinson. He would not have allowed both babies to live, for fear of the power their combined strength might wield. I was worried what would happen when Atkinson Junior arrived for the same reason, so that's why they have lived two very different lives. Tamara has always lived a supernatural life as Atkinson's Listmaker, whereas Sarah has lived and died and lived and died the way you understand. They have been kept apart until I deemed it necessary to combine their strengths, and now is that time. My partner's son will throw everything in his arsenal at you people, and for all your sophisticated weaponry, your only chance will be if the two girls combine their strengths."

At this point, Gavin realised that he was no longer talking to John Smith. He was sitting in front of him, but he had a far-off look in his eyes and his lips were not moving. Gavin slowly looked around to see if there was anybody else in the room as the voice began again.

"Stop looking around and heed my voice! Do not get in the way of what the two girls are doing...that is, if you want life as you know it to continue." The voice was silenced and the daydreaming John Smith came back to his usual senses, but still looking a bit dazed. "Mr. Dewhirst," said Smith.

"Actually, it's me, Gavin. Are you alright, old boy?"

"What just happened?" asked John.

"I think your Mr. Dewhirst was just here," informed Gavin.

"Impossible – he can't be here when I'm here," said the Reaper.

"Well, he was here in spirit, because he just told me, albeit through your good self, what was happening with Tamara and Sarah."

"Oh," said John Smith. "I hope it was helpful to you, Gavin."

"I keep wondering when I'm going to wake up from this nightmare," said Gavin.

"If only it was a nightmare..." replied John Smith.

Tamara took Sarah into a wooded area; the trees were tall and the grass was lush. All kinds of animals were grazing, trotting, slithering and scrambling. Every bird was ornate, almost like the dreams Sarah had when she was small.

"This is from your dream," said Tamara.

"How did you know what I was thinking?" asked Sarah. "Oh, I see," she continued. Tamara smiled as the realisation hit Sarah that she too had just read Tamara's thoughts.

"Wow!" exclaimed Sarah, giggling. "How did I do that?"

"The skills you will learn here are deeply imbedded in your psyche. It's just a case of remembering, and that's where I come in."

"Am I going to be like this all the time from now on?" asked Sarah, looking slightly sad.

"No, my beautiful sister, you are the lucky one. You get to feel human feelings; you can love, laugh, cry, and you can now, in the blink of an eye, become a Goddess," said Tamara.

"I wish I was a giant, gorgeous one like you," answered Slabgirl.

Tamara took Sarah's hand and led her to the lake.

"Take a look at our reflections, sister," said Tamara.

As Sarah looked down into the millpond-still waters of the crystal lake, she saw Tamara, and then she saw the reflection of herself. She was amazed at what she saw; matching Tamara in height, she stood tall and proud; her attire was stunning. Knee-length. armour-plated boots were laced up the front of her long legs, which were clad in chainmail up to her tiny gladiator kilt. Her sword was in its scabbard, hanging down by her right side, the belt loosely dangling from her waist. The chainmail continued over her body and down her arms. She wore a golden breastplate, inscribed with lettering that she could not understand, and shoulder plates of shimmering gold with large spikes protruding from them. On her right hand was a golden gauntlet. The crowning glory was the blondest of blonde hair, long and flowing, dancing in the sunshine, and a hair band that looked more like a small crown. She indeed looked like a fairy tale warrior queen.

John Smith opened the strange chest, which coincidentally resembled a square, light, skin-coloured, seamless box to the human eye. He once again perused its curious contents. It seemed odd to John that Tamara had called it 'armour'...and not just any armour, but the strongest armour in existence...when it was what looked like an old cloak.

He picked up the amulet, and as he did, he felt a tingling sensation, first in his hand and then all through his body. The feeling was not a bad feeling, it was empowering – but he still dropped the amulet quickly back into the box and closed the lid. He sat and stared at the chest for a long time, wondering what would happen if he was to wear its contents. Would it make him stronger, more powerful perhaps? Maybe it would even lead to an understanding of this whole turn of events that had led him from a peasant boy to the surrogate of a God to then becoming that God.

He pushed the chest away, and informed Braithwaite that he was going out for a while, took hold of his jacket, and left the office. He felt strangely drawn to a place just outside of town – back to where all this had started, to a simpler life, one which he wished he had never been taken from. The feeling grew more intense as the taxi drew close to the place, because he knew that storm clouds were gathering over this small part of the world...storm clouds, or maybe clouds of dust emanating from the hooves of four horses charging forward, ready to bestow their biblical promise upon an unsuspecting world.

As he drew closer to the old farm building, a sense of foreboding engulfed him. He stopped in his tracks as Atkinson Junior opened the rotting door to the sound of dry creaking hinges and a cloud of dust.

"How brave of you to make my work easy, fool!" said Atkinson with a laugh.

"I am unarmed," said Smith with his arms held outstretched.

"Even better," said Atkinson. "I take it you were going to try and kill me with boredom?" continued Atkinson.

"Go back to your father, and stop all this wasting of life."

As Atkinson drew his mighty sword, he said, "Speaking of wasting lives, I will start with yours."

With that, Atkinson lunged forward with sword raised high above the trembling John Smith and brought it down upon him with all of his hatred and power. John Smith could only look up at his imminent death arriving.

Tamara suddenly stopped talking, and felt cold.

"What's wrong, Tamara?" said Sarah.

"I'm not sure; something just happened. Did you feel it, Sarah?"

"I felt something, but I can't describe it," replied Sarah.

"I feel that we need to get back, but you are not ready. I must stay with you." With that, the two girls returned to their sword training.

In the Other Realm, the shudder was more pronounced. Dewhirst turned to Atkinson Senior and said in a low voice, "So, it begins."

Atkinson looked at his partner and said, "Could you have put your own son to the sword?"

"So that's what all this was about? You are hoping someone else will do your dirty work? I would have saved you the trouble. It would have been no inconvenience to me to dispatch that idiot son of yours!" retorted an angry Dewhirst.

"Hold your tongue! You forget who you are talking to!" screamed Atkinson.

"You're right. I have forgotten you, or rather, you have..." answered a defiant Dewhirst.

A loud clap of thunder followed by flashes of forked lightning and torrential rain engulfed the town. Chief Inspector Johnson looked out at the ever blackening sky and the roads awash with rain.

D.I. Donna Lambert joined him at the window as hail, the size of golf balls, bounced off the car roofs in the station car park. The intensity of the weather escalated, as high winds started howling and roof slates began to be ripped from their fastenings, smashing as they hit the ground below. It was as if all of this bad weather was emanating from a central point just out of town. Indeed, the vortex of this storm was just outside an old farmhouse where John Smith stood, still quite alive. An outraged Atkinson wondered why his sword had stopped an inch above his victim's head. It soon became clear to both beings that they could not venture, in any way, into each other's space, which was a relief to John Smith – but an incredible frustration to Atkinson.

As Atkinson withdrew his sword, the vortex around them ceased and the clouds gave way; the wind died down, and the thunder and lightning stopped.

"It's true! You cannot hurt me and I'm not even wearing my armour!" said John Smith, looking Atkinson straight in the eyes.

"Keep out of my way!" shouted Atkinson, as he ran off into the trees nearby. John Smith felt the same feeling of empowerment as he did when holding Atkinson Senior's amulet back in the office. As Smith stood in front of the now-demolished farmhouse, he looked around. He saw that everything from the farmhouse to the woods was totally razed to the ground, and instead of his usual fear of anything untoward, a grin came to his lips as he surveyed the devastation around him.

Back at the police station, the switchboard was jammed with calls, mostly about damage and alarms going off. But the strangest call was from a man who had been fishing on a lake nearby. The caller said that all the fish in the lake were dead and just floating on the top; there were thousands of fish of all kinds, just lifeless on the lake. P.O. Collins, who took the call, said, "It's like the seven signs from the book of Revelations."

Sergeant Simpson said, "We are too busy to discuss what books you have read, lad."

"It's not a book, as such. It's from the Bible – the seven signs of Armageddon."

"What do you mean?" enquired the desk sergeant.

"In the Holy Bible, the last book is Revelations, and it depicts the signs or seals of Armageddon. It's probably not real. It's just thunder, lightning, hail, and the sea giving up its fish. I was just making a light-hearted comment," said the red-faced young police officer.

"Keep that sort of thing to yourself. We don't want to start a panic, now do we?" snarled the Chief, as he came downstairs. Chief Inspector Johnson and DI Lambert were on their way to see what the disturbance just outside of town was.

The police station went deathly quiet as all the police inside just stared at the new police officer, who could not understand what the problem was.

John Smith was still standing in the same spot when Paul Johnson and Donna Lambert arrived.

"I thought accountancy might be at the bottom of all this," said Johnson. "What has just happened, John, and why is there so much devastation here?"

"It begins, Chief Inspector. What you just witnessed was Atkinson trying to kill me."

"How did you get away, John?" enquired Johnson.

"I didn't...I thought my end had come, but his blade could not touch me. It was when his sword drew close to me that the storm broke out; you see, we cannot be in the same place at the same time," explained John Smith.

"Lucky for you, John. Let's give you a ride back, you look quite pale," said Paul Johnson.

"I feel uncommonly strong," said John, "but I will accept your kind offer." The three people drove back to the offices of Atkinson, Dewhirst & Smith.

Atkinson's plans had taken a strange turn; he had not foreseen this problem with Smith, and wondered why Tamara wasn't with him. She should be protecting Smith at this time, and this left him wondering what could be more important. He had tried to seek out her mind but was unable to; this could only mean that she was in another realm. All this was quite puzzling to Atkinson. He started to think that there was a plan afoot to outwit him, but he was Atkinson – and he was invincible this time.

Chapter Nineteen

Tamara stood back and watched her sister wielding her broadsword as if she was dancing with a feather. She could not believe how quickly the young girl had taken on board what she needed to learn. The sword looked like an extension of her arm.

"I know you are there," said Sarah impishly, as she twirled the sword three times around and swished it into its scabbard in one move.

"I can't believe it. You are ready."

"Ready for anything!" shouted Sarah, as she danced towards her sister.

"I almost don't want to take you back," frowned Tamara.

"But I want to go back, to put things right, and then marry my Gavin!" sang Sarah.

"I'm pleased to see you still have your human emotions."

"I bet Gavin will be glad, too," said Sarah.

"Now you must meet someone before we return. Follow me into the house, Sarah," encouraged Tamara.

As they stepped through the door of what used to be Sarah's home, a shadowy figure stood in the corner.

"Don't be afraid, Sarah. He is in another dimension, but he wants to talk to you; he is not here," instructed Tamara.

"Sarah, your task is simple. Use whatever means that are available to you to kill the being known to you as Atkinson. Your weapons are only as strong as your heart. If you truly want to be with the being called Gavin Jackson, then you must kill Atkinson. There are now three of you, as Smith has finally realised his potential. Should one of you fall, the other two must carry on. Should two of you fall, the last of you has to kill him – for if all three of you fall, the seventh seal will be broken, and Humankind will be no more. As we speak, the seals are already opening. Time is short. The fate of everything you know rests in your hands. I have helped all I can. Sarah, if you fall, you will lose the side of you that is human, and everything that is human will be forgotten forever – so take care, brave girl. Keep the love in your heart; it's the one weapon that Atkinson doesn't have." With that, the shadowy figure of Dewhirst disappeared.

Atkinson Junior stood under an old oak tree in the centre of the woods. As he surveyed the area around him, he noticed the vegetation was dying in the pattern of a circle, moving slowly outwards. The old trees were left burnt and felled in its wake. To his amazement, great stones were rising up from the ground at the fire's perimeter. The huge druid stones groaned and creaked as they took their place, one after the other; in each gap between the stones stood a long-dead druid; it was as if nature itself was lending a hand in holding off this beast.

"The circle of stone and a long-forgotten religion won't stop me!" laughed Atkinson.

The druids all pointed their staffs at Atkinson, and from each staff came a bright red beam of light, all pointing towards the beast. The light engulfed Atkinson, and, for a time, held him in that spot as if frozen. As the druids pointed their staffs, they knelt down on one knee, keeping the beam of prehistoric laser light fixed on its target. Behind each druid, a witch stood with arms stretched upward, drawing down with their incantations a vast energy right onto the head of Atkinson. By now, Atkinson was feeling all the force from this primeval earth power. He had not expected this turn of events; his body was starting to feel the effects of the enormous gravity, like pressure that was weighing him down. As he fell to his knees, he took his mighty sword and struck it deep into the earth.

At the same time, in the Other Realm, his father raised his sword. At first, Dewhirst thought he was finally going to finish it, but to his horror, the old God sent his son power. At this point, all three planes merged. In the living world, Atkinson pulled his sword out of the ground, and raised it into the air. All the force attacking him rebounded to his captors, sending them back from whence they came, and the stones collapsed into dust. In the Other Realm, Dewhirst drew his sword and knocked his partner's sword from his hand. Dewhirst lunged forward with his own sword in the first-ever duel in this realm. Atkinson Senior moved out of the way, regained his sword and struck back at Dewhirst, who blocked his strike with an upward glance of his sword. Each blow of these two swords sent shockwaves through the Earth, leaving earthquakes and volcanic eruptions all over America, China, and Russia – in fact, all over the world in places that have never had seismic or volcanic problems, such as England and parts of Europe.

Every blow of the sword sparked a new eruption or earthquake somewhere in the world. The San Andreas fault opened a crack in the earth, and many cities disappeared into the sea, creating mountainous tsunamis across the Pacific Ocean. Every geological plate was now shifting worldwide and buildings were burying their inhabitants. Rivers of molten lava now flowed through every continent, for every blow from the two old Gods brought more and more destruction.

The tranquil forest of Sarah's dream had now turned into a nightmare of biblical proportions. Tamara took Sarah's hand, and in the next instance, they were transported back to the old accountancy firm. John Smith was waiting as they returned.

A confident John Smith smiled as the two girls, both still warrior-clad, arrived. "Not a moment too soon," announced Smith.

"What the hell has happened?" demanded Tamara.

"Hell itself," replied John.

The two girls ran to the window; there was destruction everywhere. The sky was red with burning buildings and lava flows. Lightning crashed to Earth, charging the air with electricity, with thunder so loud it went off the decibel scale. The inhabitants of the city were scared and confused and were scampering around, trying to find shelter.

The two Gods carried on blow after blow after blow, as more and more destruction befell the Earth. The Other Realm where they existed was getting brighter and brighter from the huge sparks flashing from their divine blades.

The building that Gavin Jackson had called home since his arrival was now in a poor state. Large pieces of masonry, steel, and glass were falling all around him as he made for the stairwell. Some unfortunate people in the building had taken the elevators, just as the main elevator in the building collapsed, sending them screaming to their untimely deaths.

As broken glass and twanging restraint steel flashed past his head, Gavin made his way down to the underground car park, only to find his Jaguar smashed under fallen concrete. The only way out was blocked. Gavin looked about him at the destruction and devastation. As he sat at the stairwell, the lights dimmed and extinguished.

As the roof caved in on the old police station, C. I. Johnson asked if everybody had made it out.

"All except D.I. Lambert, Sir," said the young police officer that he'd met only that morning.

"Get as many as you can, and try helping the people that are trapped! I'm going for Lambert!"

"No, Sir, you can't go in there, it is too dangerous! It's all falling down!"

"Do as I say!" retorted the Chief Inspector as he ran into the collapsing police station.

The epic battle in the Other Realm was drawing to a close, with both Gods wielding their blades with furious anger, crash after crash, blade on blade, God against God. Dewhirst was first to draw divine blood, as his blade tore into Atkinson's arm. Atkinson quickly retorted with a back swipe, taking off Dewhirst's lower arm. Unfortunately for Atkinson Senior, it wasn't the sword-wielding arm. With a flash of his left arm, Dewhirst's last swing parted Atkinson's head from his body. As Atkinson fell, what was left of his power burst from his body, knocking his assailant to the ground. The force of the Other Realm partially imploding on itself, and then exploding, could be felt by everything living or dead, human and animal alike, all over the crumbling world. As the dust settled at the epicentre of all of this divine demonic unrest, everybody had taken cover, or was dead. All, that is, except four giant beings, three of them at one end of what used to be High Street, and one at the other.

JOHN PAUL BERNETT

Chapter Twenty

Mayhem and confusion reigned, explosions could be heard. Screams of the sick and dying, and the constant rumble of buildings collapsing, comprised the backdrop of possibly the last battle of Humankind. It wasn't as some predicted – international-super powers with their atomic bombs; nor was it an asteroid leaving its orbit. No, this biblical holocaust was to be between three enchanted warriors and one demented God, the latter wielding power that Humankind, with all its knowledge, could not begin to understand.

Atkinson smirked as he looked at his one-time lover and confidante, his hapless surrogate, and the bitch who had stopped him last time. He shouted, "I am the power and now the God of the underworld; if you yield at my feet, I promise your death will be quick and painless." Atkinson stood with his arms folded, awaiting their answer.

John Smith turned to the two girls, almost in a huddle, as if discussing what Atkinson had just proposed. In fact, he was handing the girls items from Atkinson Senior's armour. Smith placed the amulet around Tamara's neck. He placed the gauntlet on Sarah's hand and wrapped the cloak with its hood down on himself. "These ancient weapons will buy us time while we wear him down," said Tamara. "Only our combined strength will win this day, and we must, because this time, he must die," she continued.

In the dark, silent grave of his home, Gavin Jackson waited for the emergency services to arrive. As his eyes adjusted to the dimness of his situation, he noticed a pinhole of light breaking through the debris. He carefully crept on his hands and knees, trying to avoid the crushed cars and masonry. Slowly, he made his way through to the light, and started pulling out stones and cupping dirt and loose rubble with his hands.

At the police station, the Chief Inspector had made his way back into the demolition site that used to be his work place.

"Donna! Donna!" shouted the Chief Inspector, but there was no reply. He ripped wood and bricks out of his way. He made it up what was left of the staircase to his office; inside, he saw D.I. Lambert on the floor, crushed and lifeless. He frantically tried to remove all the debris from his workmate and lover, but to no avail; it was just too heavy, and more and more masonry, roof tiles, and wood were still falling on her and him. He knew that he had to get out. He made it back downstairs as the entire building was collapsing around him. The doorway was getting smaller and smaller as he ran towards the ever-closing aperture. Just as the entire building totally collapsed, he emerged in a cloud of dust, but without his fallen comrade.

"Enough stalling!" shouted Atkinson. "Who among you will face me first?"

"Do you want me to kill you again? I've heard all I can take of testosterone-fuelled bullshit, Atkinson," scorned Sarah, as she charged towards her foe. Atkinson raced to meet her, sword outstretched, with anger and revenge in his eyes.

"It seems your training hasn't removed any of Slabgirl's uniqueness," laughed Smith, as he too charged forward.

Tamara smiled with confidence as she watched her brave sister; she shouted to John Smith, "Pull your hood on, John!" Slightly puzzled, he did what she asked, and instantly disappeared, and now was truly able to be in the same space as Atkinson.

Atkinson and Sarah met in the middle and sparks flew from their swords. Atkinson found it hard to believe that this once-tiny girl was so strong, so he swiped her legs from under her. As she fell off balance, he brought his sword down onto her head. But a flash of sparks flew from his sword as the invisible John Smith's sword stopped his blade from hitting its target. Sarah rolled sideways and withdrew as Tamara moved in on Atkinson. With his sword still raised, she thrust her sword right into his midriff.

Gavin had, by now, burrowed his way out of his tower block and realised, for the first time, the full horror of what was happening around him. It looked the way most people depicted hell. The sky was red and what appeared to be lava was flowing down the hills on the horizon. Over the road was a motorbike with its engine still running; he quickly removed the dead rider, and roared off in the direction of Main Street.

At the police station, the devastated but still-in-control Chief Inspector Paul Johnson dusted himself off and gathered his people. Police Officer Linda Harper came running from the town centre. As she tried to catch her breath, she said, "There are giants...giants fighting in Main Street!"

"Come on, people! Gather whatever you can to arm yourselves and follow me!" The police started running towards Main Street. As they ran, more and more people joined what was becoming an angry mob. By the time they arrived, they were one thousand strong.

In the middle of High Street, the battle was raging. Atkinson had dodged the thrust from Tamara's, sword and was matching his three assailants blow for blow. Streams of sparks were lighting up the whole area. He had not noticed the crowd that had built up on the fight's perimeter. The battle grew more intense as Atkinson began to back off slightly. Sarah was first to take advantage of Atkinson withdrawing. While Tamara and Smith kept up the pressure, Sarah leapt over Atkinson, catching him across his neck with her sword. He immediately turned and raised his sword, but Tamara thrust her sword into his side. Atkinson recoiled his sword to knock Tamara's away, and with the same swing, caught John Smith in the arm. To Atkinson's horror, Sarah thrust her sword into his back, but he would not fall. Again, he turned to Sarah and lifted his sword, but the best shot of Johnson's career sent his sword spinning out of his hand.

All the time this battle was raging, the weather was worsening because of the close proximity of Atkinson and Smith. The armour Smith was wearing made it possible for their blades to actually touch each other, but it was causing devastation around them.

Atkinson noticed the crowd that had built up; with a simple wave of his arm, every one of them hit the floor. As if by magic, his sword lifted from the ground and landed back in his hand. John Smith took this opportunity to swipe at Atkinson; he opened a wound deep into his side. Atkinson, as if not hurt in the slightest, turned and hit John Smith on the head with the hilt of his sword. The hit sent him sprawling on the ground. Smith pulled the hood of his cloak over his head, which rendered him invisible, and instantly healed the gaping wound on his forehead. Smith felt invigorated and rejoined the battle hooded, so Atkinson had to deal with a sword he couldn't see. Even with that disadvantage, Atkinson was getting the upper hand.

Although Tamara and Sarah were fighting with super-human strength, they were beginning to lose the battle and Atkinson seemed to be getting stronger. He was delivering blow after blow on all three of his opponents. As Atkinson gained the initiative, he knew the end was near. His three foes were beaten. All that was left was the last dispatch; he drew back his sword to deliver the last hit.

As his blade began its downward swish, suddenly, a motorbike roared through the air and the front wheel embedded itself into Atkinson's back, knocking him down and unseating the rider.

"Go get him, Sarah!" shouted Gavin Jackson, as all three warriors swiped their swords at the same time. John Smith's blade separated Atkinson's legs from his torso, Tamara's blade pierced Atkinson's heart, and Sarah's blade sliced his head from his body. All that was left of Atkinson fell for the very last time – all, that is, except for his head, which was held aloft for the gathered masses to see, most of whom had no idea what had just taken place. All, that is, except a policeman, a coroner, and a journalist...

...and as for the Reaper and the Scribe?

To be continued.

JOHN PAUL BERNETT

About the author

JP Bernett and his wife Beverly live in the North of England. JP was brought up on a council estate called Belle Isle, in South Leeds, an upbringing he is proud of.

Art and sports played a big part in his early years, although writing was always a secret passion.

The computer age arriving enabled him to start writing his poetry and stories down, as dyslexia held him back from showing his work previously.

This particular book owes a lot to the Gothic circles he keeps reappearing into every now and then, which he has done ever since he first walked down the staircase and stepped into the famous Le Phonographique nightclub in Leeds in 1976.

E-mail jonno41@hotmail.com
Twitter www.twitter.com/JPBernett
Facebook www.facebook.com/JPBernett

John Paul Bernett

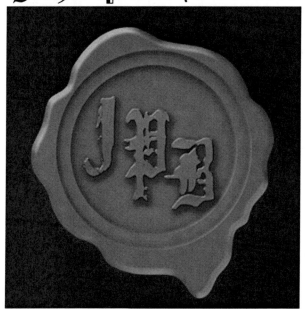

Be Happy

CPSIA information can be obtained
at www.ICGtesting.com
Printed in the USA
LVOW10s1505040418
572282LV00026B/755/P